RECEIVED

JUL 2 8 2022

ROADVIEW LIBRAR

PRAISE FOR

PRELUDE FOR LOST SOULS

"Small-town staples—no-frills restaurants and chattering busybodies—blend with the supernatural to create a unique backdrop for this paranormal mystery. Small touches, such as a haunted piano, enhance the atmosphere and are regarded with a normalcy that makes the spiritualism-steeped streets of St. Hilaire feel as American as apple pie. Working to unravel the mysteries that drew them together, three teenagers find unexpected answers in a town where not only the dead are haunted."

NO LONGER PROPERTY OF
SEATTLE PUBLIC LIBRARY

—*Foreword Reviews*

"*Prelude for Lost Souls* is a charming novel perfect for a lazy weekend. It's moody and melodramatic, the kind of story that makes you think of falling leaves and cozy sweaters and waning friendships and new lovers and finally learning to let go."

—Tor.com

"Ghost story, love story, and mystery in equal measure, Helene Dunbar's *Prelude for Lost Souls* is filled with unforgettable characters who reveal the many ways a life can be haunted. Perfect for fans of *The Raven Boys*."

—Lisa Maxwell, *New York Times* bestselling author
of the Last Magician series

D1052464

"Dunbar invokes small-town intrigue and plentiful atmosphere with this haunting, romantic tale."

—*Publishers Weekly*

"Mesmerizing and haunting, Dunbar invites readers into a world of family secrets, anxious ghosts, and a society's ruthless grasp for power that will leave you wanting more."

—*The Nerd Daily*

PRAISE FOR

WE ARE LOST AND FOUND

A YALSA 2020 Best Young Adult Fiction pick

Bank Street College of Education's
Best Children's Books of the Year

Texas State Tayshahs High School Reading List pick

Capital Choices (DC) 2020 Noteworthy Books
for Children and Teens List pick

The Nerd Daily's Best YA Books of 2019

"*We Are Lost and Found* absolutely sparkles… She so perfectly, so evocatively captures the angst, uncertainty, and shaky self-confidence of adolescence that it might make you wince."

—*Echo Magazine*

"It's a certain type of magic that Helene Dunbar managed with this story… A hauntingly beautiful, yet scarring story that captures the struggles of figuring out who you are while facing the uncertainties of the world, a story that should be mandatory reading for all."

—*The Nerd Daily*

"Michael's journey of growth and self-acceptance, with all its drama, confusion, and raw emotion, is one that many teens will be able to identify with…regardless of sexuality or gender."

—*Booklist*

"Dunbar painstakingly populates the narrative with 1980s references—particularly to music—creating a vivid historical setting… A painful but ultimately empowering queer history lesson."

—*Kirkus Reviews*

"Dunbar paints a broad and accurate portrait of the pain of the times through a series of emotional snapshots."

—*Bulletin of the Center for Children's Books*

"This YA novel provides an interesting way for youth of all backgrounds to explore a dark history that is rarely discussed."

—*Washington Blade*

"In haunting and lyrical prose Dunbar beautifully and accurately captures a generation."

—Tom Wilinsky, coauthor of *Snowsisters*

"With staggeringly gorgeous, experimental prose, Dunbar delivers a critical story about love, heartbreak, the manifestation of fear, and hope."

—Mia Siegert, author of *Jerkbait*

ALSO BY HELENE DUNBAR

THE PROMISE OF
LOST THINGS

the PROMISE of Lost THINGS

HELENE DUNBAR

sourcebooks
fire

Copyright © 2022 by Helene Dunbar
Cover and internal design © 2022 by Sourcebooks
Cover design by Erin Fitzsimmons
Internal design by Danielle McNaughton/Sourcebooks
Cover images © Patricia Turner/Arcangel Images, Sam Gmuer/EyeEm/Getty Images

Sourcebooks and the colophon are registered trademarks of Sourcebooks.

All rights reserved. No part of this book may be reproduced in any form or by
any electronic or mechanical means including information storage and retrieval
systems—except in the case of brief quotations embodied in critical articles or
reviews—without permission in writing from its publisher, Sourcebooks.

The characters, events, and places portrayed in this book are fictitious
or are used fictitiously. Any similarity to real persons, living or
dead, is purely coincidental and not intended by the author.

All brand names and product names used in this book are trademarks,
registered trademarks, or trade names of their respective holders.
Sourcebooks is not associated with any product or vendor in this book.

Quote from Robert Montgomery used by permission.

Published by Sourcebooks Fire, an imprint of Sourcebooks
P.O. Box 4410, Naperville, Illinois 60567-4410
(630) 961-3900
sourcebooks.com

Cataloging-in-Publication Data is on file with the Library of Congress.

Printed and bound in the United States of America.
POD

To Keira,

who wanted to see her name at the front of a book.

Six books later and I STILL love you more
than hippopotamuses.

*The people you love become ghosts inside of you,
and like this you keep them alive.*

—The Artist Robert Montgomery

RULES OF CONDUCT FOR MEDIUMS

NEVER CHANGE THE COURSE OF THE FUTURE
through the sharing of information.
~~This includes scenarios of life and death.~~

MEDIUMS PASS ALONG MESSAGES FROM THE DEPARTED.
We do not read minds and any attempt to insinuate otherwise
will be met with censure by the Guild.

NEVER READ A FELLOW MEDIUM OR SUMMON A SPIRIT
to that end without their permission. Mediums who have
passed on may only be contacted with explicit Guild approval.

NEVER USE YOUR GIFTS FOR SELFISH GAIN.

NEVER MISLEAD THOSE YOU COULD HELP.

ALL WISHING TO MOVE TO ST. HILAIRE WILL BE TESTED.
A full half of any family must be able to pass tests as certified
mediums and be able to support themselves as such.

ALL HIGH SCHOOL SENIORS WILL SERVE IN THE GUILD'S
Youth Corps during that school year. In the likelihood that
a student shows special promise, there exists the option for a
one-year position as Student Leader within the Corps, leading
naturally to a permanent Guild position upon completion.

HAVE A NICE DAY.

THE GUILD, GOVERNING BODY OF ST. HILAIRE,
NEW YORK, ESTABLISHED 1870.

chapter one
RUSS

In St. Hilaire, New York, everyone talked to the dead.

If you were lucky or talented, or both, the dead might listen. Sometimes they talked back. Sometimes they made sense. Sometimes they were just a pain in the ass.

I knew it was odd to live in a town filled with mediums whose primary business involved séances, healing sessions, and ghost walks. It was odd to live behind a gate that only opened to visitors—for a price—during the summer when they'd converge on our town seeking answers, comfort, and forgiveness from those who had passed on.

And perhaps it was equally odd to embrace the idea that death wasn't an end point. Even though, maybe, in most cases it should be.

But, odd as it was, I loved it. I loved the history of our town, which was founded by a group of talented mediums over a hundred-and-fifty years ago. I loved the weirdness of séances and fairy trails and people coming to walk the huge labyrinth on the other end of town. I loved feeling like I was part of something big, something that mattered, as well as the fact that I could bring hope and closure to the people who came here. And I *really* loved being chosen as leader of the Youth Corps, made up of all the high school seniors. The role put me on the path to an actual job with the town's governing body, the Guild, assuming I survived high school and some extra training courses, first.

Today's lesson started the way most spirit-related activities did, with a voice in my ear and a feeling I was being watched, a slight vibration under my chair and a chill in the air.

I shivered in my wool coat. The chill, which seemed to settle somewhere in my spine and radiate through my body like a spiderweb, was a reaction to ghosts that most mediums outgrew, but one I guess I was stuck with. I tightened the muscles in my shoulders, locked my knees in an effort to stay still, and hoped Willow Rogers didn't notice, which was ridiculous because Willow Rogers noticed everything.

"Tell me, Russ," she commanded. She sounded bored as if she'd rather be manning an off-season phone line or working the research desk at the town archives than mentoring me in conjuring the dead. More than that, she *looked* bored, her green eyes dismissive and clouded as if her thoughts were far away.

I tilted my head and searched the air around her. "There's a woman," I said. "Standing over your left shoulder." I examined the ghost's clothing: over a hundred years out of date. Her hair: a messy blond ponytail. This lesson was so easy; it was no wonder Willow was bored. The spirit could have walked out of my freshman-year textbook. "Melody Thorne," I said, identifying one of our town's founders and most frequent ghostly visitors.

Willow stared at me, perfectly still and unblinking, her lips red against her skin as she said, "Continue."

I tried to tune out the sound of my heart beating in my ear. Narrowed my eyes to focus on the syllables formed by the ghost's barely there mouth. "You have a"—I leaned forward to listen more closely to what the spirit of Melody Thorne was saying—"a class. No, a meeting. You have a meeting at four o'clock and she's worried you'll be late."

There were no clocks in the room, so Willow glanced at her phone. Her face flashed with annoyance and then cleared before she stood and smoothed down her straight black skirt. "That's all for today," she said, which meant I hadn't done anything she could find fault with. Willow was notoriously generous with her criticism.

I stood and stretched. The muscles in my neck were taut and sore. These weekly lessons were required to help me strengthen my skills as a medium, but they were dull, exhausting, and it was clear both of us were only here out of obligation. I could do this sort of thing in my sleep.

Willow walked to the door of the classroom, her high heels echoing on the parquet floor. Then she turned back abruptly, as if she were trying to catch me off guard. "I overheard Father talking…" she started, her face animated for the first time since she'd walked into the room. "Is it true that Ian Mackenzie speaks to you?"

I inhaled sharply. Willow and I never spoke directly about our lives. We'd talk about school or the Guild or general current events: the museum got a new collection of dowsing rods from the early 1920s, or did you hear Miranda had something strange happen during a reading she was conducting? But never anything more personal and for me, it didn't get any more personal than Ian Mackenzie.

I didn't talk about Ian with anyone. I hadn't talked about him when he was alive and considered St. Hilaire's hottest, young medium, even though we were friends with benefits. Or enemies with benefits. Or whatever you call it when you kind-of-sort-of like someone and kind-of-sort-of hate them at the same time and yet can't seem to stay away.

I *really* didn't talk about him now that he was dead and haunting me (and only me) and now that we actually *did* like each other. Maybe more than liked each other. When it came to Ian, the specifics were always hard to pin down.

I answered her question with a tentative nod and waited while she looked me up and down. She had a piercing stare, one I'd often emulated with some success. I knew she had to be irritated that Ian would talk to me and not her. After all, she and Ian had gone to school together and served on the Youth Corps together. And even though she was only a few years older than me, she was already a member of the Guild. More than that, she'd actually been raised by them as a type of collective adopted daughter. She even called Guild President Clive Rice "Father."

And Ian? He was a Guild legend. That hadn't changed just because he was dead.

I was only a high school senior. A senior who was currently student leader of the Guild's Youth Corps, but still, that was nothing in comparison to either of them. She had to be pissed I had a line to St. Hilaire's most elusive ghost.

"I suppose it makes sense," she said, narrowing her eyes and letting contempt bleed into her voice. "Ian was always motivated more by what was in his pants than what was in his head."

I winced. She wasn't wrong, and despite my determination to stay in control, I felt myself flush. But it was one thing for everyone to know that the ghost of Ian Mackenzie, one of the best mediums St. Hilaire had ever seen, spoke to me. It was another for them to know…assume… Hell, *I* couldn't define what my relationship with Ian had been when he was alive—much less what it was now—so there was certainly no way Willow and the rest of St. Hilaire could have a clue.

But Ian and Willow were more alike than either would have admitted, and the number one rule for dealing with both of them was the same: Don't show fear.

I coughed, regrouped, and said, "I'm sure he'd want to send his best to Colin. How is your boyfriend, anyhow?" I had to restrain myself from putting air quotes around the word *boyfriend*. Colin was Ian's younger brother. He and Ian had hated each other when Ian was alive, and Ian's death hadn't changed those feelings. Rumors about Colin and Willow had been swirling around for ages, though "boyfriend" was probably putting a pretty spin on it.

Willow's eyes flashed, but when she turned back to the door,

7

she didn't answer. All she said was, "Be here the same time on Wednesday to continue your training." Then she walked out.

———

When I got home, I booted up the brick of a laptop I'd been using for over five years despite numerous crashes, stuck keys, and burned-out pixels on the screen. My browser opened to the *Buchanan Sentinel.* Buchanan was the town that sat just outside St. Hilaire, and their big news usually involved some sort of high school sportsball or a debate on mailbox colors, but sometimes I needed to see what was going on in the rest of the world.

Today's headline read: Ghost Killers Team to Re-form and Air 2-Hour Special on St. Hilaire.

I vaguely remembered the show and its mission to visit supposedly haunted places and debunk them. It had been a hit for a while and had changed casts multiple times before it just seemed to stop, but I'd never watched it when it was on and hadn't paid much attention to it ending.

I skimmed the article, most of which discussed St. Hilaire's founding as a home for spiritualists and described how we opened for business to the public in the summer, offering to contact the dead relatives, lovers, friends, and coworkers of the often-desperate customers who came through the gates for a mere fifteen dollars a head. Stock photos showed the painted Victorians and the old-growth forests, the wishing rock and the bronzed statues of our founders.

A paragraph at the bottom touched on the always-contentious topic of how, since spiritualism was classified as a religion, St.

Hilaire received tax breaks not offered to adjacent towns and how that had pissed people off in neighboring Buchanan who felt as if they were picking up our slack.

My father and I had never had enough money to worry about tax breaks. And it was hard to get worked up about Buchanan residents being irritated, since they always seemed bothered by something we were or weren't doing.

There was little concrete information in the piece about the show. No air date or cast list or rationale other than that St. Hilaire was *Ghost Killers'* next target and that it was a "breaking story."

"Welcome to small-town America," I muttered to myself. "But it didn't even mention the Guild. How can you write an article about St. Hilaire without mentioning the Guild?"

"You know what they say about people who talk to themselves, right?" a voice behind me asked.

"That they have a captive audience?" I tossed back.

Ian Mackenzie choked out a laugh. No. The *ghost* of Ian Mackenzie choked out a laugh, but really, there was little difference between the two. Even as a ghost, Ian was bigger than…well, life.

He leaned over my shoulder to read, and I could feel a cold whisper of something like breath land deliberately on my neck. I shivered.

"Need I remind you they didn't mention the Guild because the Guild is obsolete?" he asked. "Or at least it will be once we get through with them." Then he pulled back and said, "Although they could have interviewed me. And maybe you, I guess."

I couldn't help but laugh at Ian's indignation. Aside from one conversation I'd facilitated with his youngest brother, Alex, Ian hadn't spoken to a single living person aside from me since he'd died, and here he was, wondering why the press wasn't calling and asking him to do the late-night talk-show circuit. *Typical.* "Good thing you don't have an agenda."

"No," Ian corrected me. "*We* have an agenda."

"Okay, fine." I admitted. "Technically, he wasn't wrong. The Guild had always been secretive and controlling. But Ian had told me about rumors of them actually *killing* people during the time he'd run the Corps. Plus, lately, they'd been doing ridiculous things like making all the houses put up Guild flags and running people out of town for refusing to follow some arbitrary rules. Something had to give, and we were going to make sure it did. We just didn't know how we would do that yet.

"I thought my being chosen to lead the Youth Corps would give us inside information we could use against them, but so far most of my time has been sucked up with these." I gestured to the piles of reports that threatened to take over the room.

And it was true. All high school seniors had to serve in the Guild's Youth Corps. And most years, one student was chosen to lead the Corps and possibly jump straight into a Guild-shaped career. When I'd originally dreamed of being chosen student leader, I'd assumed the role would include many things: the chance to learn everything I could from the town's most esteemed mediums, an opportunity to hone my talents, and a chance to prove I was Guild material.

I didn't think it was going include trying to take down a corrupt organization.

Or communing with Ian who, through sheer willpower, was keeping himself tethered here instead of doing…well, whatever those who have passed on beyond the ghost state normally did.

Unfortunately, neither of us were getting very far. Not with *that* goal, anyhow. Aside from my weekly lessons with Willow, my three months as student leader had included one thing: paperwork. Stacks and stacks of reports the Guild expected me to read, verify, catalog, and input into their databases. My entire position was turning into nothing more than a hellish internship.

Ian picked up the top half of a mountain of séance reports, riffled through them, and then before I could stop him, he tossed them dramatically across the room. "Why not make them go away," he said.

I watched the papers fall like snow, one after the other, the staples making tiny clicks as they hit the worn wooden floor.

Then I watched Ian watching the papers. He was more solid than most ghosts, smugger than, well, anything.

"Are you telling me they didn't make you do the reports when you were leader?" I asked, already able to guess his answer.

Ian raised an eyebrow.

"What?"

"Wake up, Griffin. This is a waste of your time." Ian crossed his well-defined arms loosely in front of him, relaxed and in control. As usual.

I considered asking how he'd gotten out of having to do the Guild's grunt work but thought better of it. It was foolish to assume I'd be treated the same way Ian had been. And even if he told me his secrets, I was too sensible and not charming enough to resort to whatever tactics he'd used to bend the Guild to his will.

"I suppose you have a better idea?" I asked.

He cocked his head and smiled a smile full of innuendo. "I have many better ideas."

If "Don't show fear" was rule number one when dealing with Ian Mackenzie, rule number two was "Don't take the bait."

Even when part of me wanted to. *Especially* when I wanted to.

"No doubt," I said and quickly began to distract myself by gathering the papers. "Weren't we going to discuss you not bursting into my room anymore?"

"I'm dead. Where would you send the engraved invitations?"

I rolled my eyes and moved the now-ordered stack out of Ian's grasp. Boundaries had never been his strong suit. "Can't we just… I don't know. Set up a time to meet?"

"Like a date? Do I need to bring flowers and make dinner reservations, too?" Ian leaned back against the bed and smirked. "Funny enough, my watch doesn't exactly work in the great beyond. What's your problem, anyhow?"

What was my problem? I didn't know where to begin. Willow had gotten under my skin, and these days, Ian seemed to live there.

But most of all, I was struggling with the fact that I'd spent years working my ass off to prove myself to the Guild and now I was doing everything I could to find a way to destroy them. It was stressing me out.

"I don't have a problem," I said.

Ian ignored my bullshit answer as he wandered around the room and, from somewhere, sourced a marble. He rolled it back and forth on the desk.

The cat's-eye rolled left, then right. I wasn't sure where it had come from. I wasn't sure why this act was worth Ian's limited reserve of energy. I wasn't sure why I cared. Except…

Ian Mackenzie was a complicated thing to be. He'd been the

darling of St. Hilaire when he was alive. He was their darling now. Or would be if he'd agreed to speak to anyone other than me. But now that he was dead, there were times when I could see cracks in his characteristic cockiness, times when he seemed oddly anxious. And, despite my better judgment, I found that, in those times, I had an overwhelming desire to do something to relieve his anxiety.

When Ian rolled the marble toward me a fourth time, I bent over and grabbed it. As if it had been his plan all along, he leaned forward and kissed me. The marble was icy where it lay clenched in my fist. Ian, too, was cold. I always forgot Ian would be cold and therefore I was always surprised. But then Ian had always been unexpected. He was an open window where I was sure I'd shut it, a road out of town that didn't exist on a map.

I pulled away to catch my breath and clear my head and remember my name. But Ian was a drug, and I couldn't help but want more.

This time he placed one cold finger on my lips.

I waited. Waited. Waited. My breath came in fits and starts, my traitorous heart pounded, looking for escape. My focus was equally divided between the marble in my hand and the strip of icy flesh against my lips. I waited as if waiting were the only thing I knew how to do. And around Ian, that wasn't far from the truth.

"Trust me," he said, holding my gaze. I found it impossible to look away and equally impossible to remember what I was supposed to trust Ian *with*. I was still wrestling with this new understanding between us after I'd refused to speak to him the entire year before his mysterious death.

My phone buzzed and broke the spell. Grateful and annoyed in equal measure, I blinked, pulled away, and stared at an unfamiliar local number before letting the call go to voicemail.

Ian reached toward my cell phone, but I slapped his hand away. "You gave up things like phones when you…" I was going to say *chose to die* because that's what everyone believed had happened. That Ian was too good of a medium, too good looking, too privileged and special to do anything as uncivilized as to just *happen* to die young. His death must have been a deliberate choice, everyone said, caused by Ian being wild and reckless and too consumed with being Ian to bother staying alive.

I'd bought into the story, too, at the time. But something about it had always unsettled me, and Ian always skirted around the subject like a spider. "Sorry. I didn't mean…"

Ian didn't look away.

"Sorry," I said again, forcing myself to glance down.

I reached over and grabbed another stack of papers, aiming to line up the staples in the upper-left corner. As I did, something caught my eye. I sorted through the pile in my hand and then looked through the ones on the table. Then I looked again.

"Seventeen?" I asked Ian. "They held seventeen séances to try to reach you in a single season?"

I knew the Guild had been oddly obsessed with contacting Ian. But I hadn't realized they had been *this* bent out of shape. In all that time, Ian had never thrown them a single bone.

"Never let it be said I don't know how to play hard to get," he said. "Give me those." He reached over for the stacks and skimmed the forms, turning pages, and turning them back.

14

I studied him. Ian was so present, so focused, that I rarely had the chance to watch him without him watching me back. But now he was captivated by the reports and I had the chance to take in the straightness of his back, the way he distractedly narrowed his eyes as he considered what he was reading, and I had the chance to think about how much easier my life would be without this connection to him that I couldn't seem to shake. And how much duller.

"Willow Rogers," he said, looking up so quickly I felt as if I'd been caught watching porn in the library.

"What?"

"Willow Rogers was part of…" Ian thumbed through the reports. "Shit. Over half of these."

"Okay. And?"

"I thought they kept trying to reach me because they were worried about marketing St. Hilaire to tourists and wanted me to be their poster boy. But now I wonder if the reason wasn't something else."

Ian's expression was unusually distorted for someone who was always concerned about appearances. I would have loved to believe that this lapse in control, this letting down of his guard, was due to us spending more time together, but like everything with him, it was hard to know for sure.

"Something else like what?" I asked, but when he didn't answer and didn't meet my eyes and the room got perceptively colder, I felt my anger rise. "Ian?"

"Just keep your distance from her," he said, still looking away.

"That's gonna be a little difficult given that she's mentoring me, don't you think?"

He rubbed the back of his neck. "Maybe you can ask for a new mentor?"

"Who did you have in mind since she's pretty much the best here, now that you're…" I paused when Ian narrowed his eyes. "Anyhow, stop being so…cagey," I demanded, although I easily could have said, *Stop being so…Ian.* "There's no point to us trying to get anything done if you aren't going to be honest with me."

Ian tilted his head at an odd angle, which was something he'd just started to do. It was a ghost thing, I guessed, and the awkwardness sent shivers racing up my spine. "You want to play that card? Really?" His voice had an edge that did nothing to put me at ease. I could bleed out from the sharpness of that tone alone. "Then let's see your arm."

"What?" I flinched against my shirtsleeves. Ian always had a special way of making me feel exposed.

He turned away.

"Ian…" I started, searching for a way to avoid an argument. Lately, I'd lost my taste for battle. I looked for loopholes in Ian's argument, but we both knew I'd deliberately done the one thing I'd promised him I wouldn't do—continue to mix up potentially lethal batches of potentially lethal herbs as directed by a crumbling old book of my grandmother's, and inject them into my arm in order to have the ability to visit with ghosts without having to hold a proper séance.

There was no way of getting around the lie; that serum had been the only way I could talk to Ian in the beginning without the whole dog-and-pony show of an illegal formal séance, since I was technically under age for holding one on my own. I had a hard time believing he could hate it that much. "I don't want to fight with you."

"That isn't a denial," Ian observed, thankfully bringing his head back to a more normal angle.

"No," I admitted. "No, it isn't a denial. But it also has nothing to do with you."

I could see Ian's shoulders tense, feel the temperature drop in waves. Although he'd never done it, it was a fair bet he had enough energy or presence or whatever-the-hell it was to damage the house. It was amazing the amount of power a pissed-off ghost could harness.

Instead, Ian stuck his hands in the pockets of his painted-on dark jeans. "Right. It's your life," he said. "I'll keep in mind that it has nothing to do with me."

"Ian," I said, but he was gone before I got the word out.

The passive-aggressive disappearing-in-the-middle-of-an-argument thing drove me nuts, and he knew it.

I sat down and tried to parse the silence. Ian was a black hole of sound and vision, noise and expectation. It always took a few minutes after he left for me to return to myself, not unlike waking up from a realistic dream. Sometimes it took a few minutes before I could tell what was real and what wasn't.

My phone lit up with a reminder of the earlier voicemail. I played the message back and then played it again, oddly relieved.

The message had nothing to do with ghosts. Nothing even to do with St. Hilaire. The real world was calling, and for once, I was more than happy to answer.

chapter two
RUSS

If you looked at the building from the street level, it resembled many of the others in Buchanan. It had the same white, chalky brick. The same one-block-long, half-a-block-wide dimensions. It sat behind the same gray concrete sidewalk.

Yet, if you looked up, the building that housed the Buchanan Science Center was topped with a many-sided silver dome. I tried to avoid spending more time than I needed to in Buchanan. Actually, aside from the occasional trip to the train station to visit my father who worked as stationmaster, or to the consignment shop that was the only place I could afford to buy clothes, I rarely even stepped outside of the gates of St. Hilaire. I'd worked too hard to get there in the first place, and leaving never failed to remind me how out of place I was anywhere else.

But every time I did have to come to Buchanan, this building was the one that caught my eye. Like me, it also *felt* out of place, like something that had wandered out of St. Hilaire, gotten tired, and then stopped to rest before finding itself at home.

I pulled my eyes from the dome and scanned the street, looking for the car I was here to buy. The position as Youth Corps student leader came with a small stipend, and my father had insisted I use the money for a car rather than something useful like food or the winter heating bill. As much as I would have liked to turn down the offer, I'd found myself unexpectedly without transportation and looking down the barrel of an upstate New York winter. So, here I was.

I glanced at my phone again, opened the SellItQuick app, and brought up the ad. The listing gave the car's model year (fifteen years prior), the color (blue), the make (Chevy), and the condition (not dead). In the voicemail he'd left on my phone, the guy who owned the car had confirmed each of those items and not much more, but that was fine. I wasn't in a position to care what the car looked like, only that it drove.

On the street, Volvos sat next to Fords sat next to Hyundais. All of them were from model years in recent memory. None of them was anything my $500 would buy.

I walked past the Wickens Funeral Parlor, which gave St. Hilaire a large amount of business, and around to the building's front door and pushed the buzzer, then waited with my hands in the pocket of my dark coat. Maybe there was no car and I'd been played. Maybe I was going to end up stuffed in the freezer of some crazed serial killer.

Just as I turned to go, the door swung open.

"Hey, are you here for the car?" Out of breath, a boy around my age held open the door. With his pierced lip and his mostly buzzed dark-blond hair, his cuffed jeans and his wide smile, he was a boy unlike any St. Hilaire could have produced or would have known what to do with.

St. Hilaire was shadows on the wall and voices in your ear. It was incense and history and belief in the unbelievable. In St. Hilaire there were no coincidences, no impossibilities. To live there was to talk to the dead more than to the living. Everyone in town had been touched by spirits in one way or another. And it showed in the people who had chosen—and been allowed—to live there. Even those who typically didn't conform showed their individuality quietly, like me. Living in a town with one industry meant playing by a specific set of rules. Also, no one wanted to be on the Guild's bad side.

In contrast, Buchanan was school and work, grocery shopping and paying bills on time, mini golf and mowing the lawn. It was guys slapping each other on the back and parents taking screaming toddlers out of restaurants. It was a place where you could be whatever you wanted, wear whatever you wanted, look however you wanted, so long as what you wanted didn't include any kind of "weird occult practices."

The boy standing in front of me was all of that and none. He radiated something I could only describe as calm, a concept I was barely on speaking terms with.

"Come on in," he beckoned and then walked into the darkness. I glanced over my shoulder. I didn't expect something bad to happen necessarily; this was just more than I'd bargained for.

All I wanted to do was hand off the check, drive back to my house, and figure out how to appease Ian. Every time he disappeared, I worried he wasn't coming back. Then I worried he was coming back. It was a never-ending cycle.

I followed the boy through the door into a room of planets and shadows and pulled my coat tighter.

"Sorry." The boy flipped half of a panel of switches into the "on" position. "I like it dark."

Lit up, the room took on a different quality. It was magical, not in the way of St. Hilaire, which could veer quickly into creepy, but overwhelming beautiful in the way the sky was on a clear night. Breathtaking. Majestic. Disorienting.

Something inside me lit up in response.

"Asher," the boy said unasked, holding out his hand. "Asher Mullen."

I stared at his hand, unsure for a second what to do. "Russ Griffin," I answered, coming to my senses. I forced my hand out and felt a jolt of warmth from where the boy's palm touched mine. It was sometimes easy to forget that living people were warm.

"This is…" I searched the constellations above me for a word. I'd made a papier-mâché solar system for school when I was in second or third grade. My mother had hung it up in our dining room. In the rush to leave, I'd forgotten to take it when I'd moved to St. Hilaire from Chicago, and I hadn't realized that until now. That realization came with a sharp pang of loss even though I'd moved here years ago.

"Cool, right?" Asher asked, waiting, I guessed, for my approval.

I hadn't thought it was possible for Asher to smile any

broader, but somehow his angular face stretched to accommodate this new expression. I nodded again.

"There are certainly worse part-time jobs," Asher said.

This is how life was in Buchanan. This is how it had been in Chicago, where I had lived until I was fourteen. School, part-time jobs, summer breaks, vacations. All very different from my life in St. Hilaire.

"What do you do here?" I asked, surprised to hear the curiosity in my own voice. I knew what people in St. Hilaire said about me behind my back. I was aloof. Standoffish, even in a place where pretty much everyone was strange. We made our living talking to ghosts, so "strange" came with the territory. But honestly, I was fine hanging with the dead. It was the living I was inherently suspicious of and uncomfortable with. The dead had rarely betrayed my trust.

Asher twisted a black leather cord that hung around his neck. His right hand was decked out in a fascinating number of silver rings. "You know," he said. "The usual stuff. Selling tickets, taking tickets, checking the displays, running the planetarium."

"Planetarium," I repeated, as if I'd forgotten where I was.

"Yeah. I was getting ready to run through a new program demo. Wanna come see?"

My left thumb ran across a rough seam inside my coat pocket. There was a pile of paperwork waiting for me that, thanks to Ian, had to be reordered. There was a report I had to write for school on the Crimean War as well as sixteen unanswered emails in my inbox. Then there was the fall planting I'd yet to do in my dead grandmother's garden.

My right hand wandered up to the Guild pin on my collar.

I still wasn't used to the pin being there, and it gave me a jolt of uncharacteristic pride every time I remembered that I'd done what I'd set out to do, followed by a crash of repulsion when I reminded myself of what the organization had done. Was doing. Would keep doing if they weren't stopped.

I looked at Asher again. There were so many reasons to say no to his offer, but I didn't want to. I didn't binge-watch shows. I rarely had time to read anything that wasn't for school anymore. I didn't lose hours scouring the internet and watching people blow shit up in their backyards. I wanted something, even for fifteen minutes, that felt like a little bit of fun. "Yeah. I'd like to see it."

Asher led the way through the museum, which was empty if you didn't count the massive planets hanging overhead, and the mock Apollo rocket sitting in the corner, and the ropes on stands, which spoke to how many people usually waited, tickets in hand, to enter the exhibits during business hours.

I waited while he unlocked the heavy metal doors and then ushered me in. I settled myself into an unobtrusive end seat out of habit.

But Asher called out, "No, you need to sit two rows from the back, kind of in the middle. Otherwise, the distortion is too great."

I surveyed the empty room and moved to where he'd pointed. As I settled myself into the reclining seat, I was acutely aware that, even though I'd never bought one before, this was not the normal way to purchase a car.

Some sort of low classical music started up. I craned my neck and watched Asher fiddle with a bunch of knobs. The huge, round projector in the middle of the room swung on its axis. The lights began to dim.

Asher appeared at the end of my row before I knew he'd moved. "Scooch over," he instructed. I scooched and realized I was actually enjoying the illicit feeling of being in a place where no one was asking what the dead had to say.

The show was about the birth of black holes. I tilted my head back and tried to lose myself in the darkness, the projections, and the announcer's calming voice. I hadn't been in a planetarium since I'd gone on a seventh-grade trip back when I lived in Chicago. It had been a disaster. Something about the dark and the movement of the stars spinning overhead along with the all-too-comfortable chairs had lulled me into a half sleep.

I had heard a voice monotonously reading off a shopping list: one can of baked beans, a loaf of bread, three boxes of spaghetti. Another sang The Beatles' "Yellow Submarine" terribly off-key. While the other kids in my class watched the presentation and pinched the arm of the person sitting next to them and, in the case of the one couple who everyone knew would end up together, kissed themselves into oblivion, I'd put my head down and my hands over my ears and tried to block out the voices. It had worked for one blissful minute. And then it didn't, and I heard Molly Rawlings's screechy and all-too-alive voice from the seat next to me sneer, "Oh lord, Russ Griffin is freaking out. *Again*."

I'd taken my hands down and given her a withering look. But I'd also decided, in that moment, to stop pretending. I heard spirits. That was who I was. That was who I had been born to be. That was, I knew as I looked at her sneering face, who I wanted to be.

My grandmother had been a medium in St. Hilaire, a good one. And I knew my mother was lying when she claimed not to see the specters hovering around the Thanksgiving table as well as I could.

I also knew there was going to only be one place where I had a chance of fitting in. I wasn't looking to be happy. Happiness was a strange foreign thing, meant for others. I didn't need life to be easy; I just wanted mine to mean something.

I'd gone home and told my parents I couldn't keep pretending. More, I didn't want to. I'd recounted the times spirits had appeared to me, talked to me. I calmly laid out this badly kept secret I'd barely hidden from my parents.

My father had hugged me. My mother had stormed out of the room. Within a month, she'd deposited me and my father in St. Hilaire and stormed out of our lives.

"Hey, are you okay? You're shivering," Asher said. I hadn't realized the lights had come back on. "They keep the air cranked in here because of the crowds. It costs too much to keep turning on and off, so the temp's always set to glacial."

I glanced down at my arms, crossed on top of my wool coat, which was pulled ever-so-tightly around me. I forced my shoulders back and my arms to unlink. The movement was more difficult than it should have been. I'd learned to protect myself when I was still in Chicago. Sometimes that meant throwing a punch, and sometimes that meant being loyal to a friend, and sometimes that meant simply folding myself up quiet and close.

Also, ghosts made me cold.

But this was Buchanan, not St. Hilaire. It was a town of air-conditioning cranked too high and lines that snaked past barrier ropes. It was fast food and twenty-four-hour drugstores. Every town had its ghosts, but here, no one was expecting me to talk to them.

"I'm good," I said, trying to convince myself as much as Asher. Then I took a deep breath. "I'm good. So, let's see the car."

———

The banged-up blue Chevy was barely a car. But it would get me from one end of St. Hilaire to the other in the dead of a New York State winter. It would allow me to drive my father to work when his bum leg was bothering him. I could drive to the dollar store in Buchanan for staples rather than debating whether to spend the money on hand-milled soap from one of St. Hilaire's trendy shops or on socks without holes in them.

Asher opened the driver's door, which squealed in protest. "Go ahead, get in."

I started to explain I didn't need a test drive. I wasn't expecting the car to be comfortable, fast, or fuel-efficient. I simply wanted it to be faster than walking. Drier than walking. Less muddy. Less freezing cold. With a trunk I could throw my backpack in, so I didn't need to lug all my books everywhere I went.

But I got in anyhow. Placed my foot on the gas, hands on the sun-peeled wheel. Moved the rearview mirror around. "Looks fine," I said and turned the key. The ignition caught and no warning lights came on. Nothing in the sound said, "will soon be breaking down on the interstate."

Asher walked around to the passenger's side and slid across the cracked vinyl.

I was suddenly aware of the blank check in my pocket. Five hundred dollars. I couldn't get over having that amount to spend on something as frivolous as a car when my legs worked perfectly well and when St. Hilaire was easily walked from one end to the other in less than an hour. "You said five hundred, right?"

Asher nodded. "Right" and then he said quietly, "I've turned down three higher offers already."

My hopes deflated as I realized I'd already started to think of the car as my own. "Why did you turn them down? If you don't really want to sell—"

"It isn't that," Asher interrupted. He sucked his lip ring thoughtfully. I wondered if it hurt. "Look, you're from St. H., right?"

I nodded. A tendril of anxiety stretched up in my stomach. *Please don't ask me to contact someone for you,* I thought. *All I want to do is buy a car.*

"Yeah, okay. So, this summer..." Asher's voice went low and conspiratorial when he leaned in toward me wide-eyed. "I had a reading done."

I surprised myself by laughing. "It's okay. I won't tell anyone."

He scrubbed his ringed fingers through the long part of his hair and winced. "Man, sorry, that was rude of me."

Everyone in St. Hilaire was aware of the reputation the town had in the outside world. I'd heard the phrases *New Age yahoos* and *airy-fairy hippies* thrown around on a regular basis, but it didn't escape us that the people doing the mocking were some of the same people we kept in business during the summer when they housed and fed and sold souvenirs to our customers.

Impulsively, I asked, "Who did your reading?" which was a question I instantly regretted; it was similar to asking someone in therapy who their shrink was.

Asher turned in his seat and leaned back against the passenger's-side window. I thought, from the way his eyes darkened, there might be some magnitude to his words, but he simply said, "I don't remember." He looked down at his right hand and spun a couple of the silver rings. Moons and stars. Ropes and fleur-de-lis. His fingers were long, his nails manicured. "It was a woman. Wearing a long, flowered skirt." He stopped and shrugged.

I couldn't help but laugh. "That pretty much describes most of the town. Where was it? The spiritual center? The archives? Someone's house?"

Asher kept spinning the rings. "It was the last day of summer. The gates were open, and I came in to wander around. See what all the fuss was about. The woman stopped me on the street. The town was about to close so maybe she took pity on me or something." He paused and stared at me as if he was waiting for my reaction, but I wasn't sure what he was expecting. Finally, he said, "If you don't have to be anywhere, do you want to come back in?"

Did I? I wasn't sure why he was asking. I wasn't sure why my answer to his question was a resounding, definite "yes" and that intrigued me, so I nodded and followed Asher through the front door. But instead of going back to the planetarium, he led me up a ladder to the roof. In one direction, the setting sun bounced off the spires of St. Hilaire. In the other, the flat roofs of Buchanan sat, concrete and industrial.

Asher walked to the edge and sat on the dark shingles, legs hanging over the edge; I followed his lead and settled down next to him, my legs folded in front of me.

One by one, the streetlights of Buchanan began to flicker on. In the half-light, Asher said, "Last summer. The day I got the reading. The guy at Hub City Books told me there was a big year-end festival going on and to check it out before the gates closed, so I wandered over. I wasn't planning on getting a reading done or anything. But this woman came up to me and offered to do the reading for free, so I figured there was no harm. Anyhow, before I left, she told me I was going to have to part with something important to me in order to get something that would end up being *more* important, and my car is really all I have, so…"

"And you just went along with the whole thing?" I asked. But I knew what it was like. St. Hilaire on festival day was a glorious circus, an all-hands-on-deck celebration of all things paranormal. It would be hard not to get sucked into it if you'd never been to town before.

Asher shrugged. "My parents are…scientists. That's why we're here. In Buchanan."

I searched Asher's words for an answer to my question but didn't find one, so I waited.

"They spend all of their time watching where they're walking and questioning things," Asher said. "I prefer to look up." I followed Asher's light-brown eyes toward the sky. Somehow, it had gotten dark. I could make out the half-moon, fuzzy around the edges and cratered. It made me wonder if I was missing anything in St. Hilaire and then decided it didn't matter. My father was at work and no one else would be looking for me. Honestly, there was no one living in St. Hilaire who would wonder where I was. I felt detached from almost everything and, at the moment, that didn't bother me.

"I had some questions, so what the hell, right? Life is for taking chances." Asher leaned back. His legs still dangled over the edge, but his back was flat on the concrete roof. He looked more relaxed than I'd probably ever felt.

"Did you get your answers?" I asked.

Asher raised himself on his elbows. He shared a lower-wattage version of the smile I'd first seen. "I'm still trying to figure that out. But she was insistent about me selling Orion. That's the car's name. And she told me to make sure he went to the right person."

"Orion?" I asked. "Am I the right person?" I ran the tip of a shoelace through my fingers. I'd scoured SellItQuick for two weeks before I found a listing for something I could afford that didn't sound like a scam. If this deal fell through, it might be snowing before I had something to drive, and in upstate New York, snow could be fierce.

Asher's eyes swept over me. His stare didn't feel heavy and intrusive like Ian's. It was hopeful, as if Asher was looking for the best in me. I wondered what he saw.

He smiled. "I think you might be the right person. Do you promise not to drive him too fast? And make sure you give him time to warm up in the winter. It's supposed to be bad this year."

I nodded, surprised to feel myself smiling back.

"You should take him for a spin first. Make sure I'm not taking advantage of you or anything."

My cheeks warmed. "Nah, I'm good," I said, and reached into my pocket for the check. My fingers latched around an errant piece of sage. I'd intended to spiritually cleanse the car after I bought it. Now I was having second thoughts about how necessary that would be.

I'd never been able to put my process as a medium into words, but I felt vibrations when spirits were near. I'd also learned to listen to my instincts. And now they were saying that Asher was unlike anyone I'd met, even if I couldn't figure out why or how. No, this car wouldn't need to be cleansed of negativity at all.

"So, there's one more thing I should show you." Asher stood and stretched. Then he held out a hand, offering to help me up. I hesitated and took his hand. Asher was slow to let go. He said, "Look down."

It took a minute to know what I was looking *for*. Then it took a minute to know what I was looking *at*.

The surface of the car twinkled in the waning night. The effect was that someone had poured a bucket of stars over the hood. White on the blue surface. Moving as if they were in a sea. The sight was disorienting in the same way as the planetarium show. I was aware of myself swaying. Suddenly shaky.

Asher reached out and put a hand on my arm.

I wasn't typically fond of being touched. Certainly not by people I didn't know well and definitely not by boys from Buchanan.

But Asher's grip on my arm helped steady me in more ways than one, and I didn't pull away.

I blinked hard and looked up at the sky, but the stars were as bright as the lights on the car. Just as disorienting. It was difficult for a moment to tell up from down.

"I think I have to sit," I said, lowering myself back to the roof's surface.

Asher sat as well and sucked on his lip ring in an intimate way that made me look away.

When I looked back, his eyes reflected the streetlights or maybe the light was from the stars. Either way, it was oddly unsettling and comforting at the same time.

"Can I ask you a question?"

I nodded, feeling drugged.

"Did you always know you could…" He stopped and reworded his question. "Did you always know what you could do?" Asher rose to his knees and looked over the edge of the roof, down at the car, not at me as if he knew that would help. He spoke carefully, his face turned to the spire of Eaton Hall. "I'm assuming since you live there…"

"Yes," I interrupted before I lost my nerve. "To both of those."

"Oh," Asher said and sat back down.

I waited for the questions that always followed, which were some of the reasons I rarely left St. Hilaire. *Really, man? You can talk to ghosts? You sure you aren't just nuts?* As if those two things were mutually exclusive.

"It's a good thing you grew up there, then," he said.

"But I didn't…" I started. "I didn't move here until a few years ago."

Asher's face softened. "That must have been hard. Before. When you were a kid," he said gently. "Everyone must have wondered what was going on with you."

"What?" My chest tightened. Coming from someone else, the words could have been weapons. But Asher was welding them in a different way. As if he was asking a question he already knew the answer to and wanted me to know he knew.

"Kids can suck," he said with a forced smile before I had to explain anything. "Was your family cool with what you could do? Are these things hereditary?"

I closed my eyes and imagined I could smell the sage in my pocket, although that was impossible. The idea of it was comforting, though. "My father was cool. *Is* cool. He runs the train station."

"Tall dude with glasses?"

I snapped my eyes open. "Yeah."

"My parents take the train into New York City all the time."

Could I get away without mentioning my mother? Perhaps I could change the subject and talk about the weather or ask what high school seniors in Buchanan studied while I was busy debating why thirty-five was the most common age for a spirit to take on regardless of how old the person had been when they died.

But of course, Asher asked, "What about your mom?"

I stared at him, trying to find a way to avoid answering. "She was less than cool with it."

Asher raised an eyebrow, recognizing there was more to the story, but he didn't press. "Yeah. I'd guess that happens sometimes."

It wasn't often I wished I was the type of person to spill

my secrets on command. To the contrary, I prided myself on being someone who could appreciate the value of a well-kept confidence. So why did I feel compelled to tell this boy I'd just met about my mother's abandonment? About the intense love I shared with my father? About how much I missed the grandmother I knew more through her notebooks than through any time I'd spent with her.

And about how I was trying to carve out some new sort of day-to-day life on my own now that my best friend, Dec Hampton, had left and moved to New York City along with his girlfriend, Annie.

Without thinking, I added, "She was a medium. *Is*, I guess, assuming being a medium still counts when you don't use a talent you have. She grew up in St. Hilaire. Coming back was her worst nightmare, so she opted out."

"I'm sorry," Asher said. "Are you in touch?"

I looked back up at the same sky she might have been looking at wherever she was, and answered, "Not often enough for it to count."

Asher stretched out on his back next to me again. This time, his black T-shirt pulled up enough to show a tanned strip of flesh reflecting in the moonlight. "You know," he said. "The footprints left by the Apollo astronauts will be there for centuries, since the moon has no wind."

Then, before I could wonder what that had to do with my mother, Asher continued. "Some things don't change. People either. You need to keep going in spite of it."

I glanced over at him, trying to be critical. Who was this boy to think he understood anything of my life? He was from

Buchanan, of all places. But instead of criticism, other feelings welled up, and I tore my glance away and back toward the stars. There was no ending, and knowing that made me feel small, in a good way. As though my worries, my fears were meaningless in the vastness of the universe.

I understood enough about astronomy to know that the light I saw was mostly from stars that had died centuries before. That understanding settled into me with a crash of perspective of how little I meant in the bigger picture.

Without warning, Asher sat up and pulled a set of keys and the car's title out of his bag and shoved them in my direction. "Take care of him, okay?"

"Oh." Confused, I wondered what the keys were for and then remembered the car. I took the key ring and dug disappointedly into my pocket for the blank check. "Yeah, let me…"

Asher shook his head. "No. You keep the money. Just…I don't know. Do me a favor sometime or something?"

"What? No." I cataloged all of the things I could do with five hundred dollars. There was some work that needed to be done on the porch that was probably more than I could handle on my own and more than Dad had time for. There would be insurance on the car and gas to pay for. I would need a new suit for Guild events.

Still, I didn't like to be on the wrong end of a favor. I was comfortable dropping everything to sort out a problem for a friend or complete a work task, even if I found it objectionable. Self-sacrifice reminded me that my mother had been wrong when she'd left. Owing someone else was something I was unfamiliar with. Something I avoided.

"It's a car," I said grimly. "I'm not going to take your car."

Asher stood and offered me a hand up. "That's okay. I have your number. I promise I'll call and let you know if I ever need to borrow it or anything. But I walk to work and don't have anywhere I need to go."

I took his hand and stared at the way our fingers sat on top of each other, transfixed by the warmth of his skin. The whole encounter had set me off-kilter. "Yeah," I said. "Let me know."

I allowed Asher to pull me to my feet. I stumbled down the stairs and, dismissed, I left.

chapter three

ASHER

I closed up the planetarium and took the long way home through Arbor Field.

It was a perfect night. The power lines vibrated and sparked with electricity, sending shocks all around me. The stars were frenetic; I could feel them humming. They were a symphony of hydrogen and helium, burning from the inside, sending their light far into the future.

You are made of star stuff, I whispered under my breath. It was something my sister, Mari, used to tell me. I spun around with my arms out, feeling connected to everything. Feeling connected to her.

Arbor Field divided our subdivision from the higher-end one next to it. Every once in a while, the trains would come by and fill the air with the noise of wheels and mechanics. But now the field was silent aside from the *crack, crack, crack* of the current.

I needed the silence and the energy in equal measure.

I needed to recharge before I went home to deal with my parents.

I needed to talk to my sister.

I took off my jacket, balled it up, and eased down onto the ground, pushing the fabric under my head to use as a pillow. Then I stretched out and looked up, up, up, my eyes tracing the stars in Orion, the hunter. As a kid, Orion had been my favorite constellation since it was the easiest to find. And because you could use it as a compass to find other dimmer constellations.

It was my touchstone.

Tonight, though, Orion felt like a stranger. I closed my eyes.

"I think I did it, Mari," I said, my voice barely above a whisper. After all, there was no need to shout to people who had died. "I think I did what they wanted."

My sister never answered. But I believed she was listening. I *hoped* she was listening. Somewhere.

The power lines above me buzzed and popped. I opened my eyes. Tiny orange sparks jumped from one line to the other.

"I guess I don't actually need a car," I said to the sky. "And I got lucky, really. I know Russ Griffin—that's his name, the guy from St. Hilaire—will take care of Orion."

I was good at reading people. Always had been. And reading people who thought they hung out around ghosts came particularly easy to me, which was good because my parents cultivated the skill. As the creators of the TV show *Ghost Killers*, it was a skill they demanded I learn early on when they realized a child could more easily charm the owners of the houses or churches or libraries that were the focus of their episodes. Being a kid, I could ask the questions they had to avoid. Poke in rooms and beg forgiveness. I was quiet and observant, and at the time, I'd relished blending into the background. But most of all, I had good instincts about people.

And those instincts told me Russ Griffin was smart. And focused. Being near him was like being near a power source. Like being here. It reminded me of that big ball in the science center you touch to make all your hair stand up. Walking next to him felt similar to walking into St. Hilaire. Strange and alien. Mysterious and chaotic.

But there was something else. His pain resonated in the pit of my stomach. I recognized the loneliness in his eyes because I lived with the same feeling of being unmoored and looking for a true place, a true person, to connect with.

"I haven't had that since before you died, Mari. That connection."

The wind blew around me and I added, "I have to admit I'm curious about him. I think he's the real deal. I know that sounds odd, but it's true." Then, because it was my sister and I'd never kept anything from her, I added, "And I know this sounds stupid, but it kind of feels like I've known him for longer than just today."

That happened sometimes. I'd know someone for months and not know how to talk to them, and then I'd meet someone and feel like I'd been around them all my life.

"The thing is," I said to the sky, and to the dead sister who

39

might or might not hear me. "The thing is, I'd like to think Russ Griffin is someone I could be friends with if things shake out the right way. I have to be really careful."

My words were only a scratch on the surface of what I felt. But I was pretty sure words weren't what was important. Even when she was alive, Mari could always see through to the heart of me. She would know how rare it was for me to meet someone I thought I could be friends with. That I wanted to be friends with.

"I didn't know what to do, Mari. I wanted to help Mom and Dad with this show, and I couldn't figure out how else to pull it off. I posted the car for sale on SellItQuick and turned down offers until someone from St. Hilaire answered my ad. I thought I got lucky when someone my age called, someone… He's really cute, Mari," I admitted and felt myself blush.

I sat up and put my jacket back on. The fabric had absorbed the chill from the ground. "I don't feel so lucky now, Mari. Mom and Dad aren't going to be happy about this."

I looked back at the sky, hoping for a sign to tell me which way to turn, or to tell me my sister was listening, or something. But all I saw were dead stars and a bright moon and a faint glimmer of the Milky Way.

As long as I could remember, I'd been told to stay away from the type of people who made their money by preying on grief. My parents had devoted their careers to trying to show how everything worked behind the scenes and how it was possible, with just a few leading questions, to make someone feel as though you knew things about them. They hoped that people would realize it wasn't that these sham mediums were being fed answers "from the great beyond" and that lots of things could be done with tricks of light.

"I don't think Russ is like that," I said under my breath as I stood up. No matter how I turned the image of him around in my mind, Russ Griffin didn't match up to the picture I had of the people my parents had been warning me about all my life.

chapter four
RUSS

It had felt surprisingly good to drive the Chevy home from Buchanan last night and park it under our rusty carport. Still, I woke slightly dizzy and out of sorts. My mind was a jumble of questions. *What the hell just happened?* pretty much summed up most of them.

I took a quick shower and then headed out to sift through the overgrown weeds in the backyard and my grandmother's garden. The area behind the house was as it was when my father and I moved here. The plants on this side of the fence, nearest to the house, were common cooking herbs: basil of four varieties, thyme, sage, verbena, dill, rosemary. The scent reminded me of my grandmother's chicken soup, which was filled with dill, and her roast potatoes, which she sprinkled with rosemary.

As I walked further into the dark and farther into the messy wood, I came to the place where Grandma had planted vervain, dandelion, and rowan. These were supposed to repel the stronger spirits, but as Ian had free rein of my house, I had my doubts as to how well they actually worked. These plants were the tools of our trade, though. It was a safe bet that most gardens in St. Hilaire contained at least some of these.

I had to dig further back and into the older growth before I found what I looking for. These plants were buried deep in tangled brush. These were ones you only found if you knew where to look and would only recognize if you studied further on your own than the standard classes at St. Hilaire High would take you.

Soon after my father and I had moved into my grandmother's empty house, I'd discovered a blue notebook under a loose floorboard. Filled with notes and recipes for serums she used to contact ghosts without a formal séance, the book had changed my life, allowing me to contact Ian without much effort, and even now, I wasn't sure if that change was for better or worse.

As I walked, I inhaled the scent of wormwood, which played a large part in many of my grandmother's recipes. I'd devoted more than a little time to researching the plant. Its primary use was in alcoholic drinks such as vermouth and absinthe. In large quantities, it was rumored to cause dizziness, seizures, hallucinations, paralysis, and even death. Grandma's recipes didn't include large quantities. Somehow, she seemed to have figured out the sweet spot between "doing nothing" and "doing too much."

The leaves rustled with memories, and the smell was both

medicinal and floral in a way I'd never encountered anywhere else. It was a scent I dreamt of as a kid and which had always calmed me, excited me, and made me miss my grandmother fiercely and my mother marginally. It spoke of heady possibility.

I collected a number of leafy bunches, pulled out the worst of the weeds, and then moved the plants back and forth simply so I could smell their aroma and remember.

When I got back to the house, I followed one of my grandmother's recipes to create a thick, noxious tea that was difficult to swallow until it wasn't. The sharp, earthy flavor quickly gave way to a sort of blissful euphoria that did a good job of making me forget my questions about what had happened in Buchanan and pretty much everything else.

The next thing I knew, something was buzzing in my ear. No, not buzzing. The sound was more like that of leaves crunching underfoot. Or paper. That was it. Paper being crumpled.

I rolled over carefully and opened one eye to see my desk chair spinning. Then I regretted moving.

"What are you doing?" I mumbled in that general direction.

Ian pushed off the corner of the desk with a boot and spun to face me. "Keeping up on current events, Griffin," he said, waving a half-crumpled newspaper in his hand. "You might want to try it."

I pulled myself up. The inside of my head sparked like lightning. I lay back down. "What is it now?"

Ian slid his hands into the pockets of his pressed black jeans. He was dressed, as always, as if he were about to head to a nightclub, one where he'd breeze past the bouncers on a wave of being Ian Mackenzie. He looked, as always, ready for conquest.

And, as always, seeing him made my chest tighten. He glanced down at me with his glacier-blue eyes and then slipped into the bed, pushing me aside with his elbow.

He settled in and pointed at an article. "Have you ever actually watched *Ghost Killers*?"

"No," I said, turning to avoid falling off the edge of the bed. "And since when do they have Netflix where you are?"

He half laughed. "You're funny. But seriously, I think you're going to have a problem."

I glanced at him. "What sort of problem am *I* going to have?"

Ian pointed wordlessly at the paper. I kept my eyes on him. Everything between us was always some sort of damned quiz or competition, and I wasn't in a losing mood. This time I was going to wait him out.

"Okay, look," he said finally. "This show isn't playing around. They even won an Emmy for some episode they did about a college theater that was supposed to be haunted, but really just had a great crop of tech kids that year who wired the place up. And they've apparently had 'great success' debunking the entire idea that ghosts exist."

"But the idea of them debunking St. Hilaire is obviously bullshit," I said to the ghost who was summarizing the article for me. The buzzing in my head morphed into a dull pain. I glanced at the nightstand where my mug sat and wondered if there was any more tea in it or if I'd drunk the whole cup.

"Well, obviously," Ian said. He tossed the paper across the room, and it landed in my ficus. "Apparently they've petitioned the Guild to be allowed into town to film here."

I tried to focus on what he was saying. *Ghost Killers*. Filming in St. Hilaire. Debunking ghosts. The whole thing didn't add up. "What are you worried about? The Guild is never going to allow that. The whole town could go under if something goes wrong."

"Again, obviously." Ian ran his hand over the edge of my pillowcase, smoothing down a rough seam. "So, what are you going to do about it?"

I shrugged, wishing I could go back to sleep. "I don't know. It doesn't sound like I'm going to have to do *anything*. Besides, this is something for the Guild's leadership to take up. I'm on paperwork duty, remember?"

Ian opened his mouth, no doubt to put up some sort of fight, but then my phone buzzed with Frank Sinatra singing "I Don't Stand a Ghost of a Chance with You." It was my ringtone for the Guild's main number; my friend, Dec, had set the song up as a joke, and that was enough of a reason for me not to change it.

"Hell," I said.

"Duty calls," Ian replied as he shoved me out of bed.

chapter five
WILLOW

I closed my eyes and listened to the dull rumble of the voices of the dead.

The clamor poured up from beneath St. Hilaire's streets and yards and houses. It sang to me like a chorus. Calling to me. Asking for my assistance. Asking to be freed. My blood rose in response.

A strong breeze rattled the window. I could see half of the city from my room on the top floor of Eaton Hall. I'd heard it was thought to be an attractive town, filled as it was with large colorful houses and well-kept lawns. But thankfully, that superficial facade was countered by a sort of wildness, an energy that flowed beneath the foundations and sang with the voices of history. This energy was reserved for those of us who could sense it, and the wildness deserved more respect than the silly fairy doors and the insipid wind chimes that filled the Buchanan gift shops and littered many of the lawns.

It was from underneath that the voices came. That place between the worlds where the dead were trapped. Where their power called out to mine to free them from their purgatory. And if I liberated a bit of their power in the process of freeing them? Well, that was the cost of doing business.

Outside, most of the houses boasted brown Guild flags beating against their flagpoles. It was an old custom, these flags. A custom from close to the town's creation in 1870 before the gates were put up. A custom from a time when knowing who was on your side was deemed important.

It's entirely possible that part hasn't changed.

I'd come across descriptions of the flags while reading minutes from the town's old council meetings, held back before there was even a Guild. And I impressed upon Father that in these uncertain times, we could benefit by identifying those who were true to the cause.

And by elimination, who was not.

It was the first step toward returning to a time when those who lived in St. Hilaire were the strongest, the most devoted, the most talented, the most dedicated. The most powerful.

Instead of what they'd become, which was the softest, the most commercial.

The time for a welcoming, quaint town filled with mediums had passed.

It was time to consolidate power. The more power we had, the thinner the wall between our world and the spirit world would be. The more power we had, the easier it would be for us to cut the ties that spirits had to our world, to free them.

The time had come for us to stop serving the living and return to our true purpose.

I turned away from the window, flipped my mask down and poured a bottle of acid onto the surface of the yew wood on the table in front of me. The pattern, an intertwined SHG, the guild symbol, began to take form as the acid ate deep grooves into the surface.

I allowed myself a minute to envision the liquid cutting a path through Ian Mackenzie's pretty face, dissolving his flesh, making him cry out in pain in regret for a life wasted. And more, for a death wasted.

Then I forced myself to refocus. It wouldn't do to get distracted and caught up in fantasy.

I'd been fine-tuning my spirit cabinet for the better part of a year, far before Ian's rumored return. I'd procured the pieces I was adding to the original and began my work around the same time I was paired by the Guild with Colin, Ian's eager puppy of a brother. *Ironic.* I didn't have to spend much time with Colin, but Father was certain that somewhere in his genes lived the talent that Ian possessed.

The concept of the cabinet was simple. So simple it almost seemed destined to fail. But the process made more sense than anything I'd heard since I'd first been deposited in St. Hilaire as a precocious five-year-old who had only spoken to ghosts and never to the living. That changed when I met Father, who had sheltered me and tutored me and taught me the ways of the mediums of St. Hilaire. I learned everything he had to teach by the time I turned ten. And then I sought out the old books and taught myself the rest.

Including this.

Spirit cabinets worked on the concept that ghosts couldn't exist without the freedom to haunt. Since ghosts stayed around to accomplish a goal, a contained ghost would, with no opportunity to work toward that goal, simply cease to exist. Their spirits would move on. They would be freed.

The process offered perks I'd never read about. Bonuses that might exist only for the strongest of mediums. Mediums like me. The most notable of this was the transfer of power from the ghost inside the cabinet to the person controlling the process.

When I began building the cabinet, it also seemed useful to learn to create an enclosure that would ensure ghosts would go back to where they were meant to be permanently. Just in case such a thing was ever needed.

And now, not for the first time, it was needed.

Ian Mackenzie should have stayed where *he* was meant to be.

Unlike his brother, Ian was elusive. Powerful. Hungry. Or at least he had been when he was alive. It was easy to leap to the idea that those qualities had only been augmented by his death.

My opportunities would be certain yet limited. Still, the thought drove me to work through the night, when only once did I allow myself to dwell on the pure waste of it all. Ian and I could have rebuilt St. Hilaire into a glorious and commanding sanctuary for powerful mediums. We could have created a force strong enough to change history. To change the world.

Of course, that had never been what Ian had wanted. Oh, he'd played with power. He'd laughed at it. He'd *owned* it. He'd just never embraced it. He never saw, as I did, that our futures could amount to so much more than what we had here. He never saw we had a responsibility to unite with other mediums across the world. To form a coalition and stake our rightful places in the world. To free the ghosts from their pain, their connections to the living.

He was a fool.

He'd died. He'd been safe. I'd called for him all summer to make sure he was really gone. And then he came back.

He shouldn't have come back.

———

I hated meetings. No matter the validity of the topic, it amounted to bureaucratic blather.

Which might have been one of the reasons I hadn't been invited to this one discussing the *Ghost Killers* TV show.

Although that didn't keep me from listening at the door to the Guild's boardroom.

"Certainly, there would have to be compensation," Father said to the assembled leadership. It took no imagination to picture the glint in his eye.

St. Hilaire was having problems with money. Or rather, the town was having problems with having no money.

Father and a couple of additional high-placed Guild members had even tried to solve their problems by calling on the ghost of Sarahlyn Beck. Sarahlyn had lived in St. Hilaire during a most prosperous time; she even funded the creation of Eaton Hall. Rumor had it that she was an alchemist who was able to change copper into gold, and the Guild thought that was exactly what they needed in order to save St. Hilaire.

The plan hadn't gone well. The Guild's greed had lost them Sarahlyn's trust. The money disappeared. Quality mediums had died under mysterious circumstances.

"How much money are we talking about?" I heard Judi Davis ask. "Because it seems as if the risks might be larger than any check they're likely to write."

A low rumble went through the room. Father gaveled the table.

Someone else asked, "What risks are we actually talking about?"

"Now, certainly there *is* the risk the show will catch us on a bad day," I heard Father answer.

"You mean their stunt will end with our town closing in disgrace?" Judi asked. "All it's going to take is us having an off night on national television. Come on, Clive. How many mediums did we have trying to contact Ian Mackenzie this summer and look where that got us."

I coughed and took a step back, holding my breath long enough to ensure no one had heard me. Then I stepped back up to the door.

"Underage mediums." I heard someone say.

"Well, we'll need all hands on deck to do this. Though I still can't imagine that no spirits will show up."

"We can force their parents to sign off."

"Yeah, but with or without the kids, that still leaves it all up to chance. What happens if we can't get a ghost to show? I'm not sure a bunch of skeptics with cameras are going to set the right tone for a successful séance."

"Shame there isn't a way to trap one of them or something, just for however long it takes to make a statement."

"Yeah if you figure out how to do that…"

"But even if we could, let's be real. Melody Thorne isn't going to make us look cutting edge, and she hasn't exactly been in top form lately anyhow. The last time she appeared at a community event, she was positively see-through. So, what do you want? Some transparent specter who is going to do nothing more than knock on a wall or ring a bell?"

I stepped back into the hallway and headed to the stairs that led to my loft on the top floor. Guild leadership was never going to agree on anything. For every person who thought the money *Ghost Killers* would pay them to shoot in St. Hilaire would save the town, another thought the risk of the town being humiliated was too great.

In the end, it was a lose-lose scenario for St. Hilaire.

Which could very well amount to a win-win for me.

chapter six
RUSS

Eaton Hall was buzzing. The building housed everything official in St. Hilaire. Office space for the Guild, séance and reading rooms, the town archives, a paranormal library, an auditorium, and even a recreation space in the basement.

The old door creaked as I opened it; a cracked plaque with the town rules slapped against the wood as it swung closed.

"Hey, hold up," a voice behind me called.

Colin Mackenzie came rushing toward the door, arms filled with books. He was dressed head to toe in green, the swirled letters SHG, which functioned as the Guild logo, embossed in brown onto his shirt. The features Ian wore so well were muted in Colin. His cheekbones were less sharp. His eyes were less blue. His bearing was less confident and more volatile.

I was glad we'd never been at odds.

"Doing a little light reading?" I asked.

"Actually, I've been writing some research reports for Clive Rice," Colin said proudly. Ian had been the strongest young medium St. Hilaire had ever seen because, somehow, he'd managed to hoard all of the paranormal talent in his family. Meanwhile Colin and their youngest and most unstable brother, Alex, had no talent to speak of, but Colin wasn't going to let that stop him from making himself indispensable.

Everyone assumed it was his ceaseless devotion to being the Guild's lapdog that was the reason he was allowed to stay in town once his mother and brother had been forced to leave. But there was also the rumor that Colin had been paired with Willow by the Guild as part of their super-creepy keep-the-medium-line-pure campaign, designed to match mediums up in hopes that they'd have kids who could talk to ghosts and would strengthen the power of St. Hilaire. The hope was, I guess, that somehow Ian's talents might trickle down through his brother in the way that talents sometimes skip a generation.

I held the door as Colin went through, and while I didn't call him a name-dropping suck-up out loud, I was surprised he couldn't hear me thinking it. "What have you been researching?" I asked, hoping Colin would be so impressed with himself that confidentiality might go out the window.

He stopped and turned toward me. For a second, something about the way the light streamed through the dirty leaded windows caught the dust of hundreds of years of books and ghosts and made the Mackenzie family resemblance unusually apparent. I shook my head and blinked hard. Colin's features re-formed back into themselves.

Colin edged me over to the wall and said conspiratorially, "They're going to tell you anyhow, so I guess I can give you a heads-up. There was an article…"

"In the *Sentinel*," I said. "I know." I had to tread carefully. Despite the fact Willow knew, I had no idea whether Colin was aware Ian and I were in touch, much less that his brother was basically haunting me. They'd never been close—far from it—and I didn't need any of the Mackenzie brothers on my bad side. It was a fair bet that telling Colin about Ian reading that same *Sentinel* article to me from my bed would send him over the edge and obliterate our finely honed detente.

"Yeah, *Ghost Killers*. Here? Can you believe it?" From the furrowed expression on his face, he wasn't a fan.

I shrugged at the shock of finding something we agreed on. The whole show kind of rubbed me the wrong way as well, seeing as how it basically told me that I and everyone I loved were frauds.

"I heard they aren't really bringing the show back. This is a one-off and then the couple who are hosting it are getting a divorce or something," Colin said in a stage whisper. "This is their last hurrah before they take the show off the air for good. I've heard this thing is going to be promoted everywhere."

"What's *their* reaction?" I asked, pointing upward toward the executive offices. It would be nice to know ahead of time what I was in for.

"You'll have to ask upstairs," he said reverentially. "They've been meeting all day."

Apparently, I'd pushed my luck and Colin obviously remembered his duty to team, city, and Guild. "Right."

I climbed the stairs two at a time but hesitated outside of Clive Rice's office. From the day I'd first moved to St. Hilaire as an admittedly whacked-out fourteen-year-old who had no idea what he was getting himself into until a few months ago when I learned how terrifying the Guild could be, I'd been in awe of Clive Rice and the organization as a whole.

The Guild members were accomplished mediums who embodied the entire history of the town.

They were everything I thought I wanted to be.

Even now it was difficult not to be enticed by the thick iron door and the syrupy scent of incense. The walls were filled with over a century of history, and that filled me with awe.

But everything had changed when I found out this same group of people had called on the ghost of Sarahlyn Beck to create gold for them and then allowed my best friend's parents to be killed in order to keep their greedy plan hidden.

Now I wanted to be something different. Something better. I wanted the Guild to be something better too.

I got that even though they'd given me a position of power, I was viewed as a necessary annoyance. All Clive Rice wanted was to get to Ian, and I was the most direct way to do that. Still, the Guild had named me student leader of the Youth Corps, which meant they were stuck with me at least through the school year. Or until Ian and I found a way to make them pay for what they'd done and put new leadership in place.

My position allowed me to bypass the reception area and head straight to the hallway of the executive offices. I knocked on Clive Rice's door, and when he called me in, I entered a room filled with plush carpet, gold lamps, and deep sofas. I always had an urge to point out that if St. Hilaire was supposedly in financial trouble, the furniture in this wing of the building alone would be worth enough to bail the town out. But of course, I kept that comment to myself.

Still, when I ran the Guild…

"Mr. Griffin. Come in and have a seat," Clive Rice directed in a way that made it clear he was used to being obeyed. He was a small, short man, who looked as though he'd stepped through a time portal in his tweed jackets and vests. But there was something unnerving about him, something I'd never quite been able to put my finger on.

I went in and had a seat.

"I'm hoping you don't mind if I cut to the chase. I've learned some disturbing news," Rice said.

"Is this about the *Sentinel* article?" I asked.

He squinted and then seemed to think better of whatever he was going to say because his face softened. "I'm sure you're aware of the difficult situation that such a show as this poorly named *Ghost Killers* might place us in, should things not go precisely to plan. What if no spirits choose to show up at the precise moment that the show is filming? What if we get some infernal prankster who prefers to simply move things around? Additionally, presenting St. Hilaire as a type of circus sideshow is not something that is going to further the cause of our town, the Guild, or frankly, yourself if you hope to have a future here. I don't believe I need to spell that out further. Am I correct?"

"Sir?" My neck went hot under my collar. "Can't you simply

tell them you won't let them into town?" I crossed my fingers behind my back. It was a stupidly useless superstition, but I would have rubbed a rabbit's foot for luck if it meant I could escape the conversation that was no doubt coming.

"Well, yes, yes, I could. But think for a moment how that would make us look in the eyes of the public. They would think we had something to hide. That we are unwilling or, worse, *unable* to address this show's accusations. No, I'm afraid we can't do anything to make it look as though we're running scared."

"Wait. We're really going to hold a séance? And let them film it?" I asked, shocked at actually hearing the words out loud.

He riffled through some papers on his desk and scowled. "Guild leadership has met to discuss that, but to be honest, I'm not sure I see another option. Plus, there are other issues. Issues of the financial sort to consider."

Of course, everything came back to money. It was always money these days where the Guild was concerned.

I waited. While it was possible he was sharing this information simply because of my role as student leader, I suspected there was more to it and I was determined not to be the one to bring up the topic of Ian.

"Mr. Griffin, the truth of the matter is, this show is going to happen whether we want it to or not. If we ban them from town, they'll certainly find Buchanan to be more amenable to their request. And then we lose not only the potential funding and any to come in the future but the chance to prove our value. Are you following me?"

"Yes, but…"

"I will again be as succinct as possible," Rice continued,

tapping his chronically nonworking watch. "I plan to get through this *Ghost Killers* ordeal unscathed, and we have been given a deadline of less than two weeks to come up with an answer." He leaned forward. "I need to meet with Ian Mackenzie and I need you, my Youth Corps leader, to facilitate that meeting."

I came in suspecting they'd want the ghost of Ian Mackenzie available to do their bidding. As if Ian had ever done anyone else's bidding. But hearing Rice say that out loud sent a chill through me. "I mean, I can try, but you know what Ian is like and…"

"We are running out of time," Rice said in a tone of voice that assumed correctly that I totally understood that this was a demand and not a request. "If you could please contact Ian and pass along that I would be pleased to meet with him at 2:00 p.m. on Sunday, I would be most appreciative."

I nodded, but my head felt as though it were filled with rocks.

"That is all, Mr. Griffin. You have almost forty-eight hours. Remember, 2:00 p.m."

As if I could forget.

chapter seven

ASHER

The foyer was stacked waist-high with books. Mari's fluffy gray and white cat, who was named Houdini after the famous ghost-debunking magician ("because he was so hairy"), sat cleaning himself on a stack made from a historical mystery series my mother used to love but hadn't read in years. My father had been talking about building a bookcase for the set ever since we moved in here, but he never seemed to make any progress on it. Par for the course. Neither of my parents were used to living any place long enough to find room for things and now that they were, they still didn't have access to those muscles. I was the only one who'd fully unpacked, but then even in hotel rooms, I'd emptied my suitcase and tried to create a temporary home.

I reached over and scratched Houdini behind the ears. "I know," I said, nuzzling my face in his ruff. "I miss her too." Houdini had basically taken over Mari's room. It was difficult sometimes to pay the cat enough attention because the knowing look in his eyes always brought my own sadness to the surface. But even though I'd heard cats could "sense" things that weren't there, he never seemed to sense anything aside from when I opened a can of tuna.

I turned and looked up through the maze of books. The walls next to the stairs were lined with faded squares and nail holes. The previous owners must have had family photos hung up. Graduation pictures of their kids or vacation shots from European trips. When we'd moved in, my parents had talked about filling in the holes, painting the wall over, putting up aging photos of their own. But they had work and were busy and then my sister had died.

"Mom and Dad are never going to hang anything there, are they, Mari?" When I was little and we were living in Salem, my parents had pictures up. Mari as a baby. Mari's first day at school. Mari holding me on her lap after I was born. Us standing in front of multiple years of Christmas trees. Now that she was gone, they'd lost interest in things like photographs, holidays, and me.

My parents' voices bumped down the stairs. They were arguing again.

I sat on the bottom step and listened to my father talking about time, profits, and losses. My mother countered with reminders that plans took time, if you were doing them right. And that they had to be carefully woven if you wanted them to succeed. And that profits and losses, in this case, weren't to be measured in dollars, but in results.

I listened to my parents bicker. The only thing they seemed to agree on was their mutual frustration with not having the permits for the show booked. At least I hadn't become the focus of their argument yet, but they always seemed to get there in the end.

Houdini meowed and hopped off the stairs, probably looking for a quieter place to sleep, which sounded like a good idea. I zigzagged my way through the books and snuck up to my room, where I could finally exhale.

Here's what you learn when your sister dies young. Time is not something that can be counted on. It's not something doled out in abundant packages wrapped with pretty bows. Instead, time is something slippery and elusive. It veers and weaves left when you expect it to go right. It sings and lures you into trusting it when it has an agenda that is impossible to read. You waste it by sleeping. And eating. And listening to your parents argue about pointless things like whether the bacon is too well done.

Mari was two when I was born. She died when I was fifteen and she was seventeen. We had fifteen years of conversations and games of Jenga, bike rides and night camping in the backyard, and pretending to be all over the world, even when we already were. I told her everything. I don't think she could have said the same. But she never made me feel as if she was shutting me out. She never made me feel as if she was stuck with me because, by the benefit of birth, I was her younger brother.

We only had fifteen years to create a lifetime of memories.

And on the second-to-last day of her life, I'd screwed that up, royally.

"Hey, Ash," my dad called as he opened my bedroom door and walked in without knocking. "What's up?"

Forget about the not-knocking part. And the fairly recent and eternally annoying habit he had of shortening my name. *What's up?* was my least favorite question in the universe.

I would happily talk about the meaning of life, the chance of humanoids existing on another planet, the laws of physics, the secret to happiness, or whether color is an absolute or something we all assign to various light fractals. I would happily analyze a poem or a painting or talk about anything so long as it was something that *mattered*. But that was never what my father had in mind.

I stared at him because nothing was "up," and I was curious to know what he thought I'd done wrong this time. His hair was messy, and his eyes were lined and red from fighting with Mom. It almost made me feel sorry for him. At one time it would have. When I was little, I would have reached up to nestle into his stubble-strewn neck, thinking I could make everything okay if only I tried hard enough.

Now I knew better. I couldn't make things okay because I wasn't the child they wanted, and I couldn't bring my sister back. Worse, it was entirely possible nothing would make things better, but I was struggling to convince myself of that. If I had, I wouldn't be trying to get to know Russ as they'd asked.

"The local paper has picked up on it," my dad said, pulling a rolled-up copy of the *Buchanan Sentinel* from his back pocket. I willed myself to keep quiet about his wasting a natural resource when he could have easily read the paper online, and took it from him, glancing at the cover story. "I expect it to hit nationally sooner than later."

I wasn't sure what had my father so bent out of shape. According to the lead story, he was getting what he wanted—press and a public request for a meeting with the people who ran St. Hilaire to discuss being allowed into town to film without having to set up outside the gates and shoot over fences.

My parents had started this whole thing, after all. Did they not think their plan would work? Did they not want it to? Why wasn't he happy about this? What was he going to blame me for this time?

He sighed and sat down, leaning his elbows on his knees and spinning his wedding ring. "Look, Ash, I know this can't be much fun for you, but this is it. One last show and then we're done. All these years we've spent trying to help other people keep from being taken advantage of, and now it's our turn."

Just over his shoulder, hanging on the wall above my desk, was my favorite photo of Mari. It was taken in Scotland by a girl I'm sure was in love with her; so in love that she didn't mind Mari's younger brother following the two of them around like a lost puppy dog since he knew no one in the entire country outside his family and struggled with the Highland accents and the unfamiliar food and currency.

The house our parents had been exploring at the time was empty but in surprisingly good shape, unlike most of the haunted places they were brought in to shoot. It was isolated, though, and the most recent owners had only lived there for a few months before claiming to be driven out by the feeling there was something in the house and the fact that all of their fish kept leaping out of their tanks and their cat kept clawing at the door to the attic.

My parents were more optimistic then. They were excited about going abroad and thought it would be a good experience for their children to join them. Maybe it *had* been a good experience. Mostly, my parents worked, and Mari fell in love, and I got lost in the brambles and spent a lot of time looking at tons of sheep and super-fluffy cows and wondering what I would do if this girl were "the one" for Mari, unlike the other girls and boys she seemed to collect at every shoot site we stayed at for more than a little while.

In the photo, Mari was wearing her hair in a chin-length dark bob, which was in motion against her pale dress and the smoky sunlight streaming in the huge window behind her. She looked ghostly to be honest. We used to joke about it. *Ghost Killers*' daughter being mistaken for a ghost, ha-ha.

"Asher, I'm talking to you."

I pulled my eyes down from my sister's to meet my father's. Their eyes were both darker than mine and my mother's. It sometimes made it hard to look at him. "Sorry."

"Ash, what about what we talked about?"

I took a deep breath and said, "I sold my car to a guy named Russ Griffin." As I exhaled, I imagined the words streaming out of my mouth like the sunlight through the window in my sister's photo. "He's a medium."

"What?" My father gasped, literally gasped.

I stood and walked to the window. From here, I could see the spires of St. Hilaire's Eaton Hall. Was Russ was anywhere close to it? I let my father simmer for a minute before I turned back to him with an answer I knew he wouldn't be able to argue with. "You told me to get real information on St. Hilaire, so I figured I needed to actually talk to someone from there. I placed an ad to sell my car on an app and waited until someone from there answered it." Somehow saying it out loud made my plan sound far-fetched, but it was too late to alter course. "Anyhow, Russ Griffin is the head of their Youth Corps. He's"—I faltered—"good. I had a car and he needed one. I got kind of lucky, I think."

I watched my father argue with himself. On one hand, he was probably pissed at me for getting rid of my car. He'd be more pissed if he knew I didn't even take Russ's money. But on the other hand, I'd done what he and Mom wanted and tried to get an "in" to St. Hilaire.

Finally, he sighed. "That isn't really how I meant for you to go about it, but I suppose what's done is done."

I nodded, because what he said was true. What's done was done. I had no intention of asking for my car back even if it *would* give me an excuse to see Russ again.

"So, what have you learned?" he asked, as if our goals were the same. I was struggling to care about enlightening the world to the plight of people who sought out mediums and psychics. "Are you going to see him again?"

I closed my eyes, and for some reason the image imprinted there was the dotted owl tattoo on Russ's wrist. I had a near-photographic memory, and it was less awkward for me to examine it here in my head than with Russ standing in front of me. Geometry. Circles and dashed lines. Dotted lines. Like the universe, it was every small thing converging to create something larger and more beautiful. That was something I *did* care about.

"Asher," my dad called. "Please focus."

This conversation was one of the reasons I avoided talking to my dad. He and my brain were somehow at odds. *It's your DNA*, I wanted to remind him. At least I assumed it was, given the similarities of our jawlines and the height of our cheekbones. Besides, I *was* focusing. I could see the owl so clearly, I almost expected it to take flight.

"I don't know anything concrete yet and I don't have any plans to see Russ, but I'll find a way," I said and then added, "I promise," which felt like more of a gift to myself than to my father.

"I'm not trying to be harsh, but we have a deadline here," Dad said. He glanced at the NASA calendar on my wall. It was September. The photo was of IC 342, a spiral galaxy 10.76 million light-years away, which was hard to see since it sits so close to the Milky Way. The picture resembled a painting but wasn't. "The film crew gets here in three days, and we really need to go into production immediately. The sooner we get into the town, the sooner this is all over. It would really help to know the lay of the land before we get the cameras in there." My dad looked desperate, and I had to fight to remember the reason he was pushing me so hard. For some reason, he couldn't let his grief live inside him as sadness; he had to turn it into action.

"She wouldn't want you to do this," I half whispered, looking at the floor.

"If places like this weren't preying on the pain of people

who are grieving, there would be no reason…" My father's words stung and he didn't need to continue. We both knew the backstory.

My sister died when she was seventeen. It was a freak thing. She was hiking with friends near Poughkeepsie and was struck by lightning. When I googled it, the National Weather Service reported there were about fifty people hit by lightning every year in the United States. About ten percent of them die. My sister was one of those five statistical deaths.

After their initial shock wore off, my parents, renowned ghost hunters and TV stars, although not in that order, put away all of their doubts and convictions about how awful mediums were and replaced them with all of their electronics, and all of their superstar friends who pooled all of their money together and tried to contact Mari.

Nothing worked. Not the séance on the knoll in Ireland, or the one run by the medium they met in LA, or the LSD I wasn't supposed to know my father took in an effort to have one more conversation with his only daughter and favorite child.

Their last resort was St. Hilaire.

We'd been living in Buchanan for about a year but had only spent a couple months in the house here and there. Mostly Mari and I were touring around with Mom and Dad on their final hurrah tour and giving them a hard time for setting their sights on the town next to St. Hilaire to settle down in. I mean, what kind of self-denial was at play there?

When the time came for them to walk the twenty minutes to the town that had been the butt of their jokes for years, they called in favors and contacts and probably paid a ton of money in order to hide their identities. It was winter. The town was closed, but my parents pulled strings and scheduled a call with some bigwig who handed them off to the medium who was supposed to be the best.

My parents did everything the medium asked. They wrote out questions and turned off their electronics. They gathered some of Mari's favorite items: a stuffed tiger she'd had since she was a kid, a poem I wrote her in school, a dried flower given to her by a boy she'd met in California. They even brought in Houdini—who, despite the presence of the medium's dog, a huge Irish wolfhound—curled up in the medium's lap, yawned, and went to sleep.

The medium told my parents Mari might not talk to them, that talking to the living took an amount of energy rarely seen. So instead, they created notes on paper and placed them under an old brass pendulum that hung over the table, hoping her spirit could swing it to the correct response. *Yes. No. Maybe. I don't know. I love you.*

And then they held a séance, assuming, of course, that one of the best mediums in St. Hilaire could contact their daughter even though they'd made a career out of proving ghosts weren't real and that mediums were wasting their time.

In an odd sort of karmic justice, nothing happened.

They didn't hear the bells ring. They didn't see the pendulum move. No one spoke to them from the other side. The medium, they reported, was young but comforting and focused. He'd looked as though he was working hard but had no luck, and ultimately he told my parents that Mari had moved on. And that her moving on was a good thing. "She isn't in pain.

She isn't angry. She isn't lost. She's where she needs to be," he said, which was *not* what they wanted to hear. *They* were in pain. *They* were angry. *They* were lost.

They wanted to talk to their daughter.

I felt most of those things, too, but more than anything, I knew her silence was my fault.

I missed my sister desperately then. I still did.

I wanted her to be at peace. And I still had—have—the feeling she was listening to me from wherever it was she had gone. Even if she wasn't talking back to us. To me.

Mom started drinking more than she should. Dad became… I don't know. Irritable. More irritable. Their fights got more frequent; their show got darker. They were even less interested in me than they had been before. I hadn't even thought that possible.

And somehow the one and only thing they could agree on was this final hurrah for the show, this plan to focus their energies on the town whose star medium had told them their dead daughter had moved on.

"Just do what you need to do, Ash. And do it fast." My father shook his head as if he was trying to avoid a fly, looked as me as if I was somehow failing him, and walked out of my room.

chapter eight

RUSS

Most of the time, I missed my father when he was at work. But lately, I'd considered it a benefit to have the house to myself. My father intellectually understood what I did—he'd been married to my mother after all—but there was a huge difference between my participating in Guild-sanctioned séances overseen by guiding adults and bantering with my dead ex-boyfriendish person about taking down the town's governing body. The latter was the only secret I'd deliberately kept from my father—because the Guild's actions would gut him.

Well, the only secret aside from my experimentation with my grandmother's recipes because if he found out about that, I sensed my father would gut *me*.

I went to my room and drew the curtains. Ian was around

more often than not these days. But my room was quiet and calling his name did nothing. I desperately needed to talk to him about Clive Rice's demand, but there was also something rare and luxurious about the silence, something that begged to be taken advantage of. I'd never minded having time alone, I just never got it anymore.

The lower left drawer of my desk was open slightly. I reached in and dug under the false bottom. My fingers wrapped around a small muslin bag tied with string. The packet could have been filled with Earl Grey tea, which my mother had loved, probably still loved, but it wasn't. I brought it to my nose and inhaled. Cinnamon and gasoline and some sort of wet-dog smell, but under that, the smell of the first sunny day of spring. Of lilacs. Of what I imagined it smelled like to walk by the sea.

I plugged in the electric kettle I'd purchased from the consignment store in Buchanan, which allowed me to circumvent the kitchen and any possible questions from my father. Boiled water. Steeped leaves. Added a packet of raw sugar "borrowed" from the school cafeteria.

There was something calming in the ritual. Something even more calming in the drinking. My anxiety over Clive Rice's words slipped away. The room swam pleasantly. The stress of the day began to blur. Under the tattoo on my wrist, my skin began to warm in a comforting way. In fact, everything was easy and comfortable, and whenever I tried to grasp onto a worrying thought, it silently grew wings and flew away.

I looked around the room and saw nothing unusual. I listened under the usual house sounds and heard nothing. No ghosts trying to get my attention. I wondered—briefly—why my grandmother had worked up a recipe for stress relief if there was nothing to be gained from it as a medium. But then I decided maybe less anxiety wasn't a bad thing regardless of your line of work.

Under the nothing, my mind kept flicking back to the planetarium. Every time I closed my eyes, I saw stars resembling the ones on the roof of the car that bled into the sky.

The huge planets hanging from the ceiling. Asher's easy smile.

The subject matter was undoubtedly a product of the tea because I lingered on that last image longer than I should have been comfortable with.

Long enough to slip into a deep, easy sleep.

—

I opened my eyes to Ian's face hovering over my own.

"*You* were smiling in your sleep," he said. "Dreaming about me?"

I jerked fully awake and rubbed my eyes. Then I rubbed my cheeks, hoping Ian would assume that was the reason for any color that had risen to them.

Be careful what you wish for. Why hadn't I learned that lesson and kept it in mind when I'd first thought that summoning Ian's ghost was a great idea? I should have known better. It was Ian, after all. Something was bound to go wrong.

I glanced at the clock, as Ian said, "It's Saturday."

Ten in the morning. I'd slept all night. *That* didn't happen often.

"I thought you could use some distraction from your paperwork," he said.

I look up into his eager expression and my stomach flipped. I didn't have time for the type of distractions he was no doubt considering. Or time for *any* distractions, for that matter. "We have to talk."

"Ooooh," he deadpanned. "That sounds ominous."

There were no ways of sugarcoating things, so I dove in. "Clive Rice is demanding to talk to you, so start ironing your good shirt because you're meeting with him at two tomorrow afternoon."

Ian froze for a beat and then pulled his shoulders back. "I'm not the Guild's little…"

"Ian," I warned. "You were the one who insisted I use you to secure a position on the Youth Corps so we could take down the Guild. You've been avoiding him all summer. I can't keep making excuses."

I waited.

"What he wants to talk to you about has to do with this *Ghost Killers* show."

"Of course it does," Ian said. He raked his hands through his hair and thought for a minute. "But there's something else as well."

I waited some more.

"Willow," he said. "I've been wondering. When they were holding all those séances to reach me, I figured it was because they were looking for Sarahlyn's missing gold from a few years back."

Ian paused while I glared at him for having dared to get sucked into a money-making scheme involving a spectral alchemist. Then he said, "I also thought that maybe they wanted to use me to help market St. Hilaire."

"Right." Repulsive as the idea was, I understood why the Guild had thought life-size posters of Ian were what St. Hilaire needed to change the town's image as boring, stuffy, and out of touch. Ian was many things, but none of those. "And now?"

Ian paused and chewed his lip, deep in thought. Then he said, "Now, I'm wondering why the hell Willow was involved in so many of those séances. I doubt she cares about either the money or marketing St. Hilaire. And how many group séances does she normally do anyhow? She isn't exactly a team player."

I wasn't sure if Ian considered Willow to be part of the *Ghost Killers* problem or if he was adding one more thing onto my plate, but my plate was full. "So what? You want me to ask her?"

Ian stiffened. "Oh shit, no. I definitely don't want that."

"Do you have a point?" I asked, feeling my blood pressure rise.

He exhaled or did something that looked like exhaling. "Look, what do you think about me blowing off this meeting and letting things with this TV show play out on their own and see where the chips fall?"

Had I not been looking directly at him, I would have assumed he was joking. But this wasn't Ian's joking face and that made me nervous. "What am I missing?" I asked. "Letting things 'play out' means the show very possibly kills the entire reason for St. Hilaire's existence, right? And you *know* they're going to ask you to do it. If you don't show up, who will? Melody? No one? How many customers are going to come to town for a reading if the show looks like it's successful in proving there are no ghosts here? Worse, no ghosts at all? What's going to happen to everyone who lives here who counts on that income? Lord, Ian. If you destroy St. Hilaire, there won't even be a Guild for me to take control of."

Ian's eyes went wide. He stared at me while I caught my breath. "Are you done?"

I glared at him and wondered if what my mother told me when I was little was true and my face could freeze like that.

He glared back in a playful way. "First off, who didn't die and made me the only ghost in town?"

"Ian, that doesn't even work as a joke. At the risk of playing into your already overinflated ego, you're the strongest ghost I've ever seen. I sincerely doubt this show is going to settle for a ringing bell or a tapping in the walls as proof that spirits exist."

For a minute, he looked smug but then his features rearranged themselves into something strange and thoughtful.

I took a deep breath. "Ian…"

"Look," he said. "I would bet my life—if I had one—that Willow is developing some sort of plan of her own. And don't ask her about that either. She isn't going to let St. Hilaire go under even if Rice does. Also, I have a hard time believing one show would destroy the whole town. You *can* prove something exists. It's much more difficult to prove that it doesn't."

He stood and wandered to the window. "People are always going to want their questions answered. But…" Peering out, he said, "Good lord, what is that piece of shit in your driveway, Griffin? Have I not taught you better than that?"

Before the conversation could get away from me further, I ignored his jab about my new car and tried to get us back on track. "Regardless of what Willow may or may not be up to, you're going to meet Rice tomorrow at two like he asked and at least hear what he has to say, right? You aren't going to fight me about that?"

He leaned in toward me and smirked. "That depends on what kind of fight you're thinking of. Is there oil involved? Jell-O, perhaps?"

I knew he was joking. He must have been. But even so, I couldn't get a word out.

He slapped my shoulder with the back of his hand. "Chill. I *still* think there's something to be said for letting this all take its course, and I'm not making any other promises but I guess I can clear my schedule and find time to have a chat with *El Presidente* if it will ease your mind."

I waited for a punch line, but there was none. Ian really did intend to help me. The idea was embryonic and a little frightening. Still, my definition of help didn't always mesh with his. "And you'll behave, right?"

"Of course." He leaned over and playfully bit my neck. "Don't I always?"

I nodded. One way or another, Ian always behaved. That's precisely what I was worried about.

chapter nine

WILLOW

I vanquished my first ghost when I was twelve.

Father was busy with the silly year-end festival. Everyone had been busy with one thing or another. The ghost in question was a sweet old lady who had died of natural causes well into her eighties but who felt so guilty about leaving her equally elderly husband that she hung around.

The husband may have been old, but his biggest issue was that he had never done *anything* while his wife was alive. She took care of their finances, their shopping, and their cooking. She planned their vacations and monitored their children's—and grandchildren's—homework.

She told me she had wanted to be a painter but was forced to give it up because married life left her no time for herself.

Screw that.

Maybe she was angry about that under the surface. Maybe her husband felt guilty and she was hanging onto his feelings as well. It takes a lot to keep a ghost around.

Even more to get them to go away.

She tried to continue the tasks she'd taken on when she was alive, but of course, she wasn't strong enough for any meaningful interactions. Oh, she'd move the checkbook to the other side of the room, which simply meant her husband couldn't find it, not that he'd know what to do with it anyhow. And she'd knock over jars of spaghetti sauce and lose the onions in the messy kitchen.

The husband, not knowing what was happening, tried to make an appointment to see Father, but the waiting list was oh-so-long, and the man was oh-so-disturbed by the loss of his wife and his misplaced objects. When I'd answered the phone, it was with the intention of taking a message, but he unleashed his story in a rush and I knew I had to help.

I was too young to do anything on the record, so I snuck into their house, which was only a few blocks outside St. Hilaire's gates, after I saw the husband leave. Once there, it wasn't hard to get the spirit's attention, given how wound up she was about her lengthy and ever-growing things-to-do list.

I offered to help her with some of the most pressing issues. Making notations in the checkbook. Opening a safe the husband couldn't remember the combination for. Writing down the password for her rickety old computer. Pulling out his favorite recipes from her crumbling cookbooks and making the corresponding grocery lists.

Then, I convinced her that leaving was best for her husband in the long run. Not to mention, definitely best for her.

And let's say, instead of waiting for her to speak with her husband and for him to make her feel bad, I expedited the process.

There are common methods for forcing ghosts to move on. I burned sage and mugwort. I boiled bay leaves in water and washed the floors with the solution. I reminded the ghost of all the reasons she needed to move along, and then I sprinkled salt water on the baseboards of all of the rooms in the house.

The ghost moved on.

The man was grateful.

But the best part was what happened after, when I learned there was an unexpected perk in vanquishing ghosts. A customer once taught me the word *lagniappe*. It meant a gift of something extra, like a free thirteenth bagel in a bag of a dozen, a gifted bag of gems in a video game.

What I received, though, was no toy. I woke up stronger the next day. Stronger, with a new vision, a new sensation when spirits were present. Had I needed to, I believe I could simply have told a typical ghost they needed to leave and they would have done my bidding.

The feeling faded a little over the next couple days, but with each ghost I dispatched, I retained a small bit of strength. I knew not all ghosts would want to leave. Sometimes they needed to be pushed, forced to move on, to be free. To do that consistently, I was going to need to obtain a great deal of strength from an extraordinary number of ghosts. Or, possibly, one extraordinarily strong one.

Ghostly Ian Mackenzie was going to be more of a challenge to vanquish than an old woman, but the power I received was going to be enough for me to take over St. Hilaire, disband the Guild, throw out the mediums who fell for all the sob stories of the living, and gather those who were also powerful. Then we would call the shots, not the commons who paid us fifteen dollars to visit us like animals in a zoo.

The key to vanquishing Ian was in figuring out his reason for staying. What, after all, did Ian care about, aside from Ian?

Unless of course he still cared for Russ Griffin.

Russ was fine. He was smart, in a quiet, guarded kind of way, and I guessed he could be considered cute if you were into the emo type. He was talented or could be if he got his emotions out of the way. He reminded me of Ferdinand the Bull in the story who could have been the biggest prizewinner if only he stopped hesitating to smell the stupid flowers.

I was on the fence about Russ, wondering if he'd prove to be an ally if I took him into my confidence. Wondering if there was a way to convince him it was time for us to stop living our lives as some sort of servant class.

He could be an asset. But there was no way he was worthy of Ian.

Ian had never gotten it. However much of a misguided jerk he was, Ian knew his way around ghosts. And now he *was* one because he'd simply been too much of a bleeding heart to do what was good for St. Hilaire. What was good for the Guild. What was good for the community of mediums he should have been protecting.

What a terrible waste of potential.

He was in my way. Russ would never see the light with Ian lurking around. And if I knew Ian, he would stay around as long as he could in order to cause trouble and be *seen*. After all, what good was it being Ian Mackenzie if you didn't have an audience?

Once gone, he wasn't supposed to come back, and now I had to get rid of him before he ruined everything.

Again.

chapter ten

R U S S

I'd sat in on sixty-four official Guild séances, mostly the big community ones. Those séances had funded my summers since the Guild actually paid student mediums minimum wage to attend. I would have gone for the experience alone, although it definitely helped to supplement my dad's salary even if he did suggest I put it away to pay for a "college" I had no intention of going to.

This year, there were lessons with Willow and the Youth Corps séances that were, by town law, overseen by Guild leadership.

But I knew today's séance with Clive Rice was going to be unlike anything I'd ever encountered. That certainty, on top of my fear that Ian was going to push his luck too far, and the nagging voice in the back of my mind that was sure there was a way to spin the idea of this show to our advantage in overthrowing the Guild—if only we could find it—was creating a traffic jam of pressure in my head.

I could see the end result. Clive Rice and everyone who'd supported him escorted out of town. A vote of all residents on whether we wanted to keep the town gated. The option for mediums to live in St. Hilaire and decide for themselves whether they wanted to work in the field or do something else. Dec could even move back here if he wanted to. The Guild flags could be torn down, and a whole lot fewer secrets would be kept by a whole lot fewer people.

When I reached Eaton Hall, I was quickly ushered up to Clive Rice's office. The air swirled with the scents of incense and herbs. It felt like the entire building was ready to welcome Ian back to the fold.

I rubbed the owl on my wrist and pulled my coat tight around me, wondering how long it would take for my teeth to begin to chatter from cold and concern. How could Ian possibly know when it was two? What if he got the time zone wrong?

I'd tried to preemptively calm my nerves with half a shot of my grandmother's serum. Then, when I was still feeling too much, still thinking too much, I took the other half. Now I was cascading between wired and catatonic. I hoped Ian would make this quick. I wasn't looking forward to spending too much time with Clive Rice.

I walked in and helped myself to a chair on the other side of the office from Rice's desk. I couldn't get far enough away. Given the choice, I'd still be in bed and someone could text me the results later.

"Oh no, Mr. Griffin. Please sit here, next to me," Clive Rice instructed, getting up from his desk and ushering me over to his more casual seating area containing a couch and two armchairs in matching blue floral patterns, and a coffee table that also served as a fish tank. "I'm expecting you to be an active participant in today's event. After all, we wouldn't be here if it weren't for your diligence in setting up this meeting."

My stomach soured. Still, I managed a forced smile as I walked over and sat where he told me to.

As I watched the fish circle in their watery world, I tried to forget how long I'd waited for—dreamed of—this moment and the chance to participate in a high-profile séance and prove myself. But calling Ian wasn't what I'd had in mind. Unpredictable, arrogant, Ian was not the ghost I wanted my role with the Guild to rise and fall with.

"Where is everyone else, sir?" I'd assumed that, at the very least, Guild leaders would be here to weigh in. So far it was just me and Clive Rice in the large room.

"Due to the sensitivity of the issue at hand and since you obviously don't need the benefit of a full team to call Mr. Mackenzie, it seemed prudent to keep this between us at the moment."

I forced myself to smile. *Great.* I'd been hoping for witnesses. I shivered in my seat. My breath crystallized in my lungs. Possibly I'd freeze to death before this whole thing was over. I wasn't sure that would be a bad thing.

Rice looked at his watch, which was permanently stuck at 10:00 a.m. "Let's begin." He stood and picked a remote off the table. He dimmed the lights, and the room took on an odd silence. Then he began his rituals. Everyone had their own way of doing things: silence, music, tambourines, incense, light, darkness, alcohol. There were as many ways of holding a séance as there were mediums.

When it came to Guild séances, the leader pretty much called the shots. And despite Rice's words about my not needing any help, it was clear he was taking charge of this meeting rather than letting me run with things.

He asked me to close my eyes. I did and listened as he took a deep breath and began the mantra he always used. "We welcome all who wish to join us. Come in. We embrace the continuity of spirit and soul. Come in. We open ourselves to the voices of the past and commit to the guidance of the future. Come in."

The room was completely silent. I kept my eyes closed.

"We invoke the spirit of Ian Mackenzie to join us in community and friendship. We, your spiritual family, request that you attend us and make yourself known."

I shivered in a type of psychic deep freeze. I couldn't quite put my finger on it, but something in Rice's voice sounded less than welcoming.

The clock on the wall struck two.

Behind me, an animal rustled through the bushes.

A breeze blew off the beach filled with the scent of brine and rain.

My skin prickled as if my entire body had suddenly fallen asleep.

I didn't know how much of the theatrics were Ian's doing. He certainly hadn't pulled out the bells and whistles for me, but I guess he hadn't been trying to make a statement then.

The room chilled further, and I pulled my coat closer. Something landed on the back of my hand and I jumped slightly. I opened my eyes a sliver and saw it was a flower petal, perfectly formed, bloodred with orange tips. I stuck it in my pocket, hoping Rice hadn't noticed.

Wind whipped up a scent reminiscent of herbs in the woods after a long, hot day.

The hair on my neck stood up.

The other blue armchair was still empty.

Rice's jaw was set in a hard line.

Everyone in St. Hilaire had participated in failed séances, ones where either the ghosts or customers were uncooperative. We'd interpreted messages wrong and unwittingly gotten stuck in the middle of family dramas. Failure of one sort or another was an unfortunate and frustrating occurrence. But this had a different feel to it, different even than the end-of-summer community séance to contact Ian, which had reeked of hundreds of mediums trying to raise one ghost and tanking. Despite the fact that Rice was leading, if this one failed, it would be all on me.

There was an uneasiness in the air I'd never felt before, a push and pull of molecules and humidity and conflicting purposes. It was like trying to reel in a large fish with a small rod. I wasn't sure if Ian was putting up a fight simply because he could, or if he was struggling to appear in front of the president of the Guild. But probably he was screwing around.

How much would Rice let him get away with before he called Ian out? What could he do if Ian refused to show up? What would *I* do?

Just as I was on the edge of a panic attack, it happened.

The wind stopped. The air cleared. And without any additional fanfare, Ian cleared his throat and simply appeared in the center of the room, looking completely pulled together as if he was walking on the set for a prearranged television interview. Or to accept an Oscar.

He stopped in front of the sofa and looked at me, his eyes bluer than I'd ever seen them. His stare moved all the way down my spine.

With a tiny smile on his face, he looked away and sat on the chair Rice had left vacant for his benefit. He leaned forward, pushed up the sleeves of his immaculate white shirt, rested his elbows on his knees, and tilted his head teasingly as if he'd just come back from a short walk and not from over a year of being dead.

"Well," said Rice in an impressed tone of voice I hadn't expected to hear from someone who spoke to ghosts on a daily basis.

"Been a while," said Ian.

"Indeed. It has," said Rice, leaning closer to Ian.

"I heard you wanted to chat?" Ian said.

"Um, yes," said Rice, visibly flustered. Apparently, he'd underestimated Ian's strength as a ghost, and Ian was pulling out all the stops. He looked positively solid.

"I know about the show," Ian said, taking charge. "Griffin filled me in. What I don't know is what you want me to do about it."

I shivered. Rice cleared his throat. Ian crossed his legs and slouched back as if he were sitting in the booth of a nightclub waiting for the waiter to bring him his much-delayed order of overpriced alcohol.

"Proof," said Rice. "I want to offer them proof. Since we aren't going to be able to stop this show, we need to beat them at their own game. Therefore, we need to offer them undeniable evidence." He shuffled in his chair, sinking slowly into it. "I have to say, it's uncanny. I've never seen anyone…any spirit…"

I looked away to hide the fact that I couldn't stop rolling my eyes. Rice wasn't wrong and playing to Ian's ego was certainly not a bad way to go, but still, all I could think of was how insufferable he was going to be after having his boots licked by the president of the Guild.

Oddly, Ian didn't buy into it. "You want me to appear on camera and debunk this debunking show and give everyone in the world proof of the spirit world." Ian wasn't asking a question. Silently, I willed him to be cautious.

"Yes," said Rice, his face suddenly pasty and pale. "If the Guild's decision is to go ahead with this, that is exactly what I'm asking you to do."

Ian turned to look directly at me as if he was trying to make a decision. I looked back, slightly unsure whether my role at this meeting involved more than making sure he showed up.

"I don't know if I agree with that idea," Ian said to Rice. "Have you thought about how world-changing this could be? Have you even stopped to think people might rush to…turn themselves into ghosts…if you prove something exists after death?"

The air in the room was heavy. The clock on the wall seemed to be ticking too fast, just like my heart. I hadn't even thought about the repercussions of sharing the knowledge that some spirits exist after death.

"It's okay," Ian said. "Don't answer that. I know you haven't actually thought about the people involved, not even your own mediums. All you're worried about is how much money the Guild can bring in."

Rice grabbed a pen off the table in front of him. I could see his knuckles turn white, he was gripping it so tightly, but he sounded in full command when he said, "Mr. Mackenzie. While I am quite impressed by your feat of strength here, need I remind you that I run this town?"

I glanced at the clock, which was now running backward, and tried to stop my teeth from chattering.

Rice looked rooted in place. I wasn't sure any of us were breathing.

"No," Ian answered. "You don't need to remind me. But thinking about it like that, I'm not going to be part of your plan." Then he stood and I did as well for lack of anything else to do. He walked to the door and hesitated, making me realize he probably couldn't open it or didn't want to take the chance of trying and then looking weak should he fail. I glanced back at Rice and then opened the door, and we stepped out.

As the office door closed behind us, I froze, watching Ian walk away. He stopped at the end of the hall before turning to look at me. "That went well, don't you think?" he asked with a wide grin.

I opened my mouth but found myself lost for words, so I shook my head and followed him out.

chapter eleven
RUSS

Ian was gone before we even left Eaton Hall, and I certainly wasn't going to sit around and wait for Clive Rice to censure me for Ian's attitude. I got out of there without wasting any time.

Instead of heading into the too-quiet house when I got home, I jumped in the car. *My* car. I was crammed with restless energy and a need to burn it off. I drove through town with an odd sense of dread. Rice wasn't going to let this go. I was both proud of Ian for standing his ground and mortified that he'd basically told Rice to go screw himself.

My anxiety distracted me so much that I surprised myself by pulling up outside the planetarium in Buchanan.

I slid into a space and looked up and down the street. Cars sped by taking workers home for the night and people who had friends and plans out for a night of fun. There was something deliberate and determined about their speed and direction, while I was grasping for something to do besides being relieved that the parking meters had stopped gobbling coins for the day.

What was I doing here, of all places? I liked to think I understood myself well, but lately it was as if I was morphing into someone else, and I wasn't sure I understood this new person. Or wanted to.

I stared at the dome of the planetarium and let the car idle while I tried to analyze my motivations.

What I craved was a conversation that didn't revolve around ghosts and that didn't feel like hard work. That I craved a conversation at all was unusual, but the thought of seeing Asher again was oddly comforting. I didn't need a friend in Buchanan. I didn't have time to develop a new friendship regardless. There was school. The Guild. And Ian.

I had enough on my plate without trying to explain my life to a Buchanan boy.

But then, I didn't want to talk about St. Hilaire, so that worked out.

But I also didn't want to sit here in the car, examining my own thoughts all night.

I grabbed the keys out of the ignition, walked to the front door, and let myself into the lobby before I lost my nerve. The door whooshed closed behind me and I hesitated, allowing my eyes time to adjust to the darkness.

"Oh, no. Orion isn't acting up, is he?"

I turned. Asher sat in the dim ticket booth, his grin both overpowering and puzzling. How could anyone be so happy in Buchanan, of all places? And how could he be so happy to see *me*?

"Behaving like a true gentleman," I said of the car. "Even made me tea this morning."

Asher laughed, which gave me an odd sense of accomplishment. "Sense of humor" wouldn't necessarily fall on my "best traits" list.

"Lucky you," he said. "All I ever got out of him was lemonade. And I hate lemonade." He leaned out of the booth and looked at the clock on the wall behind me. "Good, it's almost closing time." He sucked in his lip ring and then smiled a smile that made me want to smile too. "Actually, executive decision. I'm making it closing time now." He flipped a sign on the window, slid off his stool, and came around the wall, a blue backpack covered in stars slung over his shoulder.

What had I been thinking, coming here? What excuse did I even have? I didn't think I could come up with a plausible lie. "I don't want to keep you from work," I said, backing toward the door. I could make a quick exit and leave him wondering why I'd shown up for no reason and it wouldn't matter. I never needed to see him again.

"I wouldn't mind if you *did* keep me from working," he said and then waited for a response in a way that made me wonder— too late—if he was flirting with me. Lacking any response, he continued. "But no one has come in today, anyhow. Sundays are always quiet this time of year when the tourists are wherever they really live. Basically, I'm just hanging out and babysitting Joe." Asher walked deeper into the room, and I had to follow closely to avoid losing him in the darkness. It was too late to escape.

"Who's Joe?" I called ahead.

"The projector." His voice floated back to me from a side door. I raced to catch up.

"Do you name everything?" I asked, thinking about the car being called Orion. I found myself in a long room. Above us, the planets hung in appropriate size ratio, dangling in front of a glittering fake sky. In the darkness, the stars danced and flickered hypnotically.

I stared up at them, transfixed.

"I like to feel connected with things, I guess," he said. "Names are important. I mean, you'd be a totally different person if you were named Balthazar or Fred, right?"

I nodded, but really, I couldn't pull my eyes away from the lights.

He came up next to me and watched me watching the ceiling. "It isn't as good as the real thing," he mused. "It's better than nothing on a gray day like today, but nothing like Arbor Field."

There was something reverential about the way he said the name. "What's Arbor Field?" I asked, still looking up and making sure I didn't bring my eyes down to look at him. Why was I playing twenty questions with a boy from Buchanan? Why was I so anxious to hear his answer?

"You've never been? I'll have to take you." I could almost *feel* Asher beaming. "It's near here. Just a place I go. Don't get too excited. But…I'll take you."

My shoulders tensed at the invitation as much as my stomach relaxed. Asher didn't seem to share the idea that we'd never see each other again. In fact, it seemed as if he'd taken it for granted we would, and I wasn't sure how to feel about that.

Asher walked into the middle of the room and lowered himself until he sat cross-legged on the floor. Had I ever looked as comfortably awkward anywhere? Probably not.

I sank down onto the floor across from him. We sat there in a strange sort of silence that felt like the promise of something I couldn't put my finger on.

"So, what brings you to Buchanan on this rainy night?" he asked, fiddling with one of his many rings. I could just make out a small circle of moons. "I didn't think you'd be someone who spends a lot of time here in town."

"I don't," I admitted. I struggled to focus on something other than the vast amount of air around us. I guess I hadn't realized how often I gravitated toward the safety of walls and corners. "I just…" I didn't know how to finish the sentence, so I shrugged, glad for the darkness, and changed the subject. "Do you go to Trumble?" I asked, referencing the high school in Buchanan.

Asher rustled something in his backpack and answered, "Not really. We've moved around a lot and I guess you could say I've been homeschooled. I mean, for the last few years, I've kind of homeschooled myself. We've lived in various countries so I'm not sure what a school would even do with my credits, but I'm seventeen, so I guess you could think of me as a senior. At this point, I'm looking forward to it all being over, if I'm honest. You?"

"I'm a senior too. At St. Hilaire High," I said, amused somehow to find out we were the same age, although I'm sure that was where the comparisons stopped. It was a good bet he wasn't studying for midterms that involved contacting ghosts and comforting members of the Guild impersonating grieving family members.

He leaned forward and clasped his hands together on his knees. "What then?" he asked. "What does Russ Griffin want to do with his life?"

When was the last time anyone asked me what I wanted rather than telling me what they needed me to do? The truth ran through my head. *Well, first—with the help of a ghost who may or may not be my boyfriend—I'm going to somehow overthrow the town's leaders. Then I'm going to become a town leader myself even though I'll still be under eighteen and really just want to help people and cut out all this damned drama.* It sounded like the plot to some shitty movie.

When I didn't say anything, Asher cocked his head and said, "Sorry. I guess you have a built-in future here, right? I wasn't trying to pry."

I shrugged and ran my fingers over the owl on my wrist and turned his question back on him. "What do you want to do when you're done homeschooling?"

He looked up at the huge, fake planets above us, but for a minute they felt real. As if he and I were spinning off in space somewhere. It was a sensation that was both intoxicating and disarming.

"I want to dream," he said quietly, and then leaned back and stretched out on the floor with his hands behind his head. "I want to fall in love with the world and listen to great music and read great books when I'm supposed to be sleeping." He turned his head to me, and his eyes were shining in the electrical starlight. "I want to travel for no particular reason and make each day mean something. I want to do something that leaves a mark. I think being forgotten would be the worst thing ever, don't you?"

My chest grew cold. Asher was clearly sincere, and something about that was making it hard for me to breathe. Who talked that way? Who believed they could decide to have the sort of life where you didn't need to worry about paying for a car, or not ticking off the people you needed to help you?

I envied him.

He intrigued me.

I stretched out my legs. From there it was easy to slide myself over on the floor until I was next to him and looked up at the planets again. *One. Two. Three.* I counted nine. "I thought Pluto wasn't a planet anymore," I said.

He smiled. "Haven't you read the bumper sticker on the back of Orion?"

I considered his question. Had I even looked at the back of the car? "I guess not."

"You bought a car without really looking at it, didn't you? Anyhow it's kind of faded—the sticker—but it says, 'Let Pluto be a planet.' You know Pluto was discovered in 1930. In planetary history, that's like yesterday. It has an atmosphere only when it's close to the sun; otherwise it's covered in ice and has five moons. That they know about anyhow."

I let the collection of information roll over me, pretty sure he hadn't answered my question.

"I'm a fan." he said, "I'm sticking with 'planet.' I think the scientists will come around again too."

Our entire conversation resembled arrows moving past each other in every direction aside from the expected one.

He sat up and dug around in his backpack. The dim lights bounced off the gloss of a pack of playing cards in his hands.

He shuffled them with the dexterity of a card shark and tapped them twice on the floor before splitting the deck and shuffling them back and forth so they resembled a waterfall, a rotating fan, a constantly moving twist of hands and cards. My eyes could barely keep up.

"Are you practicing for Vegas?" I asked. "Because that doesn't seem like a place where you can dream about things that matter."

Asher slowed his hands. Split the deck and spread them out in two fans on the floor. "Pick one," he said.

I shivered. It was odd being on this side of things. I could read tarot cards and runes although I rarely had reason to in St. Hilaire. In general, we were dissuaded from doing anything that made us look like we were psychics at a state fair. I still liked to dabble for myself, though, and staring at the intricacies of the artwork helped me to focus. Normal cards were for poker. Something told me Asher had things other than gambling on his mind.

I placed my left hand an inch above the cards while I scanned them for markings or bent corners or anything that might telegraph my choice. Nothing looked out of sorts and I wasn't getting any weird vibes off Asher either. At least not in the "cheating" sense.

I kept coming back to one card, so I slipped it from the deck. It felt cold in the same way my tarot cards did when they were "on," as though its temperature was coming from somewhere else entirely. I glanced at it behind my hand. Ace of spades. The same card I'd had to identify for the Guild during their initiation test for the Youth Corps. That Motörhead song by the same name went through my head. My dad was a fan.

Asher gathered up the cards, leaving a space for me to slip the ace into. He shuffled again, this time tossing them around in a complicated pattern I've never seen.

He re-formed the deck and handed it to me. "Shuffle twice," he said. I took the deck. The cards were warm from his hands now. I shuffled them the only way I knew how—I needed to get him to teach me his tricks—and handed the cards back.

He smiled at the cards and then at me, but before I had time to react, he looked down and spread the cards on the floor, allowing his hands to wander over the cards. He stopped and pulled one. Ace of spades.

"Great trick," I said, although the hair on the back of my neck bristled.

Asher gathered the cards up and slipped them back into the box and then the box into his bag. Then he looked at me. "You have some connection to that card, right?"

"Yeah, I…" There was no way to tell someone from Buchanan about the Guild's testing practices, so I simply stopped talking. The silence between us grew.

I glanced down and watched my index finger running over the tattoo on my wrist. I felt unsettled in a way I hadn't been in a while. Spending time with Asher felt like falling over the edge of a cliff. Not dangerous in the same way as spending time with Ian, but dangerous in a completely different way. With Ian, I always had to watch my back and stay on guard. With Asher, it was hard to even put up any kind of walls and that felt equally terrifying.

"It's okay," Asher said. "Really, it is."

I found myself nodding, even though it felt like he was

reading my mind and that scared the crap out of me. At some level, I found his words comforting. That scared me too.

"Come over for dinner," Asher instructed.

The invitation, out of the blue, was so unexpected all I could say was, "What?"

Asher shrugged into his shoulders, his voice oddly serious as he said, "It's black-bean taco night. My father makes too much and then gets ticked off because he's throwing away food. My parents haven't quite adjusted to cooking for three. And they're actually out tonight anyhow so you'll be spared *that* at least. But my mom left stuff in the fridge and I hate eating alone. It would be cool if you came with me."

I wished I could read the context of Asher's racing words. I tried to pull my defenses up. Did he have some ulterior motive? Was I being hit on? Was it possible he was being sincere, again? Perhaps I'd been hanging around Ian too long and had forgotten what easy friendships felt like.

"I don't want to intrude," I said. My voice cracked and I coughed to clear it, hoping nothing was giving away my thoughts.

"I promise you'd be doing me a favor. Like I said, I don't enjoy eating alone." He looked down at the floor. "And I don't know many people in Buchanan. My parents moved us around a lot for their work and…" He let the word linger.

"And?"

He looked at me in that way people had before they confessed something that meant a lot to them. I'd heard the tone often enough from St. Hilaire's summer customers. *I loved her. I didn't mean to do it. I wish I would have…*

I swallowed hard. Normally those confessions resulted in me going into medium mode. I didn't know how to deal with those naked emotions aside from acting warm yet keeping myself distanced inside. But Asher's words wormed their way in before I was prepared and made me feel exposed too.

He ran his hands down his dark jeans. "Have you…have you ever lost someone? Like the one person you really felt understood you? Like you'd poured everything, all your trust, and effort, and stories into them and then it's just…"

"Hard to let yourself get close to anyone else again?" I filled in before I could stop myself. That was pretty much exactly how I'd felt since Dec moved to New York City.

Asher nodded and in the dim light I could have sworn I saw him blush. "Yeah. That."

I glanced around for something to occupy my hands, but I'd brought nothing aside from my wallet and keys and they were in my pocket. I pulled at a string on the bottom of my jeans until it came loose. "My best friend moved to the city a few months ago," I said. "It's almost as if my whole life changed in some ways." I dragged the string across my thumbnail until it began to fray. It was so frustrating to feel glimmers of vibration that told me Dec was in danger or needed me. But those feelings were few and far between now. When Dec first moved and I'd call him in a panic, he'd laugh and say he was getting on a subway or walking through Central Park or heading to Brooklyn.

I'd gotten better at ignoring those instincts or at least not checking in with him three times a day. I still wanted to talk to him as much. I didn't want to be annoying, and where once I'd been the one to bail him out, now I felt useless.

I didn't tell Asher any of that. I couldn't. And when my stomach grumbled and I thought about the packet of ramen I was going eat in my empty house, I considered his earlier dinner invitation.

It wasn't simply hunger that made me draw back my shoulders and look at Asher lit by the dim LED stars and shadowed by the enormity of the sized-to-scale planet models overhead. It was another kind of emptiness, another kind of appetite.

"You know, black-bean tacos are my favorite food," I lied, my voice sounding not quite my own.

He smiled broadly and hopped up, gesturing for me to do the same.

Only during the drive to his house did I realize I hadn't told him about Ian.

And I wasn't sure if that mattered or not.

chapter twelve

ASHER

My parents normally would have hated the idea of me having someone over without asking them. But I figured they'd be okay if I told them it was someone from St. Hilaire and there was a chance I could learn all the local secrets. Like about how mediums could spin things so it sounded as though they were getting things right. And whether there was some official code of conduct they had to sign, acknowledging they were all frauds. And whether they took classes in deception or in reading body language. And about what other tricks they might have up their sleeves.

Maybe my parents would be happy enough with me for a day or maybe at least a few hours and we'd go out to dinner and to a movie, like we used to. They would ask for a tour of the planetarium, which they'd never been to, and I would run through the new show for them and they'd be proud of how much I knew about the planets and how to run the donated old Zeiss "barbell" projector that could make it feel as though you were spinning dizzily through the sky if you ran it at full speed.

Then I would take them to Arbor Field and we'd walk around and discuss how much we all missed Mari and how we were going to move forward and be able to talk about her and share happy memories instead of being stuck in this odd wormhole.

Even through their grief, they'd realize that having one child was better than having none. They would pour all of their attention and pride onto me instead of simply longing for the daughter they couldn't have.

But, as I sat across our dining room table from Russ, none of that stuck in my head. All I could think about was how time seemed to slow down when I was with him. How easy it was to slip between minutes and watch as his eyes darkened in thought, and how it seemed as though there was always so much going on beneath his surface. Even though I didn't really know him, it was easy to let my guard down and sense his emotions and feel safe. It was the first time since Mari died that I'd found myself really connecting with someone. Not that I'd often had the opportunity. And not that I *should* be connecting with anyone in St. Hilaire.

Oddly, I felt nicer when I was with Russ, more out of my own head. I wasn't counting time as much when we were together. I wasn't wondering if there was something more important I should be doing. Something I needed to do before I died too.

I wasn't thinking about the average lifespan of a white male in the United States being 78.54 years and about how, since I was seventeen, that gave me over sixty-one more years if I was lucky and avoided fatal illnesses and gunshot wounds and car accidents and, of course, lightning.

Most of all lightning.

But at the same time, it was impossible to talk to Russ for more than a few minutes without remembering he truly believed he could speak to the dead. And that they spoke to him. It wasn't precisely that there was anything creepy about him. And it wasn't as if he talked about his life as a teen medium, even though I was doing my best to remember to float leading questions in his direction so I could at least *pretend* to be helping my parents.

As I'd followed *Ghost Killers* around the world, I'd met people who passed off their delusions of being haunted as some sort of mysticism, and I'd met people who were obviously up to no good and looking for whatever they could get.

Russ was neither of those.

Sitting across from him made me aware he was less afraid of…ending…than I was. He acted as if talking to ghosts was the same thing as talking to the FedEx guy. For all the people I'd met who claimed to have seen ghosts, I'd never met anyone like Russ before. I was starting to think he was the real deal simply because I couldn't bring myself to think of him as a sham. And after a lifetime of hearing there was no such thing as ghosts, which kind of meant there was no such things as mediums, I was hanging on his every word.

"It isn't that ghosts are people who haven't actually died," he explained, helping himself to a large spoonful of black beans.

"It's that their deaths aren't necessarily the end of things. Some people believe ghosts continue to grow and learn, just in a different way."

"So why aren't we bumping into dinosaurs and stuff all the time?" I asked. I wasn't trying to be argumentative. I guess I liked the way he lit up when he explained it all to me. And sometimes humor kept the anxiety at bay. My anxiety, anyhow.

Russ smiled and ran a hand through his hair. The lighter roots pushed their way up to the surface of his dark hair like flowers. It looked good on him, long and wild, and I found my eyes straying to it a little too often, studying the way his oddly transparent owl tattoo contrasted with the jet-black mane.

"Well, if everything that ever lived was still walking around on earth, it would be really, really crowded, right? But if you're going to go there… Who says we aren't bumping into spirits? I mean, you can walk through a ghost." His brow furrowed. "Most ghosts, anyhow, if their energy is low, and theirs usually is. So maybe there *is* something left here of the dinosaurs. Be careful not to step on a pterodactyl. I've heard they have a nasty bite."

"Aren't they vegetarians?" I asked, digging into a taco. Salsa ran down my chin and I wiped it off on the back of my hand, wishing I'd invited him over to eat something less messy.

"Well, I guess it doesn't matter since they're ghosts, right? Most aren't worried about eating."

"Most?" I asked.

"Well, all I guess," he said, but then shrugged and dropped his hands to his lap.

I knew he was rubbing the tattoo on his wrist. Most people had at least one nervous tell they fell back on subconsciously.

This was Russ's. Something about my question made him uncomfortable, and I wanted to know what it was. "So, ghosts aren't all alike? Like some can do things others can't?"

"Ghosts are different," he said. "I mean, people are different, so it follows ghosts would be too."

I pushed a little harder. "So, some ghosts *do* eat?" Really, I didn't care if ghosts ate or not. I mean, I couldn't imagine how that might work. But I wanted to get to whatever was at the heart of his words. He was dancing around something… I knew it. "That sounds messy."

Russ took another drink, his face suddenly serious. "Some ghosts are stronger than others. More focused. Some ghosts can do whatever they want if they're motivated enough."

"Motivated?" Did that mean Mari had no interest in speaking to me? I preferred the idea she was at peace and not simply uninterested.

"Yeah," he said. "The way we learned it in school was as an acronym. The letters that spell *ghost*, G-H-O-S-T, stand for the reasons they might hang around. Guilt. Hate. Obsession. Selfishness. Terror. They have to want something from the living. They have to want it very badly."

Mari would have loved this conversation, but I couldn't imagine her feeling any of those things. It's possible that was why no one had been able to contact her. She had simply been too happy as a person and didn't have any of those issues. Or maybe she'd been so pissed at me when she died that her anger grew and grew until it was larger than anything else. "So, you only get ghosts when one is bent out of shape? There are no happy ghosts? No Caspers or anything?"

Russ lit up. "The whole thing we're taught is that most spirits move on. Eventually. That's the normal course of things. There has to be a problem for one to stay here as a ghost— that's *our* term for them by the way, not theirs. I mean, that's just what we call the spirits that stick around. And it isn't that they aren't happy. It's that there needs to be some reason so overwhelming and all-consuming it literally stops them from allowing the typical chain of events to take place."

I took a swig of cola. Russ had pushed the sleeves of his jacket up and leaned forward, caught up in our conversation, and I wanted it to continue. Wanted *him* to continue.

"What do you do to get rid of one? Solve their problem?"

Russ smiled, and as he did, I realized it wasn't something he did much at all. I committed it to memory, wanting to wrap my hand around the smile and examine it later. "Yeah," he said. "Something like that. But thankfully that isn't our goal. We aren't psychic shrinks. In fact, we aren't psychics at all, and we can get into trouble if we even try to make people pretend we are. Besides, usually ghosts have something to say to someone. They want some sort of closure. That's true of the ones we get here, anyhow."

"Like," I said, "if they'd had a fight with someone, they might stay around to sort it out. I mean, if they wanted to?" After the words came out, I realized they hit too close to my own truth, and I got up and pretended to rummage around in the fridge. The blast of cold air felt good on my face and I waited until I heard Russ say, "Yeah, sometimes" before I went back, empty-handed, to the table.

So "ghosts" could do that, only Mari hadn't. Could she have

been so angry with me that I was the reason she hadn't stuck around?

"Honestly, forget all the bad movies you've seen. Most ghosts have harmless intentions. They just want to be noticed."

"Like most people," I said without thinking.

Russ looked at me with a complicated expression that somehow demolished our lighthearted mood. "Yeah," he said quietly. "Like most people."

The stillness of the room was suddenly heavy. I could hear the dogs barking down the block—the neighbors had taken to leaving them outside all of a sudden. I wondered if they were cold or maybe hungry. Were black beans okay for dogs? Maybe I could go after dinner and take them leftovers and check that they were okay.

I swallowed. "So, you really do go to magic school?" I said to fill the silence. My heartbeat sounded too loud in my ears.

"No, it's more like…" He stopped and paled. "I'm sorry. I'm not sure how much of this I'm allowed to tell you."

Damn. I could see he was shutting down, so I changed the subject. I'd have enough time later to analyze his words. "I know it's dark, but after dinner, do you want to walk over to Arbor Field? I'd like to show it to you, and it's way better when it's dark out and you can see the stars."

The somber expression faded from his face but remained in his eyes. "It sounds great, but I should probably get home," he said.

I'd screwed something up. I'd pushed too far and now I had to find a way to fix things. "Some other time, then, I hope."

He nodded.

"I'm sorry," I said feebly. "I really *wasn't* trying to pry. I just…"

He cut me off, which was good because I hadn't been sure what I could say to win him back. "It's cool," he said. "It's just that I live and breathe the whole medium thing in St. Hilaire, and it's nice to get a break once in a while."

I locked my lips and crossed my heart. "I promise not to bring it up again," I said, which went against every single thing my parents would want from me. "I mean, if you come with me, we can talk about sports, although I'm not a fan of any. Or music, do you like music? Or books? Or I can show you more card tricks?" I bit my lip, aware I sounded desperate and manic.

Thankfully, he laughed. "It's fine. Really. I'd like to see it, but maybe, next time?"

He didn't make any moves to go so I grabbed him another soda. And then, without trying, we talked about a million things that didn't matter and I found I was perfectly happy doing that with Russ because somehow, everything he said felt important and not once did he ask me to tell him what was "up" and he didn't actually leave for over an hour.

I really *had* planned to tell my parents Russ had been here. But when they got home and saw me cleaning up, and my mother said, "Did you have to use every dish in the house, dear?" I felt a wave of protectiveness toward Russ and my time with him so I shrugged and went up to my room.

chapter thirteen

WILLOW

I flipped my collar up to make sure my Guild badge was showing and stepped onto the porch of Hampton House. From the front, the house resembled one of the postcards that could be bought in the tacky shops of Buchanan: all columns and blazing hydrangeas.

I knocked on the door and waited until Laura Hampton answered. Everyone knew everyone else in this town. I could tell you Laura was quiet and given to unease where her family members were concerned. She was secretary of the junior class at St. Hilaire High. She was a middling medium not due to any lack of talent, but to lack of interest in spectacle.

"Willow. Hi," she said almost as if we were friends.

I looked down at the clipboard in my hands and then back over my shoulder to the front of Hampton House.

"Your Guild flag isn't up," I said. "You realize you're meant to be flying it, right?"

"Oh." She blushed and leaned out the door to look around me. "Right. Well, Harriet took it down. The season is over, and you know, we need to have it cleaned and…"

I ticked her older sister's name off on my chart and pulled a letter off my clipboard and handed it to her. "Here's a letter reminding you of the rules. The invoice for the fine will be mailed here."

Her face fell. "It's only been down for a couple of days. Can't you trust that I'll put it back up?"

I narrowed my eyes at her. "Why would I do that?"

She leaned against one of the pillars and sighed. "It's a lot of money. And it's the off-season. Please?" she begged. "I'll go get it now and put it up. You can even stay here and watch."

She was such a mild little thing, but the family had been here for generations and had a reputation for being quality mediums. Plus there was their tragic backstory. "Fine," I said. "You have a week. But I'm going to remind you that your family is already being watched. I wouldn't push our patience further."

"Thanks," she said quietly and then went in and closed the door.

I walked around the back of the house and saw the headstones of Marian and Robert Hampton.

It had been unfortunate that they died. Disappointing that my attempts to save them had amounted to nothing.

It was such a shame to lose good mediums.

I handed the sheets to Father. "I issued tickets to twelve houses," I said. "And a warning to Hampton House."

"A warning?" Father looked at me with a raised eyebrow.

"They didn't have their flag up. I gave them a day and said I'd check back. Laura Hampton claims they took it down to wash."

Father snickered. "Are you going soft?"

"Of course not," I said in defense of myself. "I also have a recommendation for you to take to the Guild. I believe we should remove the *Buchanan Sentinel* boxes from Town Square. All the paper is doing is fanning the flames of this *Ghost Killers* show. Wouldn't it be more appropriate if people were getting their news directly from us?"

Father nodded his head. "Yes, yes, you have a good point. Let me bring the issue up at our next meeting. Was there anything else?"

I tapped my pen on my clipboard. "I'm requesting again that you recommend the Guild leadership bring me on as a full member."

Father stood. "Now, Willow. We've discussed this. There will, I'm certain, come a time when the makeup of the Guild is such that they would be amenable to the idea. But the current membership..."

"Yes, I know," I interjected. "They think I'm too extreme, too radical."

Father came around his desk and stood in front on me. He

reached out a hand and then thought better of it. "Give it time, Daughter. Change comes slowly and gradually. St. Hilaire will once again be thought of with awe. We will have the best, the brightest mediums in the country—no, the world—here. There will be waiting lists for seasons in advance."

I formulated a reply but kept it to myself. Father thought he wanted change but really he wanted a return to the past where everyone worshiped Guild leaders and they never had to do anything to prove themselves.

He still considered St. Hilaire's problem to be one of finances rather than ideology. But the time would come when I would convert him to the truth. The time would have to come. Or I would simply do it on my own. The choice was his.

chapter fourteen

RUSS

The picture was blurry, which was why I never used the camera on my six-year-old phone. But blurry or not, it was impossible to deny what I'd seen as I'd driven home from Asher's house.

In the picture, Guild members all in their new uniforms walked alongside a group of twenty or thirty people I vaguely recognized. Everything got fuzzier when I zoomed in, but I know I'd seen some of the younger kids from school and their parents there.

Even in the dark, I could tell that none of them looked happy. Most were carrying suitcases or backpacks as they made their way to a line of cars parked right inside the town's back gate. I tried to figure out what the people I knew had in common. I tried to figure out why it looked as if the Guild was carrying out a military operation.

Maybe it was some sort of training drill no one had mentioned to me, even though, as Youth Corps leader, it seemed like they might have. But I couldn't imagine any training drill that would involve families leaving in the middle of the night.

And I couldn't shake the fear that this wasn't the end of whatever was going on.

———

"If you aren't going to focus, there's no reason for me to be here," Willow said, her heels clacking loudly as she paced in front of me.

"I *am* focusing," I said. The owl on my wrist itched as if to remind me of something. Maybe it was telling me not to argue with Willow. Or reminding me that I hadn't seen Ian since his performance in Clive Rice's office. Or perhaps it was echoing the reminder on my phone of it being Ian's birthday.

I wasn't sure if I should do anything about that last one because I wasn't sure Ian knew it was his birthday. Time might have been an abstract concept to the living, but it was completely irrelevant to ghosts.

I would bet, if I asked, he would know it was Tuesday. Possibly he'd know the month. Maybe the year. But I had no idea if he would put those things together in any meaningful way.

I was aware of it, though. And it was pretty obvious to Willow Rogers that my thoughts weren't on today's lesson, which was to listen to historic recordings from St. Hilaire's old phone-in line. It used to be that a group of mediums was responsible for manning a shared number so people could call in and get readings even if they couldn't get to St. Hilaire. I'd heard grumbling about the practice, but all the *Ghost Killers* publicity had given the Guild's leadership a firm excuse to stop the program, claiming it was too difficult to get a feel for whether the customers were legitimate or trying to discredit us. At least that was the reason they gave.

Still, Willow thought it would be valuable for me to review some of the older existing tapes and tell her whether I thought the medium did a good job or not and why. Kind of like those messages you got when calling your phone company. "This call might be taped for quality assurance."

The calls I was listening to were mind-numbingly dull, the customers desperate and usually anxious insomniacs calling in the middle of the night, the mediums cheesy and cloying in their delivery. The top mediums here would never want or need to sell their services over the phone, so that role was left to those with a certain amount of desperation themselves.

"...have done?" Willow finished a question I didn't hear the beginning of.

"Sorry," I said, but I'm sure it was clear I didn't mean it and I knew as the word came out of my mouth that Willow would call me out on it. All that mattered to any customer, she was fond of reminding me, were the forty-five minutes they were paying for. And all that mattered to the ghosts was that they were heard.

The option for us to act disinterested or distracted didn't exist on either side.

Willow dragged a chair in front of me and sat down hard,

crossing her arms. "What is it? Talk. I need to know if this is going to be an ongoing issue."

Ian's face, all blue eyes and tousled hair, floated in front of my eyes. Not in a metaphysical way, but in a swoony cinematic way, which frankly wasn't any better.

I shifted in my chair and focused on Willow's long, intricate braids until my vision cleared. Then I met her stare with my own and went for the low-hanging fruit. "What do *you* think about this *Ghost Killers* stuff?"

"Oh, is that what's distracting you?" Surprisingly, she looked away and seemed to be considering my question. "What I think is we might be better off if they continued believing their little fantasies about ghosts not existing. We don't exist to make commons feel better about their life choices." She looked straight into my eyes. "I'm tired of being paraded out every summer like a circus sideshow for anyone who pays fifteen dollars to get through our gates. Aren't you?"

My head spun. *Commons* was an old derogatory term from 1950s schoolbooks. I've never heard anyone actually *say* it out loud. "But isn't that what we do?" I asked. "Help people come to terms with their grief? Rid them of being haunted? What use would mediums be otherwise?"

She stood and leaned forward eagerly as if she'd been waiting all year for me to ask exactly this question. "You have this all wrong, Russ. Backwards. Don't you see? We aren't here for the commons. They have the entire world to gallivant around in while they're worrying about facts and figures. They have Buchanan," she said, spitting out the last word in a way that showed her distaste.

I winced again at the slur and knew I should call her out, but Willow's words were contrary to any I'd heard since coming to St. Hilaire and I needed to know what she was up to before I took the moral high ground. "I don't get it," I said. "Who do you think we're here for?"

"Isn't it clear?" she asked. "We exist to free the spirits who are trapped. There is no veil or door or whatever they're teaching in school these days. *We* are the veil, Russ. We exist to right whatever mistake was made that allows a spirit to become trapped. We need to free them from base human connections, from the overload of useless, primitive emotions. Ultimately, we exist to be something better. Something…higher. We need to save them."

This was probably the most animated I'd ever seen her. "Save them? Save the ghosts?"

She grabbed the old school chair next to me and sat down. "Think about it," she demanded, face glowing. "What do all those customers come to town wanting? To know where money is stored or if someone still loves them. Look at the records from last year. Virtually all of them wanted to ease their own guilt or get ahead in some way. It has nothing to do with the spirits who should be set free. The ghosts are just…trapped without us."

"Trapped," I said back. I thought of the ghosts I came into contact with most often. Ian. Melody Thorne. Neither struck me as being forced to continue on somewhere they didn't want to be. I tried to wrap my head around what that might mean in the bigger picture. "If you think ghosts should be freed to move on, what about the Guild summoning Sarahlyn Beck a few years ago so that she could use her alchemy skills to create money for St. Hilaire?"

I watched her face for any sign that my words had struck their target. Willow was so damned difficult to read. She had the world's greatest poker face. If we got through all of this on the same side, I needed to find out how she did that.

Willow's eyes moved from side to side. "That's ridiculous," she said. "Alchemy is an unproven theory. And what business is it of yours anyhow?" Her words were measured and careful, but her left eye twitched ever so slightly. *Gotcha.*

I shrugged. "Just curious."

Her jaw tightened. "If you're going to be student leader, then I suggest you start paying attention to your actual work."

"Willow…" I started. Part of me wanted to make her a confidant. She would make a much better ally than enemy. If Ian and I were truly going to fight the Guild, it would be great to have her on our side and not theirs.

The thing was, Willow had no weak spots. There was nothing—aside from this whole idea of us "freeing" ghosts—that she seemed particularly passionate about, and that included Colin. The fact that the Guild's misguided plans to use Sarahlyn's talents ended in the death of multiple mediums didn't really seem to be important to her.

I expected her to tell me again to focus on my work. But this time she fiddled with the old-as-dirt Walkman in her hand before looking up at me. "I know you didn't grow up here, Russ. But you were chosen student leader and therefore I have to assume you're smart. Be smart enough not to waste your time following the path of rumors when there are actual goals you could be pursuing."

Then she hit Play again and the lesson restarted.

When I got home, I hesitated on the porch. I was betting Ian wasn't aware of the day's significance, but what if I was wrong? I hadn't seen it, but I'd heard of ghosts damaging entire buildings on their birthdays or on the anniversaries of their deaths. I'd heard that some ghosts got pissy if either day was overlooked. Some held the day in reverence and had rituals, visiting their loved ones in dreams, moving furniture around, and generally causing trouble, just so someone would notice them. Others didn't want to be reminded of such anniversaries and stayed elusive even if you needed to reach them.

It was hard to know which camp Ian would fall into; we'd never celebrated a birthday together when he was alive, and he was twitchier on the topic of his death than any other.

I was relieved to open the door to a quiet house. After a quick glance around, I walked over to the dining room table and found a note from my father. When I was little, the notes would appear in my lunch box. Now he left them around the house for me to find.

Contrary to his usual motivational messages, this one was a joke. A train pun, of course.

Q: Why were the railroad tracks angry?
A: Because people were always crossing them.

I laughed at the corniness of the joke and smiled at the fact that, somehow, my father would have known I needed to laugh.

Since I had the house to myself, I went to my room and lit a stick of incense before I sat down in the middle of the floor. Eyes closed, I began to sing "Happy Birthday." I didn't have much of a voice, but I wasn't sure Ian could hear me anyhow or would care about the quality of my singing.

Somewhere around the "Happy birthday, dear Ian" part of my third run-through, the room cooled, but I kept my eyes closed. I hadn't actually tried to deliberately contact Ian for a while; he was just always kind of around. The whole process still filled me with a strange mix of excitement and dread, like how I imagined it would feel to go on safari and finally see a wild tiger.

"What did you get me?" Ian whispered in my ear. And even though I'd summoned him, I jumped.

I opened my eyes, but he'd turned off the lights and I could only make out shadows. "Ian…"

"So they tell me," he said. His words were slow and languid. They reminded me of the maple syrup my mother had favored. The one that always took too long to pour out of the bottle. I knew there were things—vitally important things—that I needed to talk to Ian about but I was suddenly hungry for something, for sensation, for grounding. For something so intense that it would take me out of my thoughts and allow me to lose myself.

I reached out for him, grabbed him really, not allowing him to dare to be at all insubstantial. Not allowing him to be the ghost he actually was. My nails dug through the fabric of his shirt, I heard his breath…no not breath, the facsimile of breath or whatever the hell it was, as he inhaled sharply in surprise and a million other things I didn't want to analyze. I kissed him hard and he responded in kind, understanding somehow what I needed.

"Russ." My name came out of his mouth forced in a short moment where he pulled back, sounding younger and more vulnerable than he had even when he was alive. "I don't know if I can…"

I didn't care. I swallowed the rest of his sentence in my mouth.

chapter fifteen

RUSS

I rolled over to find myself alone.

"Ian?" I called. It was odd to think Ian was out there some-where listening for his name.

I shivered, then grabbed a sweatshirt and shrugged it over the T-shirt I'd slept in. "Ian?" I called again, then licked my lips which felt bruised from our make-out session.

Behind me, I heard a suddenly there Ian yawn. I turned and watched as he made a circuit of my room.

"Looking for your common sense?" I asked.

He grinned and walked around picking up schoolbooks and pens, tarot cards, and a piece of orange rind I'd neglected to throw in the trash. Then he picked up a book of poetry I had to read for school and started reciting lines about paths diverging in a wood.

I grabbed my jeans from the floor and shrugged into them under the covers. "I think it's time we talked," I said in the direction of the wall.

Ian sat down in my desk chair. "I thought that's what we were doing."

I shook my head. "Not about the things we need to, we aren't."

Ian raised an eyebrow and leaned a worn boot on my desk. "Okay, I'll bite," he said. "What's bugging you?"

There were many things bugging me. The Guild and their ridiculous tasks. My lack of progress in making any headway into even developing a plan to get to the bottom of the death of Dec's parents. Everything Willow had said. This stupid TV show and that regardless of what Ian thought, Rice wasn't going to change his plans just because Ian demanded it. My totally bizarre yet not at all unpleasant interactions with a boy from Buchanan who *gave* me a car for no reason I could discern.

I sifted through my feelings, looking for a good starting place. There wasn't one. "There was something Willow mentioned…" I began.

"This should be good." Ian smirked.

"She has this idea…well, that we aren't here to read for"—I caught myself before I said *commons*—"people. That we—mediums—are really here to help ghosts…pass on."

"Pass on," Ian echoed in a way that made me realize, for the first time, how awkward this conversation was going to get. It wasn't that I forgot he was a ghost, it was that he was so different from other spirits and so much like he'd been when he was alive that it often slipped my mind.

"Yeah," I admitted.

He narrowed his eyes at me. "And you what? You agree with her? Are you offering to send me to my eternal rest? Gee, Griffin, I'm hurt. I wouldn't have thought you'd be *that* sick of me already."

His reaction was phrased as a joke, but I heard a whiff of insecurity behind it. Was this a ghost Ian thing? Had I gotten even a hint of that same humility back when Ian was alive, we might have…no, that didn't matter now.

"It isn't that," I backtracked. "I just… I don't know. I definitely don't buy into all of her extreme stuff and the fact she's hanging around with your brother is whacked, but her idea of us—mediums, I mean—actually helping ghosts…not you, but the others. It's an interesting concept. It makes a strange sort of sense," I ended, running out of steam. My heart hammered in my chest. I hated that this was how Ian and I exchanged information: under duress. It was always an ongoing game of tug-of-war with no clear winner.

Ian leaned his arms on his knees. I tried to tell whether his shoulders were rising and falling with each breath. Or whether it was a trick of the light. Or my vision. Or wishful thinking, maybe.

His eyes were glued to the floor as he asked, "And you're bringing this up now, why?" Then his head snapped up. His face was taut and fierce. "Why are you so fixated on my death, Russ?"

"I'm not fixated. This is Willow, and you have to admit it makes a strange sort of sense. I just…" Ian's fingers tightened on the edge of my bed. I was careful when I said, "Because you won't talk about it."

"I don't talk about global economics either, but I don't hear you giving me a hard time about that."

"Ian."

He sighed in obvious annoyance, but the muscles in his face softened. "Fine, you want the story, here's the story. I was at a party in Buchanan. At the university. Things got a little out of hand, if you catch my drift. I was… Let's say I was preoccupied. Suddenly the door burst open and there was a fight. Or something. Some commotion of the sort that always happens at university parties."

"So, what? You unpreoccupied yourself to go break it up?"

"No," he said, even more annoyed.

"Ian, what happened?"

"What happened was that I tried to stay preoccupied, but when I got up to close the door, I realized Willow Rogers had showed up while everyone else was distracted."

"What?" Even though I'd been the one to bring up the subject of Willow, her entrance into the story of Ian's death threw me. Suddenly, I wasn't sure if I wanted to hear any more. But I couldn't pull my eyes away from his mouth as he continued.

"I mean, it's possible she'd been there for a while, but frankly I can't imagine who would have invited her, given the amount of—" he mused before he stopped when he undoubtedly caught the expression on my face, which was the product of the picture I had in my head of the sort of party Ian would have gone to Buchanan to attend. "Anyhow, as I said, I was busy. Don't give me that judgmental look, Griffin. You weren't even speaking to me."

My face flushed and I looked away. There was nothing I

could say in reply. I knew Ian would let the silence build until I couldn't stand it, so I added a noncommittal and defeated "And then?"

"And then she told me the Hamptons needed my help," Ian replied, his voice softening in a way that made me miss him in spite of the fact he was sitting right in front of me. "Are you sure you really want to hear this?"

"No. Yes," I stammered. "Yeah," I lied. I wasn't sure of anything.

Ian got up and walked over to the window. "Sidebar. You know how this whole 'bloodline' thing, started right? It was Willow. I mean, that shouldn't surprise you. Her favorite word is 'purity,' and all Rice wants is a shiny legacy in the St. Hilaire history books. He isn't calculating enough to think of such a twisted, long-term plan."

I didn't call him out for the change of topic, hoping it would circle back around. "You mean Willow was *trying* to get matched up with your brother?"

Ian spun around, a bemused look on his face. "No. Not quite. Colin was never who she had in mind. Remember that for her it's about strength and...the next generation of medium babies."

I was missing something. "So, who?"

"Don't be dense, Griffin. She was trying to get matched up with *me*," Ian said with some odd tone of pride.

"Oh my god..." I couldn't keep from laughing. "Is she out of her mind?"

He smirked. "Well, clearly she was shooting for the moon," he said and laughed. "But anyhow, remember she had an agenda, and it had nothing to do with riding off into the sunset in romantic bliss."

I couldn't keep the picture of Willow and Ian out of my mind. It was absurd. And under that, unnerving. But no. That would never have happened. But was that why she was always asking about him? "Are you saying Willow killed you because you wouldn't *sleep* with her?"

Ian flinched. "I'm not saying that at all. My disinterest was a complication to her. It bugged her more that I considered being a medium what I *did*, not who I *was*. I mean, hell, I knew I was talented, but it isn't as if being a medium was the only thing I was good at." He gave me a look that made my cheeks grow hot, and I kind of hated him for knowing how to get to me so easily.

"Anyhow," he said, with a small smile of accomplishment, "she really did come to get me because the Hamptons were in trouble. She'd been part of a séance with a loose-lipped ghost… Do you remember Jerry?"

I refocused and tried to remember who Jerry was. "That old guy the Guild threatened to kick out of town after he made a pass at a tourist?"

"That's the one." Ian nodded. "Do you remember how he was always driving that ancient, rusted death-mobile way too fast through town?"

"Oh hell." I could picture it as clearly as if it were a movie in my head. Him swerving that big country-boy truck all over the road while blasting twangy music about leaving his wife and loving his dog and drinking too much whiskey. I could picture him cutting off the Hamptons and causing the accident for the price of a crappy bottle of moonshine.

"Well, apparently Jerry paid a visit to the wishing rock or something to confess his sins before it all went down. Then his brother's ghost came to Willow of all people and told her what was going to happen."

"And what? You rode in on your white horse and tried to save them?"

Ian's mouth hardened in an uncharacteristic line. "Yeah. Something like that."

Of course he did. That was the sort of stuff Ian had lived for: saving the day, making the big play, being the star.

Before I could say anything, though, his face fell to match his mouth and he said, "It didn't matter much, though, did it? They still died. I was too late."

I froze at the jagged tone of his voice. It was a ghost thing, this tone. Something I heard more and more in his voice as time went on. I forced myself to reach out and grip his bicep. The single movement felt as though it cost me something I couldn't afford to lose.

"You did everything you could," I said, trying to be comforting. The words were empty, though. I had no idea what he'd done or hadn't done.

Ian glared at me. As if he could hear my thoughts, he said, "You know better than that, Griffin. I did only as much as I thought I needed to. I told Willow I had things to finish up at the party. And I did. Finish them up. If I had taken her seriously and followed her out… Well, maybe things would have ended differently."

"What did she think you could do, anyhow?"

"I don't know. Convince the Hamptons not to go out? Not

like there was any love lost between them and her. Help her convince whoever was paying Jerry off that Sarahlyn's missing gold didn't matter? Either way, I did nothing."

"So, you're blaming yourself for the Hamptons' deaths?" I asked.

"Yes. No." The room grew suddenly hot. I felt the air shift, swirl around me in a dizzying funnel mirrored by my stomach. Ian's eyes narrowed. "Griffin, can you please fucking stop," he yelled through clenched jaws. "I'm not hanging around to work through some guilty feelings, and you don't exist so you can 'free' me. Whatever the hell that even means. Just let it go."

I pulled back fast enough that I sent a bag of runes flying off the bed.

Ian ran his hands through his hair and closed his eyes. The room stopped spinning, but my stomach didn't. "I'm sorry," he said. I could see in his eyes he wanted to step forward but knew me well enough not to. "I'm sorry." Then, "Russ?"

I took stock of myself. At my breath coming in huffs. My hand running over the owl tattoo on my wrist. I was used to Ian's quips and jabs, his intellectual games and control issues. But I didn't think I'd ever heard him yell before. Not even at his brothers. "I'm fine," I said through gritted teeth. "I'm fine."

"Death isn't great for mood swings," he said, trying to smile from across the room. I knew the distance between us was eating at him.

"Obviously," I said softly, almost under my breath.

He stepped forward slowly and placed a hand under my chin, tilting my head up, and I let him. "I'm sorry," he said again, sounding as unlike the Ian I knew as he ever had.

But I reacted as I always did to his touch. Paralyzed in a way. "Are we fighting?" he asked.

"Fighting? No…" I said.

He dropped his hand and my blood began to flow again. I collected myself. "You know what?" I said, stepping away from him and over to the window. "Let's drop this. It doesn't matter anyhow."

Only it did matter. At least to me. But even when he was alive, Ian had been made of smoke and secrets. I hadn't been able to get him to come clean about anything then, and I certainly wouldn't be able to now.

It didn't matter to him that I was confused about the events surrounding his death because why should it? That had nothing to do with why he was hanging around.

Ian could out-stubborn me any day of the week, and I'd known that since the day I first met him, so why had it been getting to me so much?

Maybe it had mattered more that he wouldn't tell me.

Now that he was willing to or at least trying to, I guess I would have to make my peace with not knowing. Or at least learn to fake it.

chapter sixteen

ASHER

"It's a bit silly to call it a family meeting when it's only three of us, isn't it?" I pointed out.

My mother rolled her eyes, but I could see my father's right hand clench. He'd never hit either me or Mari, not as far as I knew, anyhow. But I'd seen him throw a book across the room before. And once, a small stuffed toy cat of my sister's.

"Heads-up, Asher," he said. "Rick and his team are going to be here tomorrow."

"Oh," I breathed out. The syllable escaped more than I spoke it. Rick was the director of *Ghost Killers*. This was really going to happen.

Unless I could stop it.

Did I want to stop it? Maybe my parents were, at some

level, doing what they needed to do in order to move on. Maybe debunking St. Hilaire was the only logical culmination of their years-long goal to protect the people they felt were being hurt by places like this. Maybe when they were done, they would notice they still had a living kid.

I'd prefer that they didn't end up hating me more than they already did.

But I didn't want Russ to hate me either.

I couldn't imagine how I could stop the show from filming. It wasn't as if I could change my parents' minds. I had to figure out how to derail things. But I wasn't the kind of person who derailed things. Plus, in this case, derailing things meant proving ghosts *did* exist, and how the hell was I going to do that?

I could always try to convince my parents that it was actually a good thing they couldn't contact Mari, but that was even less likely, unless…

"Asher." My dad sighed impatiently.

I looked up but felt too guilty to hold his gaze. In my mouth, the metal of my lip ring tasted faintly of copper. I ran over it with my tongue to keep myself from talking.

"As I was saying," he continued. "Rick will be getting here tomorrow. He's going to head over there and scout things out before the crew shows up later in the week. If you think you'll learn anything that's going to help him, now is the time to do it. Tell Rick everything you've found out about this place, however small or insignificant it may seem to you."

I nodded and watched my mother dabbing at her eyes. Why, I wondered, for what must be the four-millionth time, couldn't we be the kind of family that simply cried together and shared memories of Mari and left flowers somewhere once in a while. Why didn't they remember or care that I missed her, too? Were they only going to take my feelings seriously if I walked around hating the world, too?

"Do you think?" Mom snuffled. "Do you think you'll learning anything from this boy?"

She let her voice trail off, and I considered letting the silence swirl awkwardly around us. But I couldn't stand the idea that it might sound as though I was hesitating or doubted Russ.

"Yeah," I said, holding her eyes. "I think so."

In my head, I heard Mari's voice: *If wishes were horses, then beggars would ride.* I almost laughed. The more time I spent with Russ, the more he reminded me of an onion: layers and layers of stories and secrets. There were more things I wanted to learn from him than I could dream of.

But none of those things were the ones my mother cared about. What she wanted was for Russ to give me a tour of St. Hilaire so I could direct Rick and his team to the cheesiest place to shoot. What she wanted was for someone who sounded confident and controlled and who looked good on camera to agree to be filmed trying to contact a ghost—not Mari, that would be too hard on her, but trying to contact someone else's random dead loved one, perhaps—and, of course, fail. What she wanted was someone who would prove their point.

Was that person Russ? Was it possible I could simply ask him to bail me out and play along?

My mother stared at me, waiting for a definitive answer.

I wanted to tell her that I was hoping to learn what made

him smile. I wanted to tell her what it meant to have someone to talk to, someone who listened.

My mother was still staring at me, so I smiled and left her with her own assumptions.

———

I closed the door to my room as quietly as I could, which was silly because my parents wouldn't be upset at me closing my door. I often got the feeling they were happiest when I was out of sight.

I stared at my phone. I had Russ's phone number from when he'd answered my car ad. He'd come over for dinner, so it wouldn't be weird for me to text him. Or would it? I had no experience with this stuff. I wondered what Mari would have done, but that was silly because people were always reaching out to her. She'd probably never had to be the one to worry about looking stupid.

Maybe I could play it safe and see what happened. I typed a text. Hi! That's it. Just saying hello. We should have dinner again sometime.

But then I deleted the last sentence and typed, I hope you're doing something fun. I just had the most ridiculous "family meeting" with my parents. Then I inserted an eye-roll emoji, hit Send, and threw the phone on the bed.

When I didn't get an immediate answer, I pulled out a beat-up shoebox from my closet, took the lid off, and dug around. Under an old worn sweater was a flash drive. In the days after Mari died, I couldn't stand to watch the video on it. Then, when I'd forgotten the sound of her voice, I forced myself to play it on my parents' computer one night when they were working and I was home alone. By the time I got my own laptop, I was able to watch it all the time without it making me feel as though I was being ripped to shreds inside.

I didn't watch it much anymore. I guess I'd seen it so many times I could play it back in my memory, projected onto the inside of my eyelids like a film. The broken stone of the building. The heat of the Tennessee summer sun. The sound of her laughter when a stray white dog ran into the frame.

The video was the only thing on the drive, the only episode of my parents' show I found at all valuable.

I plugged in the drive and pushed Play. Forwarded past the opening sequence and my father's droning introduction to the house that was said to be haunted by the ghost of some Civil War soldier.

I paused the playback when Mari came on the screen. She wasn't supposed to be there. My mother had been strict about keeping us both out of the filming aspect of the show. But somehow Stuart, the camera operator that season, had caught her running across the field in her white dress, dark hair streaming out behind her, looking ethereal and wild.

Perhaps he thought the footage could be cut out in edits if my parents didn't want it. Perhaps he was entranced by her pure joy as she spun around and around under the sunlight that seemed designed to spotlight her.

The sound was scratchy…meant to be replaced with atmospheric music or more of my dad's historical notes, but in it, the frizzle of the electrical wires created an odd type of music. Then, "Asher, come dance with me."

I usually avoided watching the next part where eleven-year-old me moved tentatively into view, never having been able to deny my sister anything. Her face lit up when she saw me; her hand pulled me into the swing dance we'd learned for some cousin's wedding. She was all grace and light. I was a clumsy accessory and I didn't mind.

I didn't begrudge my parents for wanting to talk to her again. I had so many things I wanted to tell her myself. So much I wanted to know.

I spun a tiny ring around on my finger. It had a shooting star engraved on the inside, and I'd bought it for Mari's sixteenth birthday. She'd worn it on her middle finger, but it only fit my pinky. I sometimes felt guilty for wearing it, but hell if I was going to see it donated with the rest of the stuff my mom gave away.

On the screen, the camera panned away, and the video stopped. There was no way my joyous sister would want to bring down Russ, bring down an entire town just to make us feel better. And maybe, at the end of the day, the truth was she simply didn't want to talk to us.

To me.

"I'm sorry, Mari. I'm so, so sorry. Please forgive me," I said, putting my head down on my crossed arms and listening to the unending silence that filled the room.

chapter seventeen

RUSS

I rolled over and checked my phone. I read Asher's text and smiled. What sort of normal Buchanan thing had he been meeting with his parents about? Curfew? That we hadn't left them enough tacos?

That probably wasn't fair.

I answered. I'm having a pretty whacked couple of days myself. Trust me, you wouldn't believe it if I told you.

My phone buzzed with a reply. You can try. I'm always happy to listen. But I get it if you're dealing with confidential ghost stuff.

I typed back: Ghost stuff. Yeah, you could say that. But thanks for the offer. Appreciate it.

I powered my phone down and got up to take a shower. I'd called a meeting of the Youth Corps, and hoped Rice wasn't going to corner me before I met with them and with Ian.

When I walked into the Youth Corps meeting room, Lee Holt bolted across the room, pulled his shoulders back, and said, "I pledge to always seek the truth, to form a bridge..." before I stopped him. I know I was leader of the Corps, and I actually believed in everything the pledge had to say, but I hated when other students got so formal with me. Additionally, this meeting was making me edgy enough without anyone talking about forming a bridge between life and death.

"Quite a crowd," I said. Given that I'd called this meeting at the last minute, I wasn't expecting everyone to turn up. The rumor mill in St. Hilaire was strong, though. When everyone was talking to spirits who had the potential to overhear everything happening, it was hard to keep things a secret and it was no surprise that other members of the Corps would be invested in the *Ghost Killers* show situation as well.

Someone threw a piece of popcorn, which bounced off my shoulder and onto the table in front of me. The Youth Corps might have been made up of high school seniors, but they still acted like five-year-olds when they were all together.

I tossed the kernel in the trash on my way to the front of the room and then turned around, facing the twenty-four members of the Corps. I'd known most of them for a few years since not a lot of new families had been approved to move into St. Hilaire lately. They were a good group on the whole, pretty much what you'd expect from kids who could talk to the dead and lived together in an isolated upstate town. We were all peculiar in one way or another, but there was something comforting in that accepted knowledge.

"So, you guys all know why we're here," I said, leaning back against the lectern. It didn't matter how confident I felt about my abilities to talk to spirits; I was still uncomfortable talking to anyone who was still breathing.

"Not everyone is a guy, you know," called out Cindy Hale with a laugh. She was cool. And correct. I'd lived in the Midwest too long and still called everyone "guys."

"Yeah, you're right, sorry," I said. "Anyhow, I thought it would be beneficial for us to watch one of the old *Ghost Killers* episodes and then make a recommendation to the Guild about next steps. There's no promise the Guild will follow our recommendations, but I think it would show us being proactive, and you never know, I think they could use some new input."

"I've seen one," said Mauro Ortega. "The team was sent to a telephone call center because the security cameras caught some unexplained electrical disturbance and then they thought they'd seen a ghost in the hallway. But they couldn't catch anything on camera."

"Everyone thinks they see ghosts everywhere," Cindy said. "'The door shut unexpectedly,' 'I heard a noise only no one else was home,' 'It got really cold for no real reason.' Oh, sorry, Russ."

"No problem." Everyone knew I had problems with temperature when ghosts were around, and I knew she didn't mean anything by it. "But you're right. I mean, they don't get how rare it is for a spirit to continue on as a ghost. They have to *really* want to stick around…" My voice trailed off as I thought about my conversation with Willow. *Was* Ian in pain? Or was he simply obsessed, and if so, with what? Me? The Guild? Something he hadn't even mentioned?

Someone coughed and I realized I hadn't said anything for too long. "Anyhow," I regrouped, "the *Ghost Killers* team did a lot of work in Europe, but the episode I'm going to show is one of their earliest U.S. ones. It was the only one I could find online in full. It's set in a library in Michigan. Patrons reported"—I looked at the notes I'd taken—"book pages turning without being touched, a transparent woman walking through a wall, and"—I squinted to read my own writing—"the sound of kids playing in a closed room when the librarians came to open up in the morning."

"Dum, dum, *dum*," someone hummed ominously from the back of the room. Everyone else burst into laughter.

I nodded at Lee, and he turned off the lights and started casting from his tablet. I walked over to a table in the front and sat down a few chairs from anyone else. Before I'd taken over as leader of the Corps, I might have sat with someone. But now they all treated me like I was a teacher. Whispers stopped when I walked into the room. Everyone kept a healthy distance at Corps events. It was odd and fairly horrible, and for some reason I hadn't expected it.

I turned my attention to the screen. The opening music was predictably eerie, which set the wrong tone, I think, for a show that was trying to debunk the entire theory of ghosts existing.

Fog swirled around and then cleared to display the words *Ghost Killers* in a cheesy font. A voice detailed the issues the library had been facing, while the camera showed scenes from the city, which looked like every other little town in the Midwest.

Mila Kelly, according to the banner along the bottom of the screen, was the town librarian, an impeccably dressed middle-aged woman in a red suit who looked as though she was excited about her television debut. "You hear a lot of things in my line of work," she said. "We don't just talk to our patrons about books. We function as a kind of community social center, so when I started hearing the same story from multiple visitors, I had to take them seriously."

The camera panned through the halls of the darkened library as Kelly continued. "At first we received reports of foot-steps and strange sounds coming from empty rooms whenever anyone looked inside. But then there were the books."

"The books?" a man's voice asked, dripping with scorn. "I mean, you *are* a library."

"Yes, but my staff takes even the administrative parts of their work very seriously," Kelly said, looking him straight in the eye. "Every night we ensure that books which are returned or viewed are replaced in their correct place on the shelves. And every morning, we'd return to find things out of sorts. Books on the floor. Carts overturned and such. And before you ask, it wasn't an animal or anything. We set traps." Someone sighed dismissively off camera.

"We set up to film," the man continued. "Our equip-ment will filter out white noise, so the resulting sounds will be echoey." He spoke into a black box connected to a series of wires. "Is anyone here? My name is Martin. My team and I would like to talk to you."

There was silence followed by a kind of electronic wave as he fiddled with some knobs.

He fired off a series of equally inane questions before turning to the camera and saying, "For the record, we're not getting any sort of response on either our audio or electronic equipment."

They continued down the hall and stopped in front of the room that the patrons had apparently reported hearing the children playing in. "We're going to go in and see if we can rule out any sign of paranormal activity in here," Martin said.

"Oh, good lord," someone behind me shouted out. "That isn't how it works."

"Not to mention the fact you can't actually disprove anything in that way," I said.

The *Ghost Killers* team went into the room with their night-vision cameras and their sound machines. They asked some questions and bounced on the floor to see if there were any soft spots and knocked on the walls, and then everything went dark.

"I can't watch this crap," said Lee who had obviously stopped casting. "How did this show even get on the air?"

"It ran for, like, ten years, so good question," I replied. "But the question for us is 'What do we recommend the Guild do about it?'"

I walked over and flipped on the lights and sat on the top stair leading to the stage.

"We can't just ignore it?" asked Lee.

I wished I could share the information I had about what Clive Rice wanted to do and about the Guild asking Ian to show up, but that was all confidential.

"I've heard a production crew is going to show up outside

145

the gates, so I think they're committed to addressing this somehow," I answered. "if we're going to debunk this, what do you think would be most effective?"

"I think we should invite them to St. Hilaire and let Mulvaney scare the crap out of them," said Cindy. Mulvaney was one of St. Hilaire's most annoying ghosts. From what we could tell, he'd been in his teens when he jumped into the deep end of Lake Moritz on a dare and drowned before St. Hilaire was settled. He had a habit of popping into people's readings and deliberately talking over the spirit who was trying to be contacted. It didn't matter what we did; we couldn't seem to get rid of him. Which of the five common reasons kept *him* here? There wasn't an "A for annoying" in the acronym for *ghost*.

"That would definitely get their attention," I agreed, "but probably not great for PR."

"It would be different if there was any sign of them being open-minded," said Lee. "I mean, what about Mr. Rice holding a séance to contact someone connected to one of their show's team?"

"*President* Rice," Cindy emphasized. "Didn't you see the Guild wants their official titles used now?" A low groan went through the room. "I guess we're going to have to start calling Russ 'Student Leader Griffin' now," she teased.

"Hell no, you won't," I replied. The whole idea was repulsive.

"Anyhow, a séance would be great, but it's risky," Cindy said. "What happens if a ghost doesn't show up? What happens if whoever it is from the show lies and denies everything the ghost says? They're going to be protecting the premise of their show first, right? That's where their money is coming from."

As the group bantered ideas back and forth, I started to realize there was a chance we might only have one option, and that was the one Rice—I couldn't think of him as President Rice—had already put into motion, a séance involving Ian. Mentally, I begged the members of the Corps to come up with an alternate suggestion.

"Why don't we set it up?" suggested Cindy. "Plant a ghost we trust or at least can count on to show up and be impressive."

My head whipped around to her fast enough that she called me out on it.

"What?" she asked.

I shook my head. "Nothing. I mean, that's a good idea. Who did you have in mind?" *Don't say Ian, Don't say Ian, Don't say Ian.*

"What about Melody Thorne?" Mauro suggested.

"Didn't you get enough of her this summer?" Cindy asked. "Besides, I've heard she's gotten harder to contact lately. Maybe there's a statute of limitations on sticking around just because you like a place."

My stomach rolled and I rubbed my tattoo until I caught Lee watching me. I didn't know if he was staring because he was hoping I'd offer up Ian or staring because he was hoping I'd offer some measure of leadership.

"What about Ian Mackenzie?" Lee said quietly.

The room fell silent as everyone's eyes landed on me. I pulled my jacket tighter and sat down backwards in a chair in the first row. "I'm not going to pretend that all of you don't know that Ian talks to me. So, if anyone has anything to say about that, now is the time to get it off your chest."

Some of the group shuffled in their seats and there was an uncomfortable silence before Mauro asked, "Will he show up when we need him? I've heard he's a bit of an arrogant prick."

I winced but knew he was only echoing what I was sure a lot of people were thinking.

"Would it even work?" Cindy asked. "Unless he can make himself visible not only to the show people, but to the cameras, they'll be able to write the whole thing off to electricity or lies or whatever."

"You all heard what happened when Ian came to meet with President Rice, right?" Dave asked from the back of the room. "I know no one was supposed to talk about it, but don't tell me you haven't heard how solid he was or how long it all went on for."

"That's what she said," someone else called out. Everyone laughed as I dug my nails into my palms. I knew how it all sounded, but I didn't have time for games. None of us did, and I knew I had to take control of the situation.

"Ian doesn't want to do it," I mumbled.

"He doesn't want to?" Cindy stood up. "I don't mean to be all doom and gloom, but have you given any thought to what will happen if we don't take a stand? Russ, you of all people... I mean, our grandmothers went to school together. How would you feel if St. Hilaire went out of business and you had to move somewhere else?" She didn't wait for an answer. "And Jude," she addressed a boy in the back row who had moved to town right at the gates were closing for the year. "You just got here. You told us you'd been hoping to find someplace like St. Hilaire all your life. How would *you* feel if this show succeeds and the town you've always wanted to live in turns out to be nothing except one more dull upstate town?"

My stomach curdled with the realization that Cindy would make a hell of a better Corps leader than I was turning out to be.

I raked a hand through my hair. We were supposed to be the next generation of leaders. The kids in this room were the ones who would lead St. Hilaire once Rice and his crew were ousted. I had to at least pretend I knew what I was doing.

"I'm going to be honest," I said. "I don't know if I can change Ian's mind. And I would seriously love to be able to justify going back to…" The word *President* stuck in my throat. "…Rice and telling him we think the Guild should ignore the whole idea of this show. And I'm still hoping we can come up with something better. But Cindy is right. What's really important here is to do the right thing for St. Hilaire. For everyone who has lived here and everyone who might move here someday because it's the only place they feel as though they belong."

My throat felt raw. It was the probably the longest speech I've ever made in public—or honestly in private—but this felt like a turning point. One for St. Hilaire and one for me. And in laying out my case to the Corps members, I'd started to consider that we might actually have to do this. And it all came down to convincing Ian. And convincing myself.

chapter eighteen

WILLOW

The monotony of sanding the spirit cabinet allowed me to get my thoughts in order, and I realized the things I wanted weren't so disparate after all. I wanted Ian gone for good. I wanted his power. And I wanted St. Hilaire returned to its status as a force in the spiritualist world, one that could devote itself to the true purpose of mediums. Perhaps all of that could be brought about in one spectacular maneuver. Perhaps *Ghost Killers* was the answer to everything.

I had to make it happen. And I had to make Father think it was his idea, or he and the Guild would push back.

"If you allow this, there will be trucks," I said, letting the curtains fall against the window. "Lining up outside St. Hilaire with their lights and their cameras. It's going to be the worst sort of spectacle." I drew the last word out into extra syllables. I knew Father loved nothing more than a good bit of drama.

"What do you have in mind?" Father asked. He cut a regal figure in this room of gold and burgundy, but I saw the stress in his eyes. It was perhaps presumptuous of him to assume I'd come up with an idea. But then he knew me. And he was correct.

"I was hoping you would be able to hold your ground and shut this show down, but if you don't feel as though you can do that..." I stared down at my nails, pacing myself. "I think, perhaps, we should give them what they want."

Father took a deep breath. I could feel the weight of his stare. "I'm not sure I know what you mean."

"Ian Mackenzie," I said, the name forming like cotton candy on my tongue.

Father rubbed his hands together and closed his eyes in the way he did when he was deep in thought.

"Ian seems...disinterested in helping us," he said bitterly. "And you know what he's like."

I fought to keep a smile off my face. I did know what Ian was like. I knew how charming he could be. I knew how the light danced around him when he was taking charge of a séance. I knew the power he played with when he was alive and how that power might be used in a different way now that he'd crossed over. Oh yes, I knew what he was *like*.

Ian would never simply show up if I or the Guild called him. He'd made that abundantly clear. But for my plan to work, I needed him to. And I needed Father to believe that my motives were about helping the Guild. If I planted the correct seeds, Ian would be delivered right to me.

"Everyone has a price," I said, allowing my voice to smooth into nonchalance. It amazed me how easy it was to form the lie, to lay the groundwork for my plan.

"A price?" Father asked, eager. Given the years he had led the Guild, he was surprisingly soft. Few could see through it. It was amazing how afraid the mediums were of him, when in truth all he wanted was to rule without conflict.

"Sometimes, Father," I said smoothly, "you need to turn things upside down. Threaten what Ian cares most about. You know he isn't as tough as he appears."

"His family is…"

"No," I interrupted. "Not his family. He hasn't reached out to Colin at all since he died, and neither his mother nor his younger brother lives in town anymore." I picked up the letter opener on Father's desk and waited while he figured it out. The point was razor sharp. That was good information to have.

"Russ Griffin?" Father asked, looking up. Finally.

A deep sense of relief washed over me. I nodded and watched the possibilities spread across Father's face. This was going to be a lot of fun.

chapter nineteen

ASHER

Jordan Lawler, winner of the Upstate New York Investigative Journalism Award for the past three years, according to the banner under his smiling face, leaned forward in his chair. The WKAD logo sat blinking happily in the corner of the screen as he said, "You've had previous offers—reportedly huge ones—to revive *Ghost Killers* and yet you turned them down. Why bring the show back now?"

My parents turned their heads toward each other. My father's mouth was tight and drawn, and my mother looked slightly toward the floor as if she might cry. But I could see that their eyes were blank. After a few seconds of uncomfortable silence, my mother flipped her hair back and said, "It's become obvious, in the years since our show ended, that there are still places taking advantage of good people. People who are in pain from the loss of a loved one. There was a time when I...we... assumed we'd made a difference in the extent to which these places are allowed to thrive. But I guess we're realizing that the more chaotic and frustrating the world gets, the more places such as this are preying on people's grief. The fact that the leaders of St. Hilaire have had to deliberate so long before simply allowing us into town speaks volumes."

My mother reached over and took my father's hand. I heard myself gasp. I didn't remember the last time I'd seen them hold hands.

The camera zoomed in on Jordan's face. He had a good face for TV. High cheekbones. Perfect silver hair. White, white teeth. He did something to his eyes that made the sides of them crinkle. Plus, there was nothing false about the compassion that was strewn across his face. "Forgive me for asking, but I know our viewers are curious: Do you feel as though the unfortunate loss of your daughter has changed your perspective on the existence of an afterlife?"

The camera panned to my mother who swallowed visibly. "If anything," she said softly, "it made us more committed to calling out this sort of repugnant behavior. Like everyone, we've suffered losses in our lives, but losing my...our daughter made us realize the very real responsibility we have to other families like us who don't have the platform of the technology that we do to stop charlatans such as these from taking advantage of people."

Jordan reached out and touched my mother's other hand, then he looked back into the camera and said, "I'm sure I speak for our entire viewing audience when I say that we are, all of us, very sorry for your loss. And now to Ashley McQueen with the news."

I grabbed the remote so fast Houdini hissed at me. But it felt good to hit the off button on the remote. My heart thudded in my chest. What if it were true? What if St. Hilaire was using people? What if the whole town was nothing more than some elaborate money-making scheme and none of the so-called mediums cared whose feelings they were trampling on? What if even Russ was nothing more than a sham?

No, I'm pretty sure I would know if he were scamming people. Mari used to say I was like a dog, always able to figure out who was genuine or not. But what if I was being swayed by my frustration at my parents and my own loneliness?

Or the way Russ smiled as if he wasn't used to doing so? The way he smiled at *me*.

What if I was being swayed by *that*?

I hadn't heard from him since his last text. What were the chances he'd watched my parents' interview? I had the urge to call him and confess everything, but I knew I'd never hear from him again if I did, and I didn't want to risk that.

I read his last text again. Ghost stuff. Yeah, you could say that. But thanks for the offer. Appreciate it.

No matter how hard I tried, I couldn't find the promise of seeing him again in his words. There was nothing in there that even gave me an opening, but I decided to create one.

Well, I meant it anyhow. In case you change your mind and need to get out of St. H. for a while, just point Orion toward the planetarium. He knows the way.

I hit Send before I could talk myself out of it. But damn, I wanted to hear his voice again before all of this blew up in my face.

chapter twenty

R U S S

Careful, I typed to Asher, Or I might take you up on that offer. And glad to hear Orion has a sense of direction. Mine kind of sucks.

Anytime came the reply, followed by an emoji with a smile as wide as Asher's.

I took a deep breath, enjoying the ease of it all, and then my phone rang.

This time it wasn't the Guild calling; it was Clive Rice himself. I thought about not answering but really, what was the point?

"Hello?" I answered, although we both knew I knew who it was.

"I need to see you and Mr. Mackenzie in my office in thirty minutes. This isn't a request," he said before the phone went dead.

"I get that, but when it comes down to it, I'm simply not interested in being paraded around as proof of anything," Ian said emphatically. We were all tired. Even Ian was fading around the edges, and Clive Rice had gone through three towels, wiping the sweat off his forehead.

I wondered how long Ian could hold out. His stamina was amazing, but I made a mental note not to say that out loud to him because I could only imagine how he would throw *that* comment back in my face.

Ian has been adeptly sidestepping Clive Rice's questions and demands with "That's an interesting point" and "I take your question." But I knew this meeting was careening toward a breaking point.

Rice mopped his forehead and stood, hands braced on the table edge. "The facts are what they are, and you need to decide for yourself what and whom you are willing to sacrifice…" he spit out before remembering that anger had never been the best way to approach Ian Mackenzie.

After a tense moment of silence during which Ian simply looked straight ahead as if he was admiring the tiny arrows on the Guild President's tie, Rice cleared his throat and cast a sideways glance at me. I wasn't certain if Ian was helping or hindering my cause. After all, as things stood, Rice was still my teacher. And possibly my future employer.

He tapped the dial of his watch. "Mr. Mackenzie. We are running out of time."

Ian crossed his arms and tilted his chair back as if, to the contrary, he had all the time in the world, and Rice's interrogation was, in fact, taking up none of his energy. I knew it was a lie. Rice knew it was a lie. Most importantly, Ian knew it was a lie, which gave him the upper hand.

Rice sighed. "We need you to help us stop this wretched television program from destroying everything we, everything *you*, have worked so hard to build."

Ian allowed a sarcastic laugh to burst to the surface. "Sorry? I never worked hard to build this," he argued. "Guild flags required on every house, enforced matchmaking, and mediums run out of town, including my mother and younger brother, in case you've forgotten." Ian seemed to choke on the words. I knew it wasn't simply disgust at how off-track the Guild's policies had become, and I knew it had nothing to do with his family who he'd never been close to. It was more the enormity of the impasse between Ian and Rice, because while Rice was asking Ian to risk everything to ensure the Guild's future, I was still planning to work with him to tear it all down. But also, I had to wonder if the same thing that had happened to his family had happened to those people being marched out of town the other night.

"Enough of this." Rice turned to me abruptly. His face was red and blotchy. "Are you happy here, Mr. Griffin?"

"Happy?" I parroted back. My voice felt unused, my tongue thick.

"Do you find comfort living in a place where your unique talents are understood? Is your father fulfilled in his job as railway station manager?" He leaned forward across the table. "The ebbs and flows of life are many. Things you have and appreciate can be lost at any moment. We are at a turning point in St. Hilaire. A point when our very existence is in question. A point when loyalty must be valued over everything. Even talent." He stared into my eyes in a way that made it impossible to look away. "Am I making myself clear, Mr. Griffin?"

He was making himself clear as a crystal ball. The Guild had kicked other people out of town, including most of Ian's family. The idea of my dad and I being forced to leave St. Hilaire was the plot of every nightmare I'd had over the past year. I had no idea how I'd survive if that happened.

"It would take me less than an hour to draw up the papers necessary to revoke the residency of the Griffin family," he stated quietly in Ian's direction, as if any of us could have missed his point.

Ian stared at me. What could I possibly say? Both of us understood that whether he wanted to or not, whether it was in his own best interest or not, ultimately Ian would do whatever he needed to in order to both bring down the Guild and make sure I wasn't hurt in the process.

Ultimately, as he had done with so many other things before, Ian would do it all for me, but he bought us some time by saying, "Thanks for your clarity. We'll take it under advisement. I'll have my people call your people." He and Rice glared at each other even as Ian said, "Russ, it's time to go," and I followed him robotically to the door.

chapter twenty-one
RUSS

"You must be exhausted," I said. I couldn't think of any ghost who had stuck around for over an hour. Typically, they could hang out for around five to ten minutes at a time. Fifteen, max. But of course, nothing about Ian was typical.

"Mmmmm," Ian murmured. He was stretched out on my bed with his eyes closed, his white shirt barely even rumpled. "I can manage another few minutes."

He grabbed my hand and pulled it onto his chest. I let him hold it there. I'd finally gotten to the point of not flinching from either the cold or the shock of us being close enough that he could grab my hand without a second thought. But his touch still sent chills through me that had nothing to do with him being a ghost.

"So, where do we go from here?" I asked. I had a million questions.

"I'm not going to let Rice kick you and your dad out," he said. "I'm going to have to do the damned show. We just need to figure out a way to use it to our advantage."

"How are we going to do that?" I asked. Rice's words kept ricocheting around my head. The thought of leaving St. Hilaire was devastating. And what would I tell my dad?

Ian opened his eyes slowly. I imagined his ribs rising and falling. "I'll come up with something, Griffin. I always do."

"Yeah, but you're worried about it," I said, even though I'd never known Ian to worry about much of anything. Or to admit to it. I was grateful he didn't realize that it was *this* Ian, pensive and open, rather than the usual haughty one—the one I'd seen so rarely even when he'd had a pulse—that I had the most trouble resisting.

His grip tightened slightly on my hand. "I hate that he's threatening you. And I'm…concerned. I don't trust Rice. I don't trust any of them. If he's threatened you once, he can do it again. What if the show succeeds and the whole town closes? What then? Worse, what if the show succeeds and sets Rice up as the hero? Then you'll be stuck with him leading the Guild for all eternity."

I swallowed hard, wondering if Ian had reason to think that such a thing would happen. "I guess then *I'd* have to come up with something."

"Yes," he said as his eyes slowly closed and he began to fade. "I guess you would."

chapter twenty-two

ASHER

I slammed my math book closed. I knew many homeschooled kids had opportunities to be social and play sports and join clubs and all of that. But for me, it meant my mother didn't have to reregister me for school every time we moved. She simply poked her head into my room a couple times a week to make sure there were books of some sort on my desk. It didn't matter because I picked my own subjects and liked studying. It was something I could do on my own, something quiet that no one else wanted to hear about. Or maybe I told myself I enjoyed it because it filled the hours and gave me an excuse to escape the sadness in the rest of the house.

At the moment, there was a brainstorming session going on downstairs between my parents and their film crew. My parents figured they needed to be ready if the town actually got shooting permission. Plus, most of this crew was new, the old ones having either left the business or signed on to other projects, so I assumed my mother was talking about camera angles and her "good" side, while my dad was telling them how they need to stay alert to any signs that someone in St. Hilaire was tampering with anything in the area of the séance or otherwise causing the appearance of "ghosts." Wires. Fans. Cloth. Children. Magnets. Electronics. Rodents. Blah, blah, blah. I knew the drill. They would talk and talk about anything and everything except the one topic that was off-limits: the idea there might be an actual spirit behind whatever occurrence they were reporting on.

It was an unspoken rule that had trickled down to me and Mari as well. We never discussed the chance of there *really* being ghosts in any of the places our parents set up shop, although I think we both kind of hoped our parents were wrong.

Only once had I had reason to wonder if my sister was a believer, and that was the last time I'd seen her. I'd gone into the rec room and found her bent over a Ouija board. The room was dark but she'd opened the window, letting in the summer air and a smattering of starlight that only vaguely lit up the stained wooden board.

I'd come in loud and curious and asked, "What are you…?"

"Shhhhh…" she said and cocked her finger, motioning me over.

"What are you…?" I tried again, quieter this time.

She grabbed my arm and pulled me down next to her. "I'm trying to reach Grandma Marcy."

I dropped like a rock to the floor beside her, feeling as

163

though I'd been invited into some private and unknown world of my sister's. "Is that…?"

"A Ouija board, yes," she answered. "I found it in the attic." I knew the concept. You put your hand on the triangular pointer in the middle of the board. The idea was you could summon spirits who would move the pointer around to the words *yes* or *no*, or spell things out using the alphabet displayed in the middle. But I'd never seen one before and this one brought up all sorts of questions. Had Mari done this before? When did she find it in the attic? Why hadn't she told me? Why choose Grandma Marcy, who I'd only met once when I was about two, a meeting captured in photos of a pretty older woman handing me a toy plane? Why not someone famous or more interesting like Galileo or Shakespeare, or David Bowie? Thankfully, I knew from the look on Mari's face not to ask any of my questions out loud.

"Hi Gran, it's me, Mari," she said and then, looking at me out of the corner of her eye, added, "Asher is here too."

She grabbed my hand and put it under hers on top of the pointer. The wood was smooth and worn from use. Mari's hand on top of mine was warm and slightly slippery from the tea-scented lotion she used. I held my breath, waiting to see if the—I searched for the word—*planchette* was going to move, hoping that if it did, I wouldn't feel Mari's hand shifting it in one direction or the other. I loved the idea that Grandma would show up and tell us she'd missed us and tell us we were good and tell us we were loved. I would have even settled for some funny stories of my dad as a child.

But apparently, none of that was on Mari's mind just then.

"Grandma, if you're there, can you tell me if I should go on the camping trip with Debbie?"

I stared at my sister. If Grandma Marcy was lurking around in a house in upstate New York, a place that, as far as I knew, she had never even visited, it probably wasn't to tell my sister whether she should go camping with her friends.

"Why wouldn't you just go?" I whispered under my breath.

Mari sighed. "Mom and Dad are filming this weekend. But at the same time," she added with her eyes glued to the board, "Debbie's brother, Josh, is going on the camping trip."

Ah, Josh. Mari and I were at the same disadvantage when it came to relationships—or in my case, unrequited sorta-kinda crushes from afar—because why bother? We lived in places just long enough to get intrigued with someone or for them to get intrigued with us—well, intrigued with her. And then Mom and Dad would move us again with the promise that this would be the last show, and then they'd find a nice house in a nice area of a nice town and we'd stay someplace for a while, and so on.

I grabbed her hand off the planchette and interlocked my fingers with hers. "Go, Mari. Seriously, go. There will always be another show that Mom and Dad will need help with. I'll grab this one. You should go and have fun. You don't need Grandma Marcy to tell you that. And why Grandma Marcy of all people, anyhow?"

Mari fiddled with the board, moving the pointers from *yes* to *no*. "You know how when Dad gets irritated with me, he sometimes tells me I remind him of Grandma Marcy? Mom says it's because Grandma was impulsive. Like she'd only known Grandpa a few weeks when they got married. I figured she might talk me into going," she admitted.

"Well, I'm talking you into going instead," I said.

She smiled faintly and then reached up and ruffled my hair. "Oh, Buzz. How did I get so lucky in the brother department? But, um, you *do* remember which show this is, right?" Her eyes crinkled up while I thought about it. She looked away as it dawned on me what she was talking about.

"Oh, crap. It's *that* show?" Most of the places Mom and Dad went to investigate were kind of cool. Old houses. Libraries. Schools. That sort of thing. This place was a working slaughterhouse, and I was a vegetarian. I'd fought against them doing this show altogether, and when I lost that fight, I made Mari promise she would go so I wouldn't have to. I was still pissed at my parents for even considering taking this one on.

"Sorry, Buzz. I know I..." Mari looked at me sheepishly, assuming I'd do what she wanted as always.

"Not going to happen. Sorry. You know I'd cover for you any time, but I can't do this one. You're going to have to stay here." I never said no to my sister. Not ever. But she had to know I couldn't walk around the cameramen and hold up cords to make sure they weren't dragging into animal body parts. My stomach heaved at the thought.

She squeezed my hand. "Come on," she said. "It's just one weekend. You can get through it."

I pictured myself walking into the yard with my parents. Imagined the smell, the... "Mari, you know I want to help you out. I do. But I can't *do* this one. You know what's going to happen. I'm going to freak out and the show will be ruined, and Mom and Dad are going to hate me."

Mari must have *really* wanted to go because she picked up

the planchette and dropped it hard onto the board. "Can't you hold it together for once?" she said with uncharacteristic anger. "I'm so tired of never being allowed to have a life."

I stared at her, wondering if she was possessed. "You can go camping some other weekend when Mom and Dad are investigating a cave or bookstore or something. But I'm not doing this one."

She narrowed her eyes. "You know what, just… I don't even want to talk to you right now." Then she stormed off.

Embarrassingly, I'd teared up. Then I'd thrown the Ouija board box across the room.

Going to a slaughterhouse was bad enough. Having Mari mad at me was devastating. I tried to force myself to get up and go tell her I was wrong, that of course she should go and I'd rise to the occasion and hold myself together during the show's taping.

But I couldn't do it. No matter how I turned the idea over in my head, all I saw was blood everywhere.

Mari's door was shut when I went downstairs to tell Mom I wasn't feeling well and was going to skip dinner and head to bed. Mom had nodded without a comment.

I'd gone back upstairs and hesitated outside Mari's door on my way back to my room. I didn't know how to deal with fighting with her, and I wanted to go in and sit in her papasan chair that felt like a giant hug and tell her I was sorry and have her tell me she was, too, and that she could go camping some other time.

I knocked. Quietly. But she must have had her headphones on because she didn't answer, and I didn't knock a second time.

I'd spend the night ricocheting between anger at Mari,

anger at my parents, and anger at myself both for not being able to *deal* with things and for being such a wuss that my sister being upset with me had me so tangled up.

The next morning, my parents found a note from her explaining where she'd gone and apologizing for missing the show. She never mentioned me.

Mari died on that trip and my parents put the show on indefinite hiatus. I turned my room over, looking for one last note from her, but there was nothing.

When I finally worked up the nerve to go into the rec room, I found the Ouija board, the pointer on *goodbye*. It felt like Mari's last message to me. To all of us.

chapter twenty-three

RUSS

If you aren't too busy with ghost stuff, my parents are out again. You wanna come over for dinner?

I read the words over more times than I needed to. I was behind on everything. Schoolwork, stuff at home, sleep. I hadn't had a real conversation with my dad in days.

I tried to imagine what would happen if I literally skipped out of town to have dinner with a boy in Buchanan instead of doing anything on my growing list.

Pretty much all of the pictures in my head resulted in St. Hilaire's version of the apocalypse.

THANKS. I actually have to work tonight, which sucks. Rain check? I typed and sent before I realized I'd basically invited myself to his house for dinner at some point. *Good job, Russ.*

I powered down my phone and looked longingly into my desk drawer, calculating the amount of serum and tea leaves I had left. Flipping the math conversions up and over, I tried to tell myself that a little of *something* certainly couldn't hurt and would only help to calm my nerves and help me get some of this stuff off my plate.

I reached into the drawer, pulled out the black bag of supplies and removed the syringe. My hand shook. Not what you wanted when you were holding a needle. A fly buzzed by my head. I had no idea how it got in the house. My dad was a live-and-let-live kind of guy, though, so I didn't feel any pressure to get it out.

I put the needle down and shrugged out of the left arm of my coat, matching the right side that I'd already shed. Then I got up and spread an unbroken line of salt along the door to my room. Next, the windowsill. I lit an overabundance of white votive candles. All of these were precautions to ensure that Ian couldn't pop in uninvited.

Ian. Ian agreed he was going to have to appear on television to prove ghosts existed. Ian was going to work with the Guild to save St. Hilaire. Ian was going to be on the front page of every paper in the world if he managed to pull this off with his usual flair.

Where did that leave me and our plans?

How could we stop the momentum of the Guild once they were the first people in the entire world to prove, on national television no less, that ghosts existed?

Laura Hampton, Dec's younger sister, had told me she'd received a letter from the Guild telling her to come in for a "pairing interview." How long did we have before the Guild forced her into some twisted arranged relationship? I'd promised Dec I'd look after her. I doubted that this was what he had in mind.

I was losing control of it all. I settled back on the floor and opened the pack. The liquid in the syringe seemed to flicker in the candlelight, offering me at least a little while's escape.

I picked it up and tapped the top, ensuring there was no air in the needle. What was I going to do if this all ended badly? I couldn't imagine what would happen to my dad and me if the Guild forced us to leave. At the same time, I couldn't stay in St. Hilaire and watch the Guild run every aspect of everyone's life. Run *my* life.

I took a deep breath and watched as the needle came close to my arm. I shivered in anticipation.

"Russ?"

I dropped the unused syringe and watched as it rolled under my bed.

"One second, Dad," I called as I pushed the bag and all of the other accessories under the bed next to the syringe. I grabbed my coat and threw it back on. My heart pounded. I could make a strong case for using my grandmother's serums for séances, but I'm pretty sure my dad wasn't going to be happy about me using it to take the edge off a crappy day.

I ran and unlocked my bedroom door.

"You okay?" Dad asked, looking over my shoulder. I turned my head and did a quick scan. Nothing looked out of place. I nodded.

"Why is your coat on inside out?"

I looked down. *Shit.* "Oh, I–I…" This shouldn't be so

difficult. Why would someone have their coat on inside out? *Come on, Russ. Think.* I raked my hand through my hair. "I got cold and grabbed it. I guess I didn't notice."

I watched Dad's face to see if there was a chance he was going to buy my bullshit answer. He scowled but didn't call me out. My heart shuddered in my chest.

"Can we talk?" he asked, pushing his way into my room. Salt and candles might keep ghosts out but they did nothing to deter the living.

"Sure," I said. He sat down on my bed and took his glasses off and rubbed them on his work shirt. The blue tag on the shirt has his name and the logo of the train company. I wanted a day where he wouldn't have to work so hard. The Guild was my entrance into something resembling a career. The percentage of the town profits Guild members received would allow me to take care of him for the rest of his life.

I leaned on the doorjamb, wondering if I should take my coat off and fix it. Somehow that seemed even more awkward than keeping it inside out.

"I got something in the mail this afternoon," he said. His hands were worrying the glass of his lenses, and he wouldn't meet my eyes.

I swallowed down a lump of apprehension. "What?"

He brought his eyes up to meet mine. "A letter. From your mother's lawyer."

I stared at him in shock. "Mom?" I knew as I said it that of course this was about her. Nothing else would make my father this uneasy. A rush of conflicting emotions almost brought me to my knees. I wished I'd taken the shot earlier. I would have, had I known he was coming to me with something about the mother I hadn't seen and rarely heard from in almost four years.

Dad nodded. Part of me wanted to ask if she was okay. Part of me wanted to say, "No, I don't care about anything she had to say." Forgetting myself, I glanced up to the top of my bookcase to where a tiny, framed picture of her sat. It was the only one that was up in the house and had been my grandmother's when she'd lived here. I rarely looked at it, but somehow it had felt wrong to pack it away.

"It seems," my father continued before I could tell him to stop, "that she's getting married again." A mess of tangled, angry words fought for purchase in my mouth. However much I'd resented her for abandoning me for having the audacity to share her genetics as a medium, I hated more that she'd broken my father's heart. And that she'd done it all because of me embracing the medium talent I'd inherited from her, hurt in a way I couldn't put into words.

I took a step forward to try to find a way to comfort him. Before I'd taken the second of the two necessary steps, he continued. "There's something else."

I waited. My father wasn't one to mince words. He was one of the gentlest people I knew, but he was direct. I pushed my back up against the wall, bracing myself for whatever he was holding back. He looked up and I saw that whatever concern he had wasn't for himself, but for me, and I took a deep breath while I still could.

"Of course, there is." I choked out something like a laugh. "It's Mom. There's always something else." I was trying to joke, but my voice was full of telltale fear and my dad simply knew me too well for me to pull it off.

"She's pregnant, Russ. And her new fiance, well, he wants her to cut ties with her old life. Officially."

I looked down and pulled my hand off my wrist because I realized I'd been rubbing my tattoo with my thumb hard enough to bruise my skin. I wasn't sure which of these pieces of news I should process first. She was pregnant. That meant I'd have a sibling. Half sibling. Something I'd grown up hungry for. But what if that kid had the same "problem" I did? What if he or she or they could hear ghosts and see things that weren't visible to other people? Would Mom walk away from them, too? Was she going to live with a trail of messed-up kids in her wake?

My skin prickled against my jeans and shirt. The cuffs of my coat felt caustic against the back of my hands. I wasn't sure if I was warm or freezing.

But "cut ties"?

"What does that even mean?" I asked quietly.

My father stood and walked over to my desk. As if he'd suddenly realized the room was bathed in candlelight, he picked up one of the votives and stared into it. I prayed the gap in the room's protections wouldn't alert Ian somehow. I definitely couldn't deal with him at the moment.

"She's legally relinquished custody of you. I mean, you're seventeen anyhow and it's not like she's been a part of anything, but I was hoping..." He shrugged, having run out of words that were unnecessary anyhow.

My father stared at me, but I got the feeling he was in his own head, gazing at his memories of my mom. Whether he was thinking of her in happy times or how she looked—disheveled and tearstained—when she'd helped us pack up the car and drive ten straight hours from Chicago to upstate New York before leaving us at the gates of St. Hilaire, I didn't know.

I knew he was right. It wasn't as if she had any role in my life. But like him, I guess I'd been holding out hope that she'd come around someday.

Now that door was closed. And it made staying in St. Hilaire even more important. I truly had nothing else.

I looked up at my dad, at the dark circles under his eyes, the product of his long hours at work, the work he did to keep a roof over our heads while I studied and chased ghosts, of all things and said, "I'm sorry," because had I not embraced being a medium, maybe none of this would ever have happened. He just stepped forward and pulled me into a hug as if none of the responsibility fell on me.

———

After my father left, I sat on the floor. In my hands, the syringe looked larger than it had ever appeared in my head when I closed my eyes and imagined it.

Ian once told me he equated living fast with feeling. That he needed the rush of adrenaline he'd gotten from parties and sex—and yes, even from being the best medium in town—in order to feel something large enough to force him to recognize that he was alive.

That was the biggest difference between me and Ian. I felt everything all the damned time. I'd just had fourteen years in Chicago to learn not to show it.

I rested the needle against my skin. The metal was cool and oddly calming.

I remembered Dec's grief after his parents died. The pain almost tore him in two. I fought it alongside him, dragged him out of that dark place until he'd reached a point where he could function.

This was different. Not greater, certainly not that. But not insignificant either. Dec's parents hadn't chosen to leave him. They would have done anything to be with their son, just like my dad would. I'd thought that while my mother hated being a medium and all things St. Hilaire, somewhere deep inside, she still loved me.

Apparently I was wrong.

There was no one to pull me back from the edge. It's not like I was going to summon Ian just so I could cry on his shoulder. And he wouldn't get it anyhow. He hated most of his family.

My father was downstairs, I reminded myself. I had notes that needed to be typed up tonight, or tomorrow I'd have to pull an all-nighter.

I poked the tip of the needle slowly into my skin and winced. The pain was sharp and isolated and gave my tired brain something to focus on aside from my mother's newest way of rejecting me. Or Ian. Or the Guild. Or my dwindling future.

The vein in my arm pulsed hungrily. I made a fist, pushing my nails into my palm. The owl on my wrist unfurled, opening its beak, and I shoved the serum into my arm.

chapter twenty-four

WILLOW

"You need more safeguards in place."

"Willow, please sit down," Father instructed, but I remained standing. I was too wired up about his assumption that now that Ian was on board with the show, everything would simply fall into place. "We have many opportunities here to enact change. In fact, as you asked, I have my staff putting together an additional list of those who can be cleared out of town to make way for future mediums once we begin to identify them and invite them here. As soon as this show is over…"

"That's wonderful. Really it is. But meanwhile I think we need to remember who we're dealing with."

Father chuckled. "Really, my dear? Because Mr. Mackenzie, may I remind you, is dead. He's a ghost and therefore controllable."

I couldn't believe what I was hearing. "Controllable? What do you think you have that is going to control him?"

Father flipped through some papers on his desk. He wasn't concerned about this at all, which made me all the more worried. He looked up as if he'd just remembered my question. "We have come to an understanding."

"An understanding?" I couldn't believe what I was hearing. I knew, of course, that it all came back to Russ Griffin, but to have the entire fate of St. Hilaire—no, the entire fate of *mediums*—resting on a threat seemed dicey.

Father reached out and patted my hand. "Willow, please. Ultimately, I have reason to believe we all want the same thing."

Given that Father and I didn't want the same thing, I was highly suspect. "We do? And what is that?"

He closed his book. "The survival and success of St. Hilaire," he said, hitting the book's cover. "There is nothing else."

I had never heard Father raise his voice. He had a unique ability to threaten people—when necessary—with a smile on his face. More, I'd never heard him raise his voice at me. Not even when I was a willful child.

I inhaled and let the air out slowly before replying. "And you really trust Ian, of all people, to keep the Guild's success in mind?"

"I believe he will appear when we tell him to. I believe he will be loud and extravagant and television-worthy. I believe these TV people and their show will be destroyed, and I believe we will have so many reservations next summer, and the one following, and for every summer after that. We will never again have to worry about our futures. So honestly, I don't care one way or the other what Ian Mackenzie's personal goals are, just that his actions support ours."

"You have a lot more faith in him than he deserves," I mumbled.

"Since you seem to feel that more oversight is necessary, why don't we use this as a trial run for you. You want to be a member of the Guild's leadership? Prove yourself. I'm designating you as the project manager. All requests from the show and the relevant parties shall go through you. But I urge you to move forward with caution. This is not the time to go to extremes."

"And can we agree to..." I thought quickly. My plan wasn't fully worked out but now was my opportunity. "Can we have the séance in my apartment?"

"Oh, Willow, I don't know about that. St. Hilaire has so many lovely spaces. There is the square and the healing center, for instance. Besides, I'm guessing these show people will want some input in the location."

"If I'm going to manage this process, I'd like to begin now." I stared at him. He stared back. I knew that stare. And I knew I wasn't going to get any further with him today.

But it was a start. It was definitely a start.

chapter twenty-five

ASHER

Neptune is the smallest gas giant and the farthest planet from the sun. A year there lasts 165 years on earth. Even though Saturn gets all the love, Neptune has six rings of its own. They're just super faint, and you know no one notices anything quiet these days.

It was three in the morning and I'd run through my whole insomniac drill, which revolved around the idea that if I was going to be awake anyhow, I might as well learn something.

I got up and walked over to the window. The moon was full, and all I had to do was pull back the curtain to see everything in my room without needing a light.

I opened my bedroom door and Houdini came padding in, jumped up on my bed, and fell asleep. "Damn cat," I said affectionately. It wasn't fair how they could sleep on command.

I picked up my phone and stared at it. Was Russ the kind of person who put their phone on silent when they went to sleep? Or would I wake him by texting? If I sent him a photo of a full moon, would he take it as a joke or think I was odd? Did he like cats? Maybe I could send him a photo of Houdini. But what if he was a dog person? Worse, what if he were allergic to cats and then decided he couldn't come over anymore? Although he hadn't been sneezing or anything last time, so…

I threw myself back on the bed and took a deep breath, counting to ten. Maybe I could text Russ and share that if you breathed in pure oxygen for too long, you'd eventually OD. Wow, that was useful information. *Put down the phone, Asher.*

I put the phone on the bed and Houdini rolled over on top of it, earning him a scratch between his ears. He started to purr. "Thanks for keeping me from making a fool out of myself," I said.

The clock read 3:12. In six hours, I needed to be up to get the planetarium ready for their evening 21-plus show. Just what I needed: Two hours of drunk singles and stories about love in the cosmos.

chapter twenty-six
RUSS

It was raining. Only the rain wasn't made out of water. The precipitation hitting me was hard like snowballs, only through my cracked eyelids I could see that there were words typed everywhere like on the paper. That was it, paper. It was raining paper and I was…

I opened my eyes.

"What. The. Fuck?" Ian stood over me, pelting me with pages of what? The reports I needed to type up? Pages from a book? Who knew?

I struggled to sit up, then regretted it. I needed a second to take a breath and figure out what was going on, but Ian was having no part of that.

"You're not stupid, so what is it?" he asked. "Because honestly, I don't understand why you think this is helping anything."

I rubbed my cheeks. I needed a shave and a shower. I needed him to shut the hell up for a few minutes. I shook my head. Ian wasn't even supposed to be here. I'd set up the candles and salt last night. "How did you…?"

My eyes and Ian's landed simultaneously on my desk and the space where my father had moved one of the votive candles and not replaced it, which allowed Ian to come in. *Thanks, Dad.*

"I don't really want to talk to you right now," he said. "But some of us are trying to keep you from being kicked out of town, so I don't think I have a choice."

"Ian…" I whispered, hoping he'd lower his voice in response.

"Don't," he barked. "I don't want to hear it. I don't want to hear about Willow or the Guild or Dec or how freaked out you are about your life. And I definitely I don't want to hear about you feeling so put-upon by getting exactly what you've always wanted."

I hoped my dad had gone to work and wasn't in the house to hear this. The sun roared in through the window, making Ian resemble a dark shadow in its midst. I gestured to him, "Could you move over. The sun…"

Ian turned around and ripped the curtains open so that the room was flooded by harsh light. I covered my eyes and then licked my lips, but my tongue was equally dry. "I thought you were taking a day or two off before the show."

He sat on the bed and put his head in his hands, waves of fury flying off his insubstantial form. Angry, he seemed to fill up more space than normal, which was saying something. "I thought you were supposed to be in class."

I looked around for my phone but didn't see it. I had no

idea what time it was. I grabbed one of the pieces of paper instead, saw it was the *Buchanan Sentinel*, and tossed it aside. I didn't want to know.

"I'm not feeling well," I said, realizing how true it was as I said it.

"And whose fault is that?" he asked. Then he shook his head and pulled back his shoulders, the Mackenzie blue coming back into his eyes. It was a chilling transformation. Angry Ian radiated a kind of concern and investment. This Ian was detached and insulated. "I need you to get up and get dressed. We might have an issue. As further proof of my karmic punishment, the *Sentinel* is reporting that the Guild has designated Willow as their point person for this whole *Ghost Killers* thing."

"Whose bright idea was that?" I asked. "And where did you get the paper anyhow?"

"You'd be amazed what you can find if you keep your eyes open," he said with annoyance. "And I'd like to find out what Willow's agenda is before she tanks ours."

I cracked my neck, which felt ridiculously satisfying, given that the rest of my body felt as if it had been run over by rhinos. "Fine, go."

Ian pressed his lips into a line before replying. "That crap is starting to eat your brain." He stared at me and I stared back again, too tired for whatever argument he was looking to have. "I can't just come and go. I don't have an open invitation to all of St. Hilaire. Apparently if you're stuck with me, I'm stuck with you too. You're apparently some kind of conduit for me now. Whither thou goest, I goest, blah, blah, blah."

"That's new. Great," I said, but at the same time I realized this meant Ian couldn't be running around St. Hilaire causing general mayhem. At least I could keep an eye on him.

"Yeah, well, let's not spread that information around. But in the meantime, Willow's been bellowing for me. I guess she's stressing because she and Rice are having some sort of meeting with the show's producers to come to 'mutually agreeable' terms."

"And she wants to meet with you first to make sure you aren't going to flake out." The statement could have gone without saying, it was so obvious. But given the addled state of my brain, I was proud of myself for coming up with it.

"Speaking of flaking out…" Ian said, pointedly.

"I'm not flaking out," I replied.

Ian turned around and stepped toward me so fast I had to blink to refocus. "That's what makes it worse," he said.

"Worse than what?"

He moved his hands back and forth as if there were so many things that this was worse than, that he didn't know where to begin. "Lying to me. Screwing yourself up. Skipping school. Did I mention lying to me?"

"Skipping school? Seriously, are you the truancy police now?" I hesitated, waiting to see if Ian was going to fill the silence, but when he didn't, I took a deep breath and began again. "Look, I'm not lying to you. Just because I'm doing something you don't want me to do, that doesn't mean I'm lying." Not surprisingly, my words didn't change his angry, chiseled expression.

"Fine," I said. "You want it all laid out in a pretty line, fine. Here it is. Yeah, sometimes I use my grandmother's recipes for reasons other than trying to reach ghosts. You may have noticed that my life is a little *crowded* with ghosts at the moment. But it isn't as if the living are doing me any favors either. Maybe I sometimes need a fucking break. I'm sorry you can't understand that."

My anger was simmering in a way I rarely allowed it to. I knew who people expected me to be. Russ Griffin was measured and responsible and calm. Russ Griffin never showed anger. He did what was expected of him. He was quiet and helpful and walked little old ladies across the road if his dark clothes and spiked hair didn't scare them off.

I could have told Ian about the person formerly known as my mom signing away her rights, but I didn't want to play a sympathy card. The last thing I needed was him feeling sorry for me.

"Russ," Ian said, a flicker of something like compassion flaring in his annoyingly beautiful eyes. I wasn't in the mood for his attempts at conciliation. All I wanted was everyone off my back for one single day.

"No," I said, getting up and replacing the votive. It wouldn't make him leave now, but it ensured that he couldn't come back until I wanted him to. "No. I'm done. You find some other way to meet with Willow and leave me alone." I reached under the bed, grabbed a syringe I'd left filled and jammed it into my arm.

Ian opened his mouth to say something, but I don't know what. I was gone before I could process it.

chapter twenty-seven

WILLOW

I'd learned Morse code when a customer came in four years ago to find out why their lights kept blinking on and off in an odd pattern. The customer was old. His father had been a naval gunner in World War I, and the family was discussing tearing down his boyhood home when the issue began. Classic.

But now *my* lights were blinking on and off. I recognized the scenario if not the reason why anyone would be haunting *me*. It was a gutsy move.

I watched, waiting, looking for the usual distress call: S-O-S. Three dots. Three dashes. Three dots. But that wasn't what I saw. I grabbed a piece of paper and a pen and started detailing the flickers because I wasn't quite fast enough to be able to translate the lights into letters in my head. I copied down the first word and then waited for the next, but the pattern only repeated.

K-N-O-C-K.

I looked around the room. I knew better than to say, "Come in." I was alone. Father was in the conference room five floors below me, informing Guild leadership of my new role. My rooms formed the only residence at the top of Eaton Hall. I wasn't about to invite a spirit in before I knew whose it was. Besides, it should have been easier for a ghost to literally knock against something than to take over my entire electrical system.

The flickering sped up. Knock. Knock.

Knock. Knock.

It couldn't be.

Knock. Knock.

Seriously? Fine. "Who's there?" I called.

The lights stopped.

Slowly they started again. I-N-T-E-R.

I followed the patterns, writing down each letter until the lights stopped again.

"Interrupting cow?" I read at the same time that the lights started moving again, spelling out M-O-O.

You have got to be kidding me. Of all the things I could imagine him saying to me from beyond the grave, I never would have landed on his favorite joke from elementary school.

"Ian Mackenzie?" All the lights surged brighter than I was aware that bulbs could burn. "Stop before you—" I yelled, but the bulbs popped one after one, the circuits overloaded.

"Asshole." I walked to my desk and fumbled for my lighter, which I used to light a line of three-wick candles that sat on my mantel and smelled like jasmine.

It was ballsy of Ian to contact me now. Puzzling. We had every reason in the world to distrust each other. What the hell was he up to?

"Come out, come out, wherever you are," I said under my breath. Then, louder, "You have my attention. Now stop playing games and show yourself."

A breeze whipped through the room, blowing the candles out. I guessed that Ian's stupid sense of humor wasn't the only thing that hadn't changed. He was still annoying and wanted things his own way.

I relit the candles and examined the room, wondering what else he was going to use to try to communicate with me. I ran into my bathroom and shut the door. Then I turned the shower on full blast as hot as it would go. It only took a few minutes for the mirror to steam up. "Come on, already. You know how this works."

Ian and I had worked a séance together that had gone just this way. The ghost had been too weak to appear in physical form, so Ian had the idea to steam up the mirror, giving the spirit a place to easily write its message in the condensation.

I'd heard about Ian at the séance with Father, though. There had been nothing weak about him that day. To the contrary, I'd never seen a performance like he put on in front of the Guild and…Russ Griffin.

Oh. Was that it then?

The room was steamy as a sauna. Humid and damp and

oppressive. Rivulets of water ran down the glass, making my face look as though it was covered in tears. As if Ian Mackenzie could make me cry. As if anyone could.

Slowly, letters started in form in the mist. First, my name. Then **TALK. TO. GRIFFIN.**

"I'm not your freaking messenger boy," I said. The mirror misted over again and stayed foggy for long enough I'd assumed Ian had taken my indignation to heart.

But then, a ghostly finger began writing again.

P.L.E.A.S.E.

"Ian Mackenzie *asking* for something. That's certainly new," I said. An underline appeared under the word *please*. "Talk to Russ? Whatever for?"

HELP. HIM. NOW.

Oh. This definitely *was* something new. "What am I supposed to help him with? His homework? It isn't my fault if he has no attention span these days."

The steam in the room seemed to gather in a corner. Then I heard, "Help him," only the sounds the letters made were filled with air and desperation. I probably wouldn't have understood him had I not been forced into *performing* with Ian for so many years.

"Willow."

"You really aren't joking," I said, and as I said it, I realized how true the words were. "What the hell is it with you and Russ anyhow? Oh my lord, are you in love with him or something?" I asked, hoping to incite another reaction. The room stayed quiet and nothing new appeared on the mirror. There was a sudden uncomfortable chill in what had been a hot and sticky room. I waited silently. I wasn't going to beg Ian Mackenzie for anything. For the first time in all the years I'd known him, he needed me more than I needed him.

"You want *me* to check on him?" I called out. "Really? Yeah, well, maybe I will." Slowly, a smiley face showed on the mirror. *As if.*

"But what's in it for me? What do I get for wasting my time to go check on Russ Griffin on the other side of town?"

I was still missing something. Why me? Sure, thinking about it, I was—ironically—the only one in St. Hilaire who was both a strong enough medium and knew Ian well enough to read the signs. Well, the only one aside from Father but of course that was laughable.

But why couldn't he simply appear? Was there some stupid bond between them that was so strong Ian could only show himself when Russ was there? That could change everything.

"I want you to back me up on filming this stupid show here, in my loft. I want you to insist on that as a requirement of your participation," I demanded, suddenly realizing my opportunity.

I was benefiting, I knew, from the fact that—for once—Ian couldn't start a debate and ask me to explain myself.

My hair was dripping wet, and I could feel water making its way down my back and onto the floor. Breathing was a trial, but I wasn't going to be the first to blink. A quick rush of chilled air cleared the mirror. I stared into it, seeing my face, and next to it that of Ian, unsubstantial and translucent, but his without a doubt. He smiled a victorious smile at me, full of ghostly teeth, and then gave me a thumbs-up sign and vanished.

I turned off the water and gratefully opened the door, relishing both the rush of cool air and the rare feeling that everything I needed had just dropped into my lap.

chapter twenty-eight
WILLOW

I started with a text.

Followed with a voicemail.

It was certainly possible that Russ was ignoring his phone. Or busy doing something pointless like dying his hair a new shade of black or exchanging emo musings with Dec Hampton. But the fact that unrufflable Ian had made such a fuss about him made me too curious to wait until our next tutoring session.

I called Colin and told him I needed to borrow his rust bucket. There was no way I was taking my Fiat. I grabbed his car, then drove over to Russ's house, which sat in an area we called Cardboard Village because the houses were cheaply made and poorly designed and looked as if they'd topple over in a strong wind.

I got out of the car but hesitated before walking up to the house.

The door was worn. The porch was worn. Even the garden was worn. But at the same time, it felt as if I'd walked onto a photo shoot set that specifically called for a home rather than a house. It was only Russ and his dad who lived here, though. How could it feel as if I'd walked onto the set of the goddamned *Fosters*?

I knocked because there was no bell. Then, I knocked harder because there was no answer. The door swung open. I'd seen enough horror films; I knew the story this one would tell. I was going to take four steps inside and then the door would swing closed and the monster would leap out and grab me.

Then again, they never filmed those scenes from the point of view of the monster, so this was uncharted territory.

I walked in, my heels making enough noise on the wood floor to wake the dead. *Ha! Medium joke.* I waited, in case Mr. Griffin was going to come blazing in with a shotgun—although he hardly seemed the type—or a towel-clad Russ would step out of the shower—although he probably showered in that ratty old coat of his. I was probably safe.

"Russ. Russ Griffin," I called. My voice echoed back to me, not in a haunted way, but because there was so little in the house for it to be absorbed by. The house still had the homey feel it exuded from the outside, but it looked more like a museum piece. Still life. A house untouched and forgotten the card would have read.

I called out again and heard…something…from upstairs. A cat jumping or a box being dropped. Something landing on the wooden floor without intending to. Then a groan.

I was curious but not up for anything messy. I turned around to leave but couldn't shake the vision in the glass, Ian Mackenzie's uncharacteristic "please." And really, what did I have planned for today, anyhow? I dug out my phone and dialed Russ's cell phone. Upstairs I heard it ring—"Sympathy for the Devil." Funny. Is that how he thought of me? I didn't need his sympathy.

My call went to voicemail.

A chill went through me for no logical reason. I would certainly go upstairs and find that Russ had gone out and left his phone on a table and that the sound had come from the wind coming through an open window and blowing something off a table.

Or he'd be sleeping at—I looked at my phone—two o'clock. Maybe he was meditating or studying or reading cards or something else dull but predictably responsible.

There was an umbrella stand behind the front door. I grabbed a yellow one with a long handle and let my heels announce my way up the stairs, which brought me to a small landing. There were three doors, one obviously a bathroom, one closed, and the far one open. I made sure my grip on the umbrella was strong and stuck my head into the open door.

Of all the things I could have expected to find, the scene in front of me wouldn't have made the list. Unlike the rest of the neat and austere house, this room resembled a crime scene that had been cleaned up by a careless murderer. The perimeter of the small room, including a desk and two bookcases and bed, were neat. More than neat. Perfectly made bed. Perfectly stacked files on the desk. Perfectly green plants leaning longingly toward the sun coming through perfectly clean windows.

The only thing that wasn't perfect was Russ Griffin's crumpled body in the middle of the floor, which lay next to a black bag and some obviously used—and by nature messy—syringes.

Well. Well.

I bent down and watched his chest rise and fall. He was still breathing. At least I wouldn't have to clean up *that* mess. I needed to rouse him enough to figure out what Ian needed me to speak to him about so I could claim the favor Ian owed me. So that I could get rid of him.

I slowly extended my leg and put the toe of my boot into Russ Griffin's ribs. I pushed once. Twice.

Russ groaned. It was the same sound I'd heard downstairs.

"You have a lot of explaining to do," I said loudly. The last thing I wanted to do was get any closer in case he freaked out or puked.

Predictably, Russ bolted to a sitting position before turning an unhealthy shade of green. His mouth opened soundlessly.

"Don't you dare throw up on me," I warned.

He made an undecipherable noise and then licked his lips and croaked, "What are you doing here?"

I drew the desk chair over, brushed it off, and sat down. "Funny you should ask. But I have some questions for you as well. What the hell is all this? Are you trying to kill yourself? Because if you are, let me know now. I'd prefer not to waste my time trying to teach you if I don't need to."

Color surged back into Russ's cheeks. It didn't make him look healthy, just embarrassed. In truth, he looked so pathetic and overwhelmed that I considered withdrawing my question. But what fun would that be?

"I'm…" he started and stopped. He pushed his hair around for a bit before saying, "My grandmother studied herbal enhancements. She hated having to organize full séances in order to talk to spirits, so she found other ways. She wrote it all down in a book." He struggled to his knees and then his feet. I watched as he swayed and then steadied himself. He reached over to his desk but withdrew his empty hand and sat on the bed. "I know how this looks," he said.

"You mean you're aware I could have you drummed out of St. Hilaire for this? The Guild puts up with a lot, but intravenous drug use from a high school student? One word to Father or any of the executive council and you'd be gone before you knew what happened."

Russ's glassy eyes went wide. "Willow. It's all herbal, I swear. I—"

I waved him off. "Save me the explanation. You want to fry your brain, I'm not going to stand in your way. But tell me one thing. This has something to do with why you can communicate with Ian Mackenzie, right?"

He blinked in surprise and then his shoulders slumped in defeat. "Ian? Well, I mean, it's how I contacted him the first time and it might allow him to visit me unasked now, but…"

"He haunts you?" I asked. Suddenly so many things were coming into focus.

"Yeah, but…"

"Tangibly?"

"Yeah, but…"

"So, it never mattered that the most powerful mediums in St. Hilaire were calling for him through all those séances. It only worked for you?" I wasn't asking a question as much as coming to terms with the details. It explained why all of the séances we'd tried previously had failed.

"Well, yeah, but…"

"Stop," I commanded. He stopped. The anxiety in his expression made him look young, eager to please. Maybe that was what Ian saw in him. Someone pliable—although I'd never seen that trait in Russ Griffin and I'd never figured Ian Mackenzie as someone who wanted a bootlicker.

I waited. There was something almost enjoyable about watching Russ squirm inside his dark coat, watching his well-practiced control slip away. He cracked his neck, circled his right wrist with his left hand, and rubbed the place where his tattoo lived. An owl. It was the totem for being able to see behind masks. What did Russ see when he looked at me? Whatever it was, I doubted it was the full truth.

"Would it surprise you to hear I had a visitation from him myself this morning?" I asked slowly, drawing out each word so I could watch him squirm.

"What?" Russ's head jerked up and then he winced, obviously regretting the movement. He was a mess. "How?" he asked, quieter this time. There was pain in his voice, but I doubted it had much to do with his neck.

"Your *friend* decided to come and mess with the lights in my apartment." I deliberately left out the Morse code. And the steam. The fewer details I shared, the better the odds Russ would share some additional information of his own.

His face crumpled in confusion. "Your lights? Ian's the strongest ghost I've ever seen. He wouldn't need to resort to that sort of stuff."

"I believe you believe that. And I'll admit I would have as well, but I'm going to guess you're not the only one who benefits from your grandmother's little concoctions. Have you considered that Ian can only become tangible when you're present?"

Russ looked irritated, which made me think it *was* something he was aware of but hadn't wanted to share.

"This morning he *begged* me to come talk to you. And I don't know what Ian begs you for, but it's certainly not a behavior *I've* seen from him in the past." I examined my nails. I was going to need a manicure sooner than later. If I had anything to do with showing this TV program the back side of the gate, I needed to cut a smart figure.

"Ian begged you to talk to me? Why would he do that?"

"Perhaps your line was busy?" I said, pointing to his phone. "Look, I'm presuming it was because he was wasting valuable energy by wanting me to save your life. Does that sound plausible?"

Russ closed his eyes. When he opened them, they flashed with anger. "I don't need you to save my life, Willow."

I kicked at a bunch of tubing on the floor and glared at him until he looked away.

"Ian is a meddling mother hen," he said after a beat. "He keeps telling me to quit."

"But?"

"Don't you ever think this should be…easier?" He rocked up and then stopped, obviously thinking better of it. "Like, we have this ability but can't use it without all this song and dance."

"It doesn't matter what I think. Since you asked, though, it seems as if you've replaced one sort of ritual with another. But the biggest question is why he even went to all the trouble to get me to come here."

Color rose into Russ's pale cheeks, and against his black hair it made him look a bit like those creepy dolls they had in the St. Hilaire museum, the ones with the glass eyes that followed you around the room. Apparently the dolls weren't the only things haunted. "Oh dear. You actually care for him, too, don't you? And what? You thought he cared enough for you to be virtuous and allow you to use him to increase your standing here with nothing in it for himself?"

Russ stood and seemed to shake off his fugue. He pulled his shoulders back, and I could see a glimmer of the leader he could become if only he stopped being concerned about the wrong things.

He looked me in the eye, giving away the truth behind his next words. "You know what? Yeah. Yeah to all of that. I mean, not virtuous. Not Ian. But…he was—is—definitely sincere."

I reached over and picked up the syringe. The liquid inside was pearlescent, if pea soup could look pearlescent. "He's a ghost. You remember that part, right? Ghosts are many things. 'Sincere' hardly sits at the top of that list."

Russ's hands curled into fists before he released them, stretching out his fingers and staring at them as though he'd never seen them before. "Why are you here, Willow? I know what you said about Ian showing up and asking you to check on me, but why would you do it? It's not like you care about me so much you'd lower yourself to trek all the way over here. If it isn't about me, it must be about something else. And the only something else in this case is Ian."

"I didn't expect you to be someone who sees things in black and white. We—you and I—have one purpose here, and that is to free these spirits who have been trapped by their oppressive human emotions."

"So I've heard." He rubbed the crook of his arm. I wondered if the shots hurt and if he liked the pain. Like anything, pain could turn into an instrument of desire once you'd gotten used to it. "But what does that have to do with Ian?"

I got up and walked over to his window ledge. There was a candle whose pale wax had melted down to the sill and a space where another had obviously once sat. My eyes scanned the edges of room. I recognized the pattern of a protection circle. Such things were rare in St. Hilaire. We courted ghosts rather than trying to dispel them. I picked at a piece of the scorched wax and held it to my nose. *Sage.* Perhaps I wasn't the only one trying to get rid of Ian Mackenzie.

"Did you ever run a séance with him?" I asked.

Russ shook his head. Of course, he hadn't. Their age gap was slight, but large enough to have stood in the way of any Guild-sanctioned bonding.

"He worked fast. It never took much time for a ghost to take notice of him. But he was able to compel almost any spirit to give him the information the common was looking for without much of a struggle. What he lacked was humility, an understanding of where he fit into the larger picture, the larger community. Subtlety."

Russ's dark eyes, only slightly less glassy than they'd been when I'd first woken him, followed me across the room. His bookcase, rickety though it looked, was stocked with an impressive selection of texts. Books of every color and thickness were jammed in front of and on top of others. I felt a strange sense of pride to find that my student was as much of a student of the art as he professed to be.

I turned around quickly. Only refusal to look weak kept Russ from jerking backwards. "People don't gain tact once they die. He must be quite a handful for you, Russ. He must be brimming with grandiose ideas and emphatic pronouncements. He must see you as the answer to all of his unfinished goals."

Something in Russ's cheek twitched. Was it anger? A sudden understanding? Agreement? I wasn't certain. But I knew I was gaining ground.

"Ian Mackenzie is a disruptor, Russ. He's going to go on that show and give everyone a reason to believe in ghosts. And then, eventually, he's going to go away and, after he's gone, every time anyone looks at you, all they're going to think about is Ian. Not that *you* are talented or that you were able to save St. Hilaire by getting rid of this show, but that you were Ian's lapdog."

Russ looked at me before bolting up and running from the room. I heard the door to the next room open. Then I heard retching.

I stood. Replaced the candles on the windowsill and headed back down the stairs. I was pretty sure my work was done.

chapter twenty-nine

RUSS

I stomped through the garden.

Willow. Here at the house. In my freaking room.

I tramped around the edible herbs. The basil. Rosemary. Sage. The mint that threatened to destroy everything else. I kicked at them, releasing a scent that made my stomach grumble. Not like I was going to be eating again anytime soon, after my embarrassing performance earlier.

I couldn't believe she'd seen me lying on the floor looking like a junkie or something. And sent by Ian? What the hell was he up to?

I nearly stumbled over a tree root and forced myself to stop. Take a breath. But I couldn't hold myself in place. I took a few determined steps deeper into the woods and then turned and headed back toward home. No. If I stayed here and Ian showed up, who knew how things would end.

I felt like a fuse looking for a lighter. Had I not overdone it last night, I could have made some tea or taken a shot or something. At this point, I'd eat the herbs whole. Anything to take the edge off this simmering rage. But I didn't dare. Even after throwing up, I still felt the shot's effects dancing around the edges of my brain.

Maybe I needed a break after all. It would be months before I had to do any sort of formal séance. It could be these herbs built up a tolerance in your body so you needed more and more, and I didn't want that. I'd only started messing around with them a few months ago anyhow.

I had so many items on my things-to-do list for today. Some of them were mundane (clean up my room and descale the coffee maker), some were things I actually wanted to do (call Dec, re-dye my hair), some were things for school or the Guild, but all of them faded away the more I thought about Asher's offer.

Did he mean it? I guess there was only one way to find out. I sent him a text and asked if he was working.

He replied as if he'd been sitting and staring at his phone. Working might be pushing it too far, but I'm at the planetarium and think I might have counted all the stars in the atrium to try to stay awake. Come save me?

It surprised me how easy it was to say yes. And it surprised me how much lighter I felt once I had. I never felt light.

And then I was there, and we were eating tortilla chips with some sort of super spicy cheese sauce from the closed concession stand. The planetarium had been painted and was closed to the public while the walls dried. It only smelled vaguely toxic. Asher pulled two Cokes out of his backpack and offered me one. I said no because I was still feeling the effects of last night, and I was already worried I would freeze up or say something stupid or be too serious. It didn't seem like a great idea to add caffeine to the mix.

"There's something I think about from time to time. Well, something I try not to think about. Only someone brought it up and now I can't stop thinking about it." My grandmother's serums typically either put me in a kind of meditative state or put me to sleep. This one was making me jittery as a Pekingese and, oddly, talkative. I was tempted to call Dec because *talkative* was definitely not a word anyone would use for me and I think he'd get a laugh out of it.

I gasped for breath and then started to laugh when I realized Asher's hand was on my arm. "Sorry," I said, feeling my face burn. "Super sorry."

"Sorry? Why?"

"I–I'm rambling," I admitted and then started to laugh some more, which made Asher start to laugh. The way the side of his eyes crinkled up made me want to keep making him laugh, and I had to work to focus on his words instead of the length of his dark lashes.

"You don't need to apologize to *me* for that. I do it all the time in case you haven't noticed. But what is it you're trying not to think about? Elephants? The distance between the center of Saturn and her rings? It varies by the way, you know, gravity and all. Or are you wondering about the odds of guessing ten coin flips in a row, because that's…"

"No. Ghosts," I interjected. "It's always ghosts, actually. They…I mean…some of our teachers firmly believe ghosts never stay here by choice even if they say that's why they're here. We had to study all of these acronyms and it makes sense. Like if the afterlife is peaceful or anything good, then why stick around as a transparent specter? But then again, maybe it's fun to haunt people. Maybe some spirits think it isn't their time yet, and it's fun to be invisible and knock things over and leave in the middle of conversations."

The room shifted interestingly. I stretched out on my back and watched the planets hanging over my head. I wonder what they were made out of. Would it hurt if they fell on someone? Was the planetarium insured against such things? It had to be.

Asher sat next to me. His legs were crossed in his faded jeans, and he seemed lost in thought. I realized the back of his hand was leaning on my leg, but I wasn't sure how or when it got there. Suddenly, that was all I could feel, though, the heat from the back of his hand burning its way through my jeans.

"Do you think it's like…the end?" he asked. "Like we live until we die and then that's it? Unless we become a ghost or something, of course. But before that. Do you think that we're just here looking for the people we're supposed to find? You know in books they call it 'insta-love' but maybe it isn't. Maybe there are people your cells are trying to connect to. Like magnets."

I sat up. He was staring at the carpet, his hand still on my leg, and there were so many ways to take his question, but I let myself wonder if he meant that he had to find me—and then had to remind myself to breathe.

Asher shook his head as though he were reconsidering his

words, and then he sucked in his lip ring and said, "Or maybe ghosts stick around because they miss someone. Maybe dying wasn't something they'd considered and then something unexpected happened and there were things they still needed to do, people they still needed to look out for. Or…maybe someone missed them so much that they were…stuck."

He grabbed his hand back and rubbed it across his eyes.

Okay, not about me, then. And I was *not* going to think about Ian, but now that I'd thought about him, I had to consider he was being sincere when he'd told me he was sticking around for me…and to, well, help me dismantle the Guild. But still for me. Only I wasn't going to think about that right now. I couldn't. Besides, I knew what Asher was leading up to. I knew it very well.

When I looked back at Asher, the air twitched in a familiar way and so did my stomach. "Have you lost someone?" I asked, enunciating carefully.

His eyes opened wide as if he'd just realized he'd spoken out loud. I heard him swallow deeply. He shrugged in a noncommittal way and stared into his drink like someone trying to appear casual. "Who hasn't?"

Even in my fugue state, all my schooling washed over me. Everything I learned in class, everything I learned from the Hamptons and from Dec, and even from Ian…and damn it, why couldn't I stop thinking about him? Asher looked sad in a familiar way, weighted down by memories. I didn't need to go looking for things to fill my time with, and I certainly didn't need to do anything to draw any more attention from the Guild, but something in me leapt at the idea of showing him

I wasn't just someone living in a haunted town who couldn't afford a decent car.

"You can talk to me, you know," I said. But why would he know? What had I done to prove myself to him in any way?

The whole rigmarole was easier with a customer I knew I'd never see again. And it didn't matter how much I'd watched Dec or Willow or Ian or the Guild members run séances because I sucked at small talk and wasn't comfortable connecting to people I didn't know or, really, even to people I did know. But I liked Asher. Absurdly, I wanted to be his friend and that wasn't something I'd felt in a long time.

And I felt his pain.

"I mean, you can," I reiterated, aware that I was suddenly and unfortunately sober.

He smiled and it made the hair on my arms stand up. *Okay. Maybe not that sober.*

Then he stood and put out his hand.

I took a breath and felt the air fill my lungs.

I reached out and took his hand, feeling the pressure from each silver ring, allowing him to pull me up.

"Do you want to go for a walk?" he asked, waiting, our hands still clasped.

I nodded.

And he smiled.

———

"This is totally wild in the best of all possible ways," I said, looking around.

Overhead there were six sets of power lines that ran through the field, which was lined with evergreens of some sort. I'd always thought that power lines took away from the scenery, intruded on nature. But the way the wind blew through them and the way they crackled back in a conversational response was something I'd never experienced. It was a haunted sound in a less than haunted place.

My skin felt electric too. Shivery, but not in the cold ghost way. More as if I could feel the blood racing through my body and feel every hair on my arms. I felt energized in a way I never could have imagined. This was way better than coffee.

We both stood in awe. Looking up. Listening to the sparks.

"It's energy," Asher said. "Energy plus air plus water." He took a step forward and raised his arms and spun around a couple times. When he stopped, he stumbled, falling to the grass as if he was drunk.

"This is my very favorite place in the world," he said.

I looked around. It was getting dark, but distant house-lights made it possible for us to see each other. I lowered myself to sit next to him. The sound of the place was unlike anything I'd ever heard, and it felt...alive. I wondered, for a second, if it could be my favorite place in the world, too, which made me aware how close we were sitting to each other, which made me wonder how it would feel to kiss someone with a lip ring, which made my whole body twitch.

"Look," he said and pointed to the sky. I followed his finger with my eyes to see the last of a shooting star.

"I don't think I've ever seen one before," I said, my eyes scanning the horizon for more.

"You see them all the time here," he said. "You know, you're supposed to wish on them."

I pulled my eyes away from the sky to see him grinning. "Well, I didn't really see the whole thing." I was suddenly unsettled.

"I'm sure the wish fairies will give you a pass if you want to make up for it now," he said, bumping his shoulder into mine.

I sat up straight and looked at the ground. "I don't really know what to wish for. There are too many things out of sorts right now."

He looked at me for a long time, and all I could think of was *this could be something to wish for*. But then he said, "Mari," still looking at me through his lashes. "My sister's name is… was…Mari."

The tone in his voice, one I recognized, pulled me back. It was a tone filled with loss, regret, and sadness. Asher's grief was suddenly so huge and so evident that I didn't know how I'd missed picking up on it before. I didn't know how he managed to hide it behind his ever-present smile.

When he told me his sister was gone, I'd assumed she was at college or something. I'd let myself get distracted and had missed the cue.

"I'm sorry," I said. The words were too small a gift, but I'd learned what people most wanted was permission to feel what they felt. And to know that someone wanted to listen. "You were close?"

He nodded. "She was like…my person," he said. "We traveled a lot when we were little. Our parents were always working, and they never quite got me anyhow—they still don't—but

Mari… We were close in age and she was always there. She made me feel safe."

In the time since I'd met him, I'd been trying to sort out what it was about Asher that both intrigued me and made me feel as though I was eavesdropping on some private conversation. Now I realized what it was. I'd never met anyone who was as comfortable being vulnerable, and I wasn't quite sure what to do with that. We were polar opposites.

I reached down and pulled at a stalk of grass. Then I took a deep breath and asked the question I least wanted to ask. "What happened?"

He blinked and said, faltering, "Freak accident. Lightning." He fell silent, and I had a sudden realization that the same electricity that was coursing over the wires in this field had killed his sister. I wondered if he'd made the connection. Were we here because of that coincidence or in spite of it?

His words settled around us before he continued.

"She was hiking," he explained. "She wasn't supposed to go, but there was a guy she really liked, and she…went. We had a fight about it. Maybe had we not…"

"Don't." I jumped in because I knew where he was heading. "You can't blame yourself. You have no way of knowing how things would have worked out otherwise." I'd said those words to countless people already. And I would say them again and again in the future. This time, though, I honestly didn't want Asher to beat himself up, and it was clear that he was.

I glanced down at the grass in my hand to find it wasn't basic grass at all, but witch grass, a protective crop. It felt symbolic to find it here under this electrical umbrella. I wouldn't have to wait for my plantings to take after all, a thought that made my pulse race in anticipation. Who knew what I could do with the bounty in this field?

Still…

"I'd like to say I could try to contact her for you," I said. "But that doesn't always work out the way you hope it will."

He looked up at me and smiled. "Thanks. I… Thanks. No. I mean, I talk to her all the time anyhow. Just out here. She always liked how John Lennon said he'd send his son Julian a white feather if he could, after he died. I think if she were reachable, well, I might have heard from her by now."

"But what if you *could* talk to her? I mean, what would you want to say?" I felt a sudden *need* to absorb his sadness. It was an odd feeling, this compulsion to take away someone's pain.

He sucked on his lip ring, and my stomach twisted with a type of desire that felt more like guilt given that we were talking about his dead sister.

"I'd want to make sure she wasn't hurting, I guess. I'd want to… I guess I'd want to say goodbye, but really that's the last thing I want to say, if that makes any sense. I'd want to say I'm sorry for not being there. I'm sorry for all the shitty little-brother things I did, the times when she invited me to go places and I was too busy reading or thinking, too much in my own head like always. And I guess I'd want to say I'm sorry it was her and not me."

"Asher, you…"

He shook his head from side to side, and the blond swoop of his hair fell back and forth like a pendulum. "Oh, no. No, no, no. I don't mean I wish I would have died or anything. Just

211

that…" His voice hitched, and he pushed his hair out of his eyes. "I wish she hadn't. You know, Mari made friends everywhere. All she had to do was look at someone and they wanted to be her friend. It was never like that for me. I kind of waited until she was done with her new friends and took what I could get."

Lord, this boy was something. I gave in to the yearning in the pit of my stomach and said, "If you wanted to try… I mean, we could. I could."

He rubbed his neck in a way that made me wonder if maybe he didn't actually want to contact her. Maybe he was afraid of failing, maybe he was afraid of what she might say, maybe he didn't want to do it in front of me. Some clients were like that. Picky about who they allowed to get that close to a situation they couldn't control.

Somehow, that didn't sound like Asher.

But then there was the other side of things. The fact that I wasn't sure I could contact a ghost on demand, let alone on my own—not that he knew, but still.

"We wouldn't need to tell anyone," I said in spite of myself.

His head snapped up. "Really?"

"No guarantees. I mean it may not work. But then again, it might." It sucked that I couldn't give him more assurance than that. But I liked the idea of a shared secret between us.

He looked around. "Do we need to go somewhere else?"

I looked around and then got up and led him over to a grouping of trees. "How's this? Many mediums believe trees have power. That's why there are so many in St. Hilaire."

He nodded and shuffled before he sat down.

"It's okay," I said and sat down across from him.

I took a deep breath. Then another. "I open myself to those who came before in curiosity. In friendship. In safety. I offer fairness and accuracy and ask that you join us here in Arbor Field," I said, reciting the request for spirits to visit. The words were awkward in my mouth. I'd never needed to invite spirits in when I lived in Chicago and couldn't get them to stop talking to me. Now that I was in this place that was supposedly a magnet for ghosts, I had to send them a verbal invitation.

I reached out my hands and then pulled them back. It wasn't necessary to touch someone in order to read for them, but there was a theory that "closing the circle" was more inviting for the spirit. I wonder if that was true and if spirits cared about such things. I made a mental note to ask Ian about that later.

I reached out again, and Asher took my hands in his own. Something in me calmed in an odd way. I tried to release the tension from my shoulders and focus on my breathing.

"Think about her," I suggested.

"I always do," he replied.

I waited and put out feelers of vibration, hoping something would come back. Asher ran his thumb over my knuckle, which was distracting and making me feel buzzy. I tried not to focus on it and failed.

The wind picked up. I hoped it might be her, but the fact that I was aware of it and thinking logically made me certain it wasn't.

The breeze smelled fresh the way it does before it rains. We waited.

I didn't have siblings. I wasn't sure what it would feel like to

213

grow up with someone around my age who shared my DNA. If I had a sister, would we get along? Would she be able to speak to ghosts, too? Maybe she'd be better at it than I was and be able to get spirits to speak when she needed them to.

I opened my eyes and looked around, watching for anything that shimmered or moved unexpectedly. My eyes kept landing on Asher. On how relaxed he seemed. Most people who came to contact someone were either nervous or skeptical or excited. Some emotion was always obvious. But Asher was just there. Trusting me. I didn't want to let him down.

Suddenly, Asher shook and jerked his hands back. His expression grew anxious as he pointed at a row of dark clouds rolling in. He shivered, and I could tell he was panicking. It was a stark difference from the calm he'd showed from the minute I'd met him. "I'm sorry," he said. "I need to go. I…"

I tried to figure out what I'd done wrong, but then the sky rumbled. The storm was still far away, but it was coming. Then I got it. "Lightning?"

"Yeah," he said, breathing hard. "I'm sorry, ever since…"

Of course. That made sense. "It's okay."

"I'm sorry," he said again. "But thank you. For trying and for coming here and just, thanks."

"No, I'm the one who's sorry. I'm sorry I couldn't…" I said, wondering if Asher would let me try again and then questioning my own motivations. Was it to help him talk to his sister? Or maybe I wanted an excuse to see him again.

A breeze picked up and thunder rumbled ominously in the distance.

Neither of us made a move to leave.

"You need to go," I said.

"Russ, I…" He grabbed my sleeve and instead of pulling away like I normally would, I caught myself. *Damn it*. I didn't want to pull away. That was a first. I didn't understand why Asher elicited totally different reactions from me than anyone else ever had.

I started to say something like "I know" or "It will be okay" or some other platitude I've uttered a hundred times before at séances that have gone nowhere. But I didn't want to hand Asher a bunch of bullshit. I wanted him to know I *was* sorry. I wanted to tell him I understood his pain and wanted to do something to take it away. I wanted to tell him I cared.

But I didn't know how to do that and I kind of hated myself for that.

The sky rumbled again, and a mist of rain fell over us, a warning of what was to come. But Asher's hand was still on my arm and he looked rooted in place by…not fear, but something I couldn't name.

"Asher," I reminded him. "The storm."

He looked over his shoulder at the clouds and then back at me. "I know," he breathed out. "If I stay out here, I'm going to have a panic attack and you're going to think I'm a mess, and I mean, what seventeen-year-old is afraid of a bunch of rain? You know there's a guy who was hit by lightning seven times and is still alive, but even so. I always think that if you understand something you shouldn't be afraid of it, but I can't seem to shake this."

"Do you want me to walk you back?" I offered, more selfishly than not.

"See?" He laughed nervously. "Now you *do* think I'm a mess."

215

"No," I said. He was sucking in his lip ring and drumming his fingers on his pants, and okay, maybe I thought he was a bit anxious, but more, I hoped he'd take me up on my offer. "I don't think you're a mess at all," I said. "I get it. Come on, let's go." *I'm not really ready for this to end.*

He laughed and tilted his face up to the rain. "No, no, I just…" The thunder clapped again, and a bolt of lightning lit up the field. Then, before I could even process it, he leaned in toward me.

The rain was misting off his shoulders as he put his palms flat on the lapels of my coat. His hands were warm enough for me to feel through the cloth, or maybe it was that my heart was racing against them. I tried to still it as he leaned in and kissed me, and my heart seemed to stop on its own.

I kissed him back, suddenly warmer than I could ever remember being. Dead of summer hot. Air conditioner on the fritz hot. Bonfire hot.

His lip ring nestled against my skin, but it was surprisingly not an issue either way, and shit, I was thinking too much and breathing too hard and his hands were in my hair and I wanted them to stay there, but then we pulled away at the same time to breathe.

Panting, we stared at each other and then he smiled, turned, and sprinted away, not looking back. Leaving me standing in the rain. Neither of us saying another word.

chapter thirty

ASHER

By the time I got home, the storm had died down, the rain had stopped, and I was soaked to the skin. I hesitated before going into the house, glancing back over my shoulder at the path that led to Arbor Field.

I had to know. Was Russ still there? Was he still standing where I'd left him with the rain running off his shoulders and down the length of his black coat like some model in a Victorian London postcard?

No, that's ridiculous. He wasn't going to spend the night out in a field in the rain.

But what if he had? What if he'd taken refuge under one of the larger trees and was waiting for the storm to clear, even a little.

What if he was still there and I could go back and kiss him again so he knew I meant it. Maybe it really *was* like magnets.

I ran into the house. The TV was on in the living room and turned to sports, which meant my dad was home. I raced up the stairs, pulling off clothes as I went. I threw my wet stuff into the closet and grabbed the first things I could find before heading back downstairs and out the door.

This was stupid. He wasn't going to still be there.

But maybe he was standing there under the crackling wires thinking about my kissing him, and holy hell, what had *I* been thinking?

The air was the odd kind of after-the-rain fresh that was so awesome they even had a perfume that tried to capture it. And that was good because I thought I was going to hyperventilate, I was breathing so hard, even though the field was only a few blocks away.

First, I checked near the trees where Russ has tried to contact Mari. Next, I ran around the perimeter in case he'd taken cover under some others to avoid the rain.

Then I had to admit he wasn't here. Okay, that was fine.

I pulled out my phone and typed in a smiley face.

Then I held my breath and pushed Send on my phone.

The wind was blowing the trees around, but the sky had cleared enough so I could see the stars through the branches. There was a poetic dance to it all. I'd read trees could talk to each other and warn each other of danger. But they could also share nutrients with the trees around them that needed it the most. The best was the theory that there are mother trees that nurture younger trees and can share all they know with the trees in their care before they die. Maybe in my next life, I'd be lucky to come back as a tree within a whole community of other trees who were looking out for and learning from each other. It would make for a nice change.

I glanced at my silent phone and pushed the power button to make sure it was still on. My screen saver, a photo of the Big Dipper, came up. No new notifications. I shouldn't have sent the text, I guess.

I leaned against a giant oak and told Mari how I'd been thinking about that day with the Ouija board. "Maybe you *did* believe in ghosts after all. Or maybe you knew something was going to happen." I stopped myself from remembering her words, her anger at me as she'd stalked off that day. I pictured the pointer, solid in the middle of the word, *goodbye*. At first, my parents had given me a hard time for even considering that it was a message from her. They refused to believe she knew she was going to die. At the same time, they were afraid she'd been suicidal, that maybe she'd planned it. As if you could deliberately get hit by lightning. Once they got over the shock, though, they remembered no one had loved life as much as my sister. And that's when they took the step of trying to contact her ghost.

"Do you think I can still be Russ's…friend? Even with Mom and Dad trying to discredit the whole town?" I asked the sky. Out loud, the question sounded young and desperate, like some kindergartener trying to make friends over a shared box of crayons. And I was pretty sure now that friendship wasn't all I wanted from him. Not in the slightest. Not from the way my whole body was buzzing.

I put my phone into my pocket and closed my eyes. With

the light blocked out, I could feel the wind blowing over me, hear the rustle of birds returning to their tree-bound nests. The power lines went quiet. None were crackling or popping. The air must be drying up. Good. I didn't trust storms.

I wanted everything to stop moving so fast. I wanted more time before *Ghost Killers* turned the whole world upside down by proving that everyone in St. Hilaire was a fraud. I wanted a window where I could take stock of things and figure out what to do before it was too late. I wanted more time to get to know Russ and for him to get to know me so when he found out who my parents were, he would know, without a doubt, that I hadn't been trying to do anything to hurt him.

I took one more look at my phone. At the lack of any new text messages, and I powered it down. I never should have texted Russ, anyhow.

chapter thirty-one

RUSS

I reached into my pocket for my phone.

Asher.

I couldn't bring myself to read the text. I wasn't sure what I wanted it to say. I wasn't even sure how I felt or what I'd been thinking when he'd kissed me. Or when I'd kissed him back.

That was a lie. I couldn't deny what I'd been feeling. What I had no right to feel. I had a boyfriend, or at least I thought I did, if you could be committed to a ghost. One thing Willow was right about was that Ian was going to disappear at some point, though. However strong he was. However much he decided he was going to stick around; he was still dead.

But he was also still here.

Asher had been so…alive. The field and the storm and the lightning. It had all been so damned alive.

But there was no way a boy from Buchanan was an option, even if I had time. Which I didn't. Even if I wasn't tied to Ian and didn't have plans with him that were more important than I was. Which I did.

Asher wasn't an option, but hell if I didn't wish he was.

I didn't delete the text, but I couldn't read it. I had to get my head on straight first. *Fat chance.*

———

I rolled over in bed. The wall was cool, and the room was blissfully quiet until I heard, "I've got it."

Crap. Ian's timing, as usual, left a lot to be desired.

"Isn't there a pill you can take or something?" I mumbled.

"Oh, funny," Ian said and smirked. "Have you been waiting for a long time to use that one?"

"Has no one taught you to use a door?" I asked, pulling myself up, relieved that we still seemed to be speaking to each other.

"Why walk when you can ride in style?"

"What the hell are you even talking about?" I rubbed my eyes. "And by the way, in what universe did you think it was a good idea to send Willow to break into my house?"

Ian crossed his arms. I knew from his expression I wasn't going to get any sort of honest answer from him. "I don't have a lot of addresses in my little black book these days."

I waited.

"I knew how to reach her," he admitted.

"But why…"

"Griffin, you had your little salt-and-votives routine going.

222

I couldn't get in. Besides, you were pissed at me. Anyhow, you're obviously alive so she did her job, and if you think I'm letting you off for being so stupid, you have another guess coming. But stop talking for a minute and listen. I have the real names of the people behind this stupid show, and I know why they're doing all of this."

I rubbed my eyes again. I needed to be fully awake. My hand strayed down to my lips and I remembered Asher's pressed against them, his lip ring odd and enticing.

I heard myself sigh. *Crap, again.* I'd stared at his name in my phone for too long late last night in the dark. And I vowed not to see him again rather than lead him on. He could do better than to be involved with a medium. "Yeah? Who is it?" I asked Ian. I tried to focus and to remind myself I really did want to know what he had come up with.

Ian glanced down at the paper in his hand. "One of my few failed contacts, actually. Bereaved parents trying to contact their daughter who died suddenly. I remember it because the whole setup should have worked. She was young and wasn't estranged from her family. Her death was unexpected and quick. She had a sibling she was very close to. It was kind of the perfect storm for contact. But I got literally nothing. Not even energy trails. I mean, I pulled out all the stops, but nada. No idea why she'd skipped on into the afterworld. And when I told the parents, same way I always had—explained that she must be at peace, felt her life had been completed, et cetera, the parents went ballistic. Not just weepy and sad, but they acted like it was my fault. They even lodged a complaint with the Guild, but of course I'd done nothing wrong."

"Of course."

He reached out and swatted me with the back of his hand. This banter with Ian was easier than baring myself emotionally with Asher. I knew how to do this. Both of us full of bluster, looking for the next comeback. "It was frustrating," he said. "I even tried on my own later… Wipe that grin off your face, Griffin. Anyhow, we never heard from them again."

"Until now?"

"Right."

It all made sense. Except for one thing. "And how exactly did you find this out?" I asked.

Ian gave me a charming shrug. "I watched over Clive Rice's shoulder when he was going through the information."

I bolted up. "You what?"

"Good lord, Griffin. What's the point of being a ghost if I can't work it? I can't become corporeal around anyone but you, but I can still lurk. Besides I spent a whole night waiting for him to actually get around to reading something that mattered, so a little gratitude, please." The idea of Ian haunting Guild offices made my stomach turn. But I had to admit he had a point.

"Wait. Have you ever lurked here?" I thought of all the things Ian might have seen. *Oh, hell.*

"Wouldn't you like to know," he said and wagged his eyebrows.

I gave up. "Whatever. What are their names?"

He held out a single piece of paper, and I grabbed it from his hands, skimming Clive Rice's perfect script. The story was as Ian had said, and I was about to hand it back when I saw the names at the top and my lungs twisted themselves into knots.

"Paula and Martin Mullen," I read out loud, unable to believe what I was seeing. I scanned the sheet to the end and found the names I knew—and dreaded—would also be there: Mari and Asher.

chapter thirty-two
ASHER

I stared at my phone, debating whether to leave Russ another voicemail or to send a text or a carrier pigeon or to actually suck it up and *go* to St. Hilaire.

Russ didn't seem like the type to kiss and run. Maybe I'd been reading him wrong. Maybe he was busy.

Maybe he *was* the type to kiss and run.

Maybe I should have asked first.

Maybe he was straight.

But no. I couldn't have been that far off.

Unless I had been.

Shit.

chapter thirty-three
RUSS

"Forgive the pun, but you're white as a…you know," Ian said, sitting down next to me on the bed. "What is it?"

The concern in his voice made something in my stomach curdle. Well, that and seeing Asher's name on the séance intake form.

"I know him," I said quietly.

"Him?" Ian repeated.

"Or I thought I knew him." I closed my eyes. It was suddenly clear that I'd allowed myself to believe in the possibility of something with Asher. That I'd let my guard down and allowed myself to hope. "The son," I admitted. "Asher. Mullen."

"Back up. You know the son of the couple running *Ghost Killers*, and you're just telling me this now?"

"I didn't know he was tied to the show," I said, my voice choking. "I swear. I had no idea. He… I bought his car."

Ian looked relieved in a way that made it clear he wouldn't welcome hearing about the rest of what I'd done with Asher. "That's one hell of a coincidence," he said.

"In St. Hilaire, there are no coincidences," I intoned back. The phrase had become a type of tagline. There were even plans to have T-shirts printed with the slogan on them to sell during next summer's tourist season.

"Exactly," said Ian.

"So what? You think he planned to sell me a beat-up Chevy?" I asked, only thinking the remaining sentences in my head: *You think he planned to have me over for dinner? You think he planned to make me feel like he was my friend? You think he planned to kiss me?* What if he had?

"I don't know," Ian said too seriously. "Maybe the car is bugged or something? I'm sure there's a way of checking that out. Or maybe there was some info he thought he could get from you during the transaction. Do you remember anything odd?"

There was no way I was telling Ian that Asher didn't take my money. "No," I said. "He…he's a kid. My age. And I don't think…" My words evaporated. How could I possibly trust anything I thought?

"But you only met with him once, right?"

Ian stared through me with narrowed eyes. I felt transparent. Every minute I'd spent with Asher played through my head. Every minute felt like a lie.

"Griffin?"

"No," I said, flatly. "I thought we were friends."

"Friends," Ian repeated, knowing as much as anyone how seriously I took that concept. When I didn't reply, he sighed and switched tactics. "Let's focus on damage control. Figure out where to go from here."

Damage control. What did that mean? We needed to get back to our plans. Refocus. Forget that I'd been stupid enough to allow myself to be used.

I rubbed my eyes with the heels of my palms. Enough. I was through being distracted. I had a job to do.

"Ian?"

"Yeah?"

I thought of Asher. Of his easy smile and how he'd trembled when the lightning started. I thought of his supposed love for his sister and the feel of his hand on my jeans. I tried never to hate anyone, but something sharp and brittle was forming inside me, something dark enough to block out those thoughts of him, those memories. My hands clenched into fists. I could feel the tips of my nails piercing the skin on my palms. "Let's take this show down," I said to Ian. "I want this over with, and not because Rice is threatening me or anything else. I just want...I just want it done."

He looked at me, studying me as if he knew everything I hadn't told him, and grabbed my shoulder, his grip sure and tight. My heart was racing too fast. I forced myself to remember to breathe and regroup. I had my father. I had Ian. Screw Asher and my mom and everyone else who was working hard to make me feel like crap.

I shrugged out of his grasp and grabbed my phone, deleting

Asher's text unread. Then I sent one to Clive Rice, reminding him that Ian and I were ready to do whatever he needed.

I'd gotten distracted, but I wasn't going to let myself stray any further. I had a future to take ownership of and a mission. I was going to save St. Hilaire.

chapter thirty-four
WILLOW

"You don't need to be here," I told the boy. He was dressed in an army uniform. One from another country. And probably from another century.

He blinked long and slow out of watery brown eyes. Sometimes spirits lost the ability to speak. Sometimes they sang. Sometimes they screamed. I hated the screamers. I wasn't sure yet which of those categories this particular ghost fit into.

"Walter," I said, looking down again at the card in my hand to verify his name. "There is no one left here for you. Aside from your great-granddaughter, Joanna, your family is gone. And that girl has no interest in talking to you. She doesn't even believe you exist. It's her boyfriend who reached out to me. She doesn't even know."

I'd placed an advertisement in a local paper, some hours away. It needed to be close enough that the commons might have heard of St. Hilaire, and yet far enough away to guarantee they wouldn't show up at the town gates. Also, if I was going to test my new spirit cabinet, it was important to find out its effectiveness.

The ghost moved toward the wall. Nearer to the cabinet. *Yes,* I thought. *Go in. Save me the trouble. Let me test my work.* But when I opened the cabinet door, the room grew colder.

"None of that, now," I said.

He blinked like a dying battery. I had to change tactics.

I reached out a hand. He wasn't solid. Nowhere near solid. But some ghosts register feeling in their memories the same way people do when they've lost a limb. Phantom pain, they call it. He moved slightly closer to me. I took a step back.

"Walter. Think about how good it would feel to rest. Think about how you can give Joanna the greatest gift of knowing she can come home and not wonder if her mirrors will be broken." *Think about how happy she'll be when she can have her boyfriend spend the night without the lights blinking on and off and the cat yowling at something it can't see. Think about how happy I'll be to deposit her boyfriend's check into my bank account.* "You don't need to scare her in order for her to remember you. She never knew you after all. But her boyfriend said he was going to get her one of those genealogy memberships. You know, kind of in your honor."

I opened the door and a soft breeze of sea and rain drifted out. "You lived a good life, Walter. It's time to sleep now."

The ghost took a step closer to the cabinet but twisted his

head around to an unnatural degree. He looked scared, which I never understood because he was already dead. He'd drowned in a flood. There wasn't much worse that was going to happen to him.

"She will remember that you did this for her," I said, not knowing if it were true and not caring if she remembered or not, but there didn't seem to be any compelling reason for him to be stuck in the middle, haunting a girl he'd never met. And I had to take this last chance at convincing him because if I tried to push him, my hands would go right through. I hated this part, the negotiation, the needling.

He pointed a finger at my phone, and for a minute I wasn't sure what he wanted. Surely, he didn't mean to call Joanna. But then he mimed snapping a photo with an old camera. I opened the door to the cabinet and pointed inside to where I'd taped up a photo of a pleasant-looking girl with a purple buzz cut and a small stud in her nose.

He peered in, then looked at me quizzically.

"Fashions have changed," I said, stepping behind him and wishing I could shove him in. "It won't hurt. All you need to do is step inside." I didn't know that precisely. But it had to be better than an eternity of hauntings.

He took another step closer to the entranceway, then he put one foot inside, stared into the darkness for a moment, turned to salute me, and slid inside.

I shut the door and put my ear to it.

From inside I heard—not nothing, but a heavy silence. The walls of the cabinet seemed to exhale. There was a shift in the air of the room; it felt boiling hot and freezing cold at the same time. There was a pressure and then…

Nothing.

Blissful nothing.

A small surge of energy pulsed through me. It wasn't a lot, but then Walter was weak and insignificant. Just the thought of what I would gain from vanquishing Ian Mackenzie brought a smile to my face.

Another one bites the dust.

I was ready.

chapter thirty-five
ASHER

"Hey, kiddo." Rick Healy had been working with my parents since before I was born, before Mari was born. He had helped create the show and was kind of an adopted uncle, but this time, I wasn't particularly happy to see him. Or happy to see anyone, really. "That must be some book."

I allowed my eyes to focus on the page in front of me. It was a fantasy bestseller I'd been looking forward to since reading the first book of the series over a year ago. I hadn't turned a page in an hour. All I could think about was Russ. It was one thing for my parents to totally screw up things for *everyone* in St. Hilaire. Now I've made a total fool of myself on top of it. I didn't know what the hell I was going to do about either of those.

"Yeah. I guess." I forced myself to look up at him. None of this was his fault.

"You ready for your parents to do one last show? I've heard the network has some high-paying advertisers lined up."

I shrugged. There was nothing to say.

He fiddled with a bunch of wires that fit together to form some type of EMF machine. That was the thing my parents used to measure electromagnetic spikes, which are said to be a sign of spirit activity. Apparently there is something in your mind that includes an EMF field that doesn't go away when someone dies. That's the theory anyhow. "Your dad said you could take me over to the town. I want to get the lay of the land."

I dropped my book and the pages unfolded like it might take flight. "Me?" I couldn't believe my parents had volunteered me for this without even asking. Well, yeah, I believed it. I just hated it.

"If you don't mind," he said, putting down the equipment and sitting down next to me.

"I can walk you to the gates. I guess."

He put his hand on my knee, which I'd just noticed was jiggling a million miles a minute. "Are you okay, Asher? I keep thinking your parents are going to get some closure from all of this, but I guess it isn't working like that for you."

I stood up so fast my head spun. "Closure? No, I wouldn't say I'm getting closure. I don't understand why they can't stop and let her go." My eyes prickled with tears and a wave of guilt about letting Russ try to contact Mari overwhelmed me.

Rick pulled me into a hug. "I know this is hard. People process grief differently, and in your parents' case, I guess their way of dealing with it is to turn it around and try to keep other people from being hurt."

He had such a generous take on things that I didn't bother to correct him.

"I can walk you over now," I said because it was easier than talking about my parents and grief.

Rick squeezed my shoulder and began to collect his equipment.

"I'm not sure I can get you inside, though," I warned him. "And I'll have to leave. I have"—my voice trailed off—"stuff."

I wanted to see Russ so badly that I didn't have words for it. But I couldn't let him see me with Rick and his big-as-a-house camera.

"No problem. They've agreed to let us in. They kind of had to. It would make them look bad to deny us. I mean, what do they have to hide anyhow?"

I shrugged.

"Speaking of which…I've been getting some extra footage. You know, the usual. Night shots. The spires. Entrance signs. That sort of thing. And, I don't know. I know nothing about this place, but this green-shirted security force made up of kids that I keep seeing doesn't seem right. And the other night…I don't know. A bunch of families were being marched out of town, and it didn't seem as if they were doing it by choice. You sure this place is on the up-and-up?"

I stared at the carpet. The security force was their Youth Corps. I knew that from what I'd read online. But people being marched out of town? Now *that* was creepy.

When I didn't reply, Rick said, "Look, promise me you'll be careful, alright?"

"Yeah," I said. "Of course." *Too late.*

We walked over to the town in silence. I'm sure everything would make sense if I asked Russ about it, but it didn't seem like I was going to get the chance.

I wondered where the show was going to shoot. It was odd that they were going to allow *Ghost Killers* to come in and bad-mouth their town. I wonder if Russ knew. I wondered what he thought about it. I wondered what he thought about *everything*.

———

The perimeter of St. Hilaire was surrounded by a decorative iron gate topped with pointed spikes.

After I sent Rick in the right direction, I leaned my back against the fence and stared pathetically at the gatehouse.

I'd only been inside once. That time I'd done what everyone else did and waited my turn to get in before wandering around enjoying the sense of community, the kitschy signs, the sounds of wind chimes and the smell of incense, and the general atmosphere of a welcoming party.

I'd thrown some change in the wishing well and gone to a couple of public readings and listened to the town leaders talk about their plans for the future. This time though, the ticket booth was dark, and my desperation wasn't going to get me through the gates.

I turned back around to stick my face through the fence and watched a group of older women walk down the path, laughing at a story one of them was telling. Here, only ten minutes from my house, everything seemed different. It wasn't just the old

Victorian houses or the flower-lined pathways, or even the signs advertising various services or directions to the sweat lodge or inspiration areas.

It was the air, which felt heavier, but not in a bad, oppressive way like before it rains in the summer. More like it was substantial, a curtain you could part and walk through.

I knew it was ridiculous to stand here and hope Russ walked by. I mean, even if he did...what then? What exactly was I going to say to him? I could say I was sorry for kissing him, but I wasn't. I could apologize for my parents, but that was assuming he'd put the pieces together, and if he had, I'm not sure an apology would be enough. Better he didn't know I had any connection to this stupid show. I wanted to see him.

Still, I couldn't leave. The *thump, thump, thump* in my head that had been bothering me ever since I'd tried to call Russ and he hadn't picked up was a little quieter here. Any one of these people walking by might know Russ or know where I could find him. If only I could get in...

I followed the fencing around to the back of the school, the crunch of leaves echoing my movements. Only when I stopped, the crunching didn't.

"Who's there?" I asked. I wasn't expecting an answer, so I wasn't surprised not to get one. But there was something. A breath or... "Seriously," I said. "I know you're there."

Something ruffled my hair. A breeze that didn't seem to come from anywhere, really. *Okay,* I told myself, *stay cool.* Wasn't like this was the first time I'd felt something odd around a haunted place. I'd just never felt it on my own before. Mari had always been with me. *Mari.* Was it possible?

My heart jerked. No, this was my parents' thing, not mine. My sister wasn't going to show up with her angel wings.

I looked up to see a storm rolling in. The air chilled too quickly. I'd looked at the weather on my phone this morning, or at least I thought I had. I hadn't seen anything about a storm. In the distance, I heard a crack of thunder. *Shit.* I forced myself to take a deep breath. It was fine. I would be fine. The statistical odds of being hit by lightning were so small—one in 1.2 million in any given year and one in 15,300 in your lifetime. The odds of dying from it, even less.

A bright flash struck in the direction of Buchanan. I followed the path of the fence and pushed myself under the awning of the St. Hilaire ticket booth. Then I counted. The thunder clapped sixteen seconds later. The storm was close, and I wasn't going to make it home.

I ducked down. Put my hands over my head and reminded myself to breathe.

chapter thirty-six
RUSS

This was why I didn't get close to people. An acidic feeling of betrayal crawled under my skin and through my veins. It settled itself next to the guilt I was already feeling for not telling Ian about Asher and not telling Asher about Ian, It wrapped itself around my… No, I had no use for a heart. My blood would have to figure out another way to be pumped through my veins.

Work. Work would be my salvation. I powered down my phone and grabbed my grandmother's notebook. Somewhere in its worn pages was the key to making me forget, and if I was lucky, it would also hold the key to destroying *Ghost Killers*.

Rice had replied to my text, letting me know that he and Willow were busy putting things in motion. It couldn't happen soon enough as far as I was concerned. I was ready for this whole mess to be over.

"You're sure you don't need the car?" my father asked. He rarely asked to borrow it, preferring to walk to work in Buchanan, but today he had to take some plans for station renovations into town and didn't want them to get waterlogged.

I considered the rip in the hood of my rain jacket and the hole in the bottom of my boot and how deeply into the now-muddy woods I was going to have to walk to collect herbs if Grandma's notebook came through with an idea. "No," I said. "You take it."

"Drop you somewhere?" he asked. I considered his offer, then shook my head. So far, I'd been able to keep all of this from my father—the herbals, Ian, even most of the issues with *Ghost Killers*. And certainly Asher, although there was no longer anything to tell. My father had enough on his plate. He didn't need to worry about my drama.

Dad dug his coat out of the closet and turned back to button it up. Then, as if he'd thought better of it, he sat down on the edge of the table.

I busied myself by rewashing a clean plate. My father, one of the most patient people I'd ever met, waited. I flipped the plate over and squirted soap on it, trying to buy myself more time. Pointless because I knew he could outlast me if he felt like there was something he had to say.

"You know I'm not really one for hovering, particularly when it comes to all this ghost business."

I took a deep breath and held it until it hurt. "But?" I asked.

"But I know you think I have my head in the sand most of

the time and, well, you'd be right to some extent. But pretty much everyone coming through St. Hilaire ventures into the train station at one time or another. Sure, it's quiet this time of year when the tourists aren't here, but that makes the ones who do come through the station stand out more, if you catch my drift."

I stared at the bubbles going down the drain, wishing I could follow them. Anyone else would have gotten a cold shoulder from me, but this was my dad and he didn't deserve that. I turned to face him. "You know about the show?"

"Hey." He half-grinned. "I know I don't have a college degree with a bunch of letters after my name, but I can still look stuff up on the internet. And yeah, a TV crew stands out in a crowd."

Without waiting for me to respond, he added, "Well, not like it's really my area of expertise, but that sounds like it could be a lot of work. A lot of pressure. And that on top of your mom…"

"What mom?" I asked under my breath.

My father gave me a rare expression of rebuke before his face softened into one I recognized. "It isn't like you to be bitter," he said. "But I guess you have the right to in this case. And I get why you're hurt. But honestly, well, you're almost eighteen anyhow. And you have a way of landing on your feet. It just seems like it might be a lot for one person to be dealing with at one time."

I nodded at his understatement.

"Okay, I get it, kid. Just know that I'm here if you want to unload anything." My father stood and ruffled my hair. "I don't tell you enough how proud of you I am," he said. "I hope you know."

He turned and left, leaving me feeling guilty for not being more appreciative. It sucked how sometimes it was so easy to take the people who *were* there, for granted. My dad deserved better.

I looked out the window. It was raining hard and I wished we had a second car, which was a super-greedy thought, given that we were lucky to have one. Still, I was glad I'd convinced Dad to take the Chevy.

My phone buzzed from the table. I rushed over, thinking it might be someone calling from the Guild with an update, but saw Asher's name on the screen. *Seriously?* A flash of lightning lit up the window for dramatic effect.

I wasn't one to run and hide from confrontation, but this was on another level. Still, it…*he* was going to be a distraction until I got this conversation over with. Blocking him wouldn't do much, given how closely tied he was to the show, and I needed Asher Mullen off my plate. One less thing to give my dad cause to worry.

I answered.

chapter thirty-seven

ASHER

My teeth were suddenly chattering. Maybe it was the dampness in the air that had worked its way under my NASA sweatshirt. Maybe it was fear of the lightning. Maybe it was that I hadn't expected Russ to answer after I'd tried so many times, and now I had no idea what to say.

And "answer" was probably pushing it. He pretty much grunted into the phone in such an irritated way that had I not been freaking out in the middle of a lightning storm, I probably would have mumbled back that I was sorry for butt-dialing him or hitting a wrong number and then I'd turn my phone off for awhile, hoping he'd somehow forget I'd called.

I'd made it as far as Sinema, the Buchanan art movie house, before the sky opened up again. Now, the rain was pouring off the awning, and I was crouched down watching the water pool on the sidewalk as if it could magically sweep me away home and away from this brewing electrical storm.

I tried to fight off the thoughts that told me I was going to die out here in the storm without ever clearing things up with Russ.

I also couldn't think of anyone else to call. Not my parents who were off somewhere figuring out the details of their St. Hilaire smackdown. Not my boss at the planetarium who was giving a tour to four classes of first graders. And obviously not my sister whose own storm experience was the cause of all of these stupid panic attacks anyhow.

All I had was the very last person I wanted to hear me like this.

"Russ, I…" My teeth gnashed together. I hated that I had to deal with the fallout of my stupid, rash actions before I could even grovel and ask Russ to come get me. Maybe I could turn it into some kind of shared joke and remind him he owed me a favor for giving him my car. "I'm sorry." I rocked back on my heels to avoid a new river of rain pouring through a hole in the gutter above.

"What's your game, Asher? That's what I want to know. Why me?"

His voice was hard. Distant and unlike I'd ever heard it. I closed my eyes and tried to will myself back to Arbor Field. I conjured the scent of the trees and the feel of the breeze. I heard the *buzz, buzz, buzz* of the electrical wires, and in my head, I could see the Russ I'd gotten to know. His willingness to help me try to reach Mari was the icing on the cake. If I was being honest with myself, I'd been attracted to him the first time I saw him. But it was his kindness that had compelled me to kiss him.

A crack of thunder shook through me, and I heard myself whimper over the line even though I tried to cover it with a cough. "I'm not playing," I said. "I wasn't. I mean, I should have asked. I know."

Russ laughed an ugly laugh. "You should have asked? In what universe do you think it would have been okay?"

My cheeks burned even though the day seemed to be turning colder. My sleeves were wet now, and I knew I should pull myself together and suck it up. Stand up. Walk home. Dry off. I knew my chance of being struck by lightning was slim to none.

But I couldn't move.

"I thought…" *Just say it*, I told myself. *Spit it out and get it done and brave the storm and crawl under the covers and you can sleep for a week.* "Well, I kind of thought you wanted to kiss me too."

"I did," he exploded. "I did. I didn't realize it, but I did. But what difference does that make now?"

He did. He did.

Off in the distance, thunder rumbled. I stopped myself from counting the seconds. "I don't get it," I admitted. Two realities flashed through my mind. In one, Russ and I were… well, were. And in the other, I was plodding through my days at the planetarium, aware of what I'd lost. It was crystal clear to me what was at stake. "What changed?" I asked. "Was kissing me that bad? I mean, is it the lip ring?"

There was a heavy silence on the phone. The sort of silence made famous in horror movies right before the killer jumps out of the shadows.

"I know who you are, Asher," he said.

Tell me, I longed to say, *tell me who I am.* I opened my mouth, but no words came out.

"What I don't know is why," Russ continued. "Why would you do this?"

"Why would I kiss you?" I asked stupidly. Was he so clueless about the way his eyes glowed when he talked about anything having to do with being a medium? Or the way something in my stomach curled pleasantly when he rubbed the beautiful white owl tattoo on his wrist without even knowing it? Did he not know what it meant to me that he'd tried to talk to Mari even though so many others had tried and failed, and that it almost didn't matter that he'd failed. It had mattered that he'd tried. "That's kind of a silly…"

"No," he snarled. "Why would you lie to me? Why do you and your parents want to destroy St. Hilaire so badly?"

I couldn't breathe while his words sorted themselves out in my head. "You know."

"Yeah, I know." If words could sneer, his did.

"How did you find out?"

"Does it freaking matter?" he asked. His words were dismissive, but his voice was softer now. Full of pain. And regret. Probably regret. I'd ruined everything.

A loud clap of thunder rattled the window behind me as if the sky was also trying to tell me I was a jerk.

"No," I admitted. "No, it doesn't matter at all. All that matters is that I've screwed everything up. But Russ, you have to believe me. It's not that cut-and-dried and…can we meet up maybe? Just to talk? I'd like to explain, and then if you still hate me, I guess I'll understand, but…" My words faded out and then there was silence.

"No," Russ said finally. "No. I have this stupid show to deal with, and I have too much on my plate right now. I don't think us being in touch is good idea."

"I'm sorry," I said. And I was. I suddenly wanted the lightning to find me. I wanted to cry. I wanted to smash the glass of Sinema's window. I stepped away from it to make sure that didn't happen.

I waited while Russ pulled his response together but all he said was, "Goodbye, Asher," and clicked off his phone.

chapter thirty-eight

RUSS

I couldn't get Asher Mullen out of my mind. Not the feeling of his lips on mine or the sound of his repentant voice on the phone. It all played over and over in one slightly obsessive loop, not helped by the fact that his parents were filming their show today.

Would Asher be there? Did I want him to be? Would I launch myself across the room and...what? Throttle him? Was that even a thing?

I weighed my options as I walked into town. I'd assumed we'd set up in the square with all of St. Hilaire's mediums gathered in support. The town lent itself to visuals given its tree-lined streets and painted Victorians. Not even the rain would ruin that.

But apparently something else had been in the works all along because while Clive Rice had offered the auditorium, which had been vetoed by the film crew due to its faded beige wallpaper and a nasty and unattractive leak coming from one corner of the ceiling over the stage and *Ghost Killers* had asked for the séance to take place somewhere other than St. Hilaire, which made a kind of sense given that they didn't trust us, somehow the negotiations had crashed into the idea of filming in Willow Rogers's loft.

I didn't understand why she'd offered her place. She was almost reclusive, and she had no friends. I doubted that Colin Mackenzie had even been there prior to the last day or so when he and a few other members of the Corps had moved some of her furniture into storage in Eaton Hall's basement while some of the film crew had been scouring the place for hidden speakers and false walls.

When I asked Ian about it, he shrugged and changed the subject. One more set of deflections that, while true to character, got under my skin. The feeling that Ian had plans for the taping that he wasn't sharing with me was growing with every hour. Would he show up in costume? Was he going to do some kind of striptease (oh lord, please, no) or some other shocking thing that proved ghosts existed but that would render the film unusable?

In truth, that wasn't a half-bad idea, but I certainly wasn't going to suggest it to Ian, who would more likely than not put it into action.

I ran up the stairs to Willow's rather than taking the elevator. The door was open but it was still kind of odd to just let myself in. It didn't feel like someone's home, though, since very little was left in the room. A few chairs. Heavy drapes. Tables. Lamps. A kind of solid wood cabinet into which someone had etched the Guild symbol.

What it did feel like was…rich. Willow definitely wasn't eating ramen for dinner *again*. It made Clive Rice's complaints about the town running out of money seem more than a little overdramatic.

As part of the negotiations, the Guild had allowed only one cameraman to attend and the director stepped up to take that roll. He was introduced to us as "Rick" before rushing around setting up lights and checking levels and speaking into headsets. Challenging him was the lightning outside that keep brightening the room, while rain pelted the roof, pinging off the metal gutters.

Lightning made me think of Asher and I wondered if he would be here. Then I tried pointlessly to distract myself by watching the cameraman scurry around taking light readings and sound readings, setting up some sort of electrical field reader, and generally looking as though he'd rather be somewhere else.

Clive Rice had asked the show for two days to prepare, and after a lot of grumbling about what "prepare" actually meant, they'd agreed. Ian and I had confirmed all things were in place, but he hadn't been around much afterward. He was resting up or playing hard to get or doing whatever it was he needed to before he changed the world.

In the meantime, I'd prepared a small syringe. I'd found myself having to use more each time just to get the same jolt, so I'd kicked this one up with something from the back of

Grandmother's book. Now I needed to find somewhere to use it. Not like I could pull it out in the middle of Willow's loft.

I hadn't even seen Willow since she'd come to my house. She'd canceled all my lessons, and all I could do was hope she was making her peace with the fact that St. Hilaire was always going to be in the public eye whether she wanted it to be or not.

I looked around the room. This would be an abnormally small séance for one with such major stakes. Rice, me, Willow, the one producer, and the Mullens.

And Ian.

I would have expected Guild leadership to demand to be there, but in truth they weren't really needed to run the séance. Ian was going to show regardless because he'd promised he would. I was his entryway, and even a hundred mediums calling for him wouldn't make a difference if he didn't want to appear.

I searched the room for a clock since mediums weren't allowed electronics at a séance. Then I gave up as the couple who had started this whole thing were ushered in.

The Mullens.

Paula and Martin.

Asher's parents.

How could I not have recognized them from the news articles? How did I not see Asher's high cheekbones in the sharp face of his father or his pale-brown eyes in those of his mother? I hated them at once and then felt a wave of guilt until I remembered that Asher had simply used me to get to St. Hilaire. I wasn't sure I'd ever read someone so poorly.

And yet I found myself itching to lean out the window to look for him.

I was still fighting that craving when Clive Rice came over to talk to me.

He put an odd fatherly arm around my shoulders, and I felt myself shrink. Then his hand tightened on my shoulder as if to hold me in place. "This is it," he said. "Do or die, as they say. And I'm assuming you have done what you've needed to do in order to ensure our success?"

Ensure? Where Ian was concerned? "Of course," I mumbled. My right hand reached into the pocket of my coat. My thumb ran over the plastic edge of the syringe. It was the only insurance I had.

Rice looked at his nonworking watch and said, "We have fifteen minutes before this circus begins. I suggest you go rest your mind and prepare yourself."

I nodded although "resting my mind" wasn't on my list of things to do and shrugged off his hand.

"And Mr. Griffin," he called as I stepped away. "I expect you'll remember that I'm holding you responsible for making sure Mr. Mackenzie is ready to do his part."

———

I ducked out the door and down the back stairs to the library in the building's basement. It was many degrees cooler than the apartment, thanks to the old stone walls. I leaned back against one of them in the spiritualist history section. Maybe the old mediums and ghosts of our past would step up to make sure I didn't screw everything up.

There was a heavy quiet in the room as I drew the needle

out of my pocket, an eerie silence as I flicked off the cap, made a fist, and found a vein.

In the past I'd looked at my grandmother's serum as an experiment, a tool. I'd used it to prove a point and meet a goal and to gain status.

It seemed somewhat fitting that now I was going to use it to save St. Hilaire.

chapter thirty-nine

ASHER

There had to have been a brief time—I'm sure there had—when I'd enjoyed the anticipation, excitement, and energy around a new show. I know Mari did, and I'm sure I followed her lead in this like I had in so much else. I remember being in charge of making the popcorn when we gathered to watch *Ghost Killers* air at 8:00 p.m. on Tuesdays. Mom would make caramel and Mari would melt butter and Dad would grab some sort of sugary soda that we normally weren't allowed to drink. We'd pile into the den or rec room or living room of wherever we were staying, and Mari would keep up a running commentary on Mom and Dad's performances. We'd laugh at that, and the bizarre assumptions made by those who were sure they'd been haunted by ghosts, until the final credits.

I wasn't that kid anymore. Nothing about this excited me. The idea of watching Russ and St. Hilaire discredited wasn't anything I could find a way to take any pleasure in. I'd tried to get out of coming. I'd made so many mistakes on my own that I didn't need to be a part of my parents'. But that hadn't gone over well. "Do this for your sister," my father had insisted, and it was all I could do to keep myself from sharing the snarky retort that sprung up in my head.

I could have driven over to St. Hilaire with my parents, but I'd obstinately told them I'd walk. Then, a crack of thunder rattled the windows and made my heart skip. I wasn't exactly regretting my choice, but the weather wasn't what I would have hoped for, with the wind whipping my umbrella inside out and the promise of lightning in the distance again.

A guy at the gate asked me for my name and checked it off a list. "Just keep walking until you hit the center of town," he told me. I was half-disappointed not to be turned away.

I tried to take everything in as I passed. That Russ lived here and must have walked along these sidewalks every day made me feel closer to him and more aware of what I'd lost.

To my right was a statue of a woman with a joyous smile and a large umbrella. It was oxidized green by the weather of obvious decades. Storms weren't going to turn *her* umbrella inside out. There was something uplifting about her face. She looked like a friend. A kind spirit if you believed in such things, and I surprised myself with how badly I *wanted* to believe in such things.

Over the past two days, I'd weighed my options for disrupting the filming. Disabling the EMF meters would only help to prove my parents' point, and I couldn't come up with anything else that would stop the show. Definitely, cutting two eyeholes in a sheet and scampering around the room like a kid on Halloween wasn't going to cut it. Although it might make Russ laugh.

I stopped in front of Eaton Hall. *Was stopped* by a line of teens in uniforms looking like they were playing dress-up. They were honestly creepier than the idea of actual ghosts.

One of them stepped forward. He was tall, and even though he was probably older than I was, he looked as though he hadn't grown into his limbs yet. He stuck out his chest and said, "Where do you think you're going?"

A whole bunch of retorts came to mind, but for some reason, all I could think of was that the earth spun a thousand miles a minute and it was amazing how few people actually thought about that.

I rubbed a ring against a callus on my finger. "I'm part of the…" I couldn't say it, so I pointed upstairs.

"You're the kid," he said, and looked me up and down as we stood in the rain. "Prepare to be humiliated."

"That's my usual state of being," I said. "Can I go?"

He smirked but let me walk by him. I got to the door of Eaton Hall. I knew I had to climb the stairs to the top floor, and while I was eager to get out of the rain, it all felt a little too large and intimidating. "I'm sorry, Mari," I said. "I hate that everyone is going to know about you and our dysfunctional family."

I took a deep breath and put my hand on the worn wooden door, ignoring the kids playing army behind me. There was a plaque hanging on the door that read "Rules for Mediums," and

I was dying to read it, but a crack of lightning lit up the sky and I yanked the door open and bolted up the stairs, following the directions my parents left me.

The loft was on the top floor. I walked through the only door in the hall, shaking some of the water out of my hair. My parents were posing for Rick's camera as he got some test shots to check the lights and levels. They were alone in the room aside from an old guy who kept tapping his watch and looking around suspiciously and a beautiful girl in a military-style skirt suit who looked irritated by everything going on around her.

Was Russ not here or not here *yet*? What would have happened had I told him who I was sooner? Or had he not found out until today? Or had he not found out and I'd managed to skip out on the taping and found a way to keep it all a secret?

I was brimming over with questions. What would my parents do once this was over? Were we going to leave for somewhere I had no chance of ever seeing Russ again? Stay in Buchanan where I'd be forced to be reminded of Russ and St. Hilaire for all time? How much bad karma had I earned that both of the most likely options sucked?

I'd never realized before that it was as easy—easier maybe—to be haunted by people who were still living, than it was by those who had died.

chapter forty

RUSS

I got back to the loft just as the shot slammed into my system. The recipe I'd used, one from the back of my grandmother's book in a chapter called "Heavy Hitters," wasn't playing around, and I already felt the world shifting slightly off its axis. My legs felt rubbery and too long, somehow. My fingers kept trying to grasp something that wasn't there. I reached out toward the doorframe and felt every bit of texture on the wood. My senses were souped up, like they had been in Arbor Field with Asher when we'd kissed under those wild power lines and everything seemed to be cracking with life. My lips played the memory back in shocking, wonderful, and guilt-filled detail.

I took a deep, ragged breath and tried to steady myself. There'd be enough time later to process everything that had happened. I'd have to tell Ian about kissing Asher—I owed him that. But I could hear him laughing in response. Ian wasn't the jealous type. He'd probably be impressed I'd managed to get myself into a situation where someone would kiss me. *Probably.*

But first I needed this show out of the way. I stepped toward Clive Rice, who was waiting for me with an impatient glint in his eyes. My feet seemed to sink into the floor. I stopped. Stretched my arms up. Everything felt insubstantial. Angled.

It struck me that the shot might have been too much for my weight or the wrong mix or that I should have eaten something for breakfast instead of just downing a cup of too-strong coffee. But all I could do now was roll with it and attempt to act normal. Whatever "normal" was. It didn't matter what shape I was in, anyhow. It was Ian they wanted, Ian who was going to save us. I was simply the bait.

Rice was watching me from across the room, and something about his expression made me laugh. He stood alone under the ornate crown molding. Even here, he seemed out of time, out of place in his tweed jacket, the Guild pins on his collar gleaming like stars.

I leaned against the wall and closed my eyes. It would be so nice to let myself sleep for five minutes.

Something behind me hit the wooden floor with a clang, and I snapped to attention as Rick, the *Ghost Killers'* production guy bent down to pick it up. My breath hitched when I saw that Asher was behind him. He must have arrived while I was out. He was alone, sitting on an overstuffed chair of faded red crushed something, his legs pulled up so that the heels of his black Vans were resting on the edge of the seat.

If things were different, I'd go over and sit next to him. Maybe sit too close. Maybe place my hand on his back. Maybe let his broad smile fill me up. But aside from the flutter of my hands inside my coat pockets, I was paralyzed.

"Mr. Griffin," Rice said, walking toward me, polished shoes clacking on the overpolished wooden floors. "I urge you to remember that many, many people are putting their trust in you," he said under his breath, only for me. "I know I have no need to remind you what is at stake."

Normally his tone of voice would have scared the crap out of me, but I was too numb to be afraid. I might have nodded. I might have stared straight ahead at the rings on Asher's fingers. I wasn't sure. Either way, I allowed him to guide me to where Willow was coming out of the bedroom.

We'd already discussed that we weren't going to put ourselves on full display. No prayers to the dead. No begging words or threats. No incense or clanging bells or holding hands. No introductory demonstration that could be used against us or appropriated later. After all, it was only Ian we were after and he was waiting around in the wings. Somewhere.

"We're ready," Clive Rice announced to the room.

The guy running the camera counted back from five. It seemed to go on forever.

Rice bowed his head. Willow and I followed.

The room was long with a separate bedroom and kitchen aside from this wide-open space with high, high ceilings that reminded me of the planetarium. It had three pillars running down the center, and I leaned against one of them as a hush went through the room and Asher's parents stepped forward.

We already knew that a lot of the show's opening, closing, and voiceovers would be added in during production, but this part was going to be filmed live. Asher's dad's voice was loud and strong, and he didn't need a microphone as he began speaking about his daughter. He spoke about Mari in the same way I'd imagine that my dad would talk about me. It wasn't hard to see that his grief was real. I'd had enough experience with customers who had other motives to know the real thing when I saw it. I caught, too, the single mention of his son, only in the context of how much Asher missed his sister. I got it. I mean, it was obvious that Asher's grief was also real—even if his friendship with me hadn't been. But something in his father's demeanor made it clear he wasn't finding solace in his remaining child.

I took a step to the left so that I could see Asher better. I was curious how he was reacting to this public mourning but he was staring down at his hands, not even looking at his father, and I couldn't get a read off him. After a minute, Martin Mullen stopped talking and motioned to Rick. The men conferred, and nodded to each other before signaling to Clive Rice, who then nodded to me.

My stomach heaved. *You can do this*, I told myself. I only had to hold it together long enough for Ian to show up, and then I could slink off somewhere to be sick in private.

The light from the camera was hot on my face, and a trickle of sweat ran down the back of my shirt. Ian might have loved being the medium at the center of attention, but it was way outside my comfort zone.

I flexed my hands. Shakes or not, I had to get through this.

Rice cleared his throat.

I took a deep breath and held it until I was sure I'd pass out. I exhaled, mentally counted to ten, and whispered, "Ian, now."

There was a dramatic pause that lasted long enough for me to wonder if Ian would actually show up. What would I do if he didn't? I'd promised myself long ago that I wasn't going to put my future in his hands, and here I'd handed him not only mine, but also the future of St. Hilaire.

Time was skipping around in my head. Did I need to call him again? Had I done it? I closed my eyes and swayed, then opened them to at least put up the appearance of being in control.

A whine came from the corner of the room. It reminded me of Ian's dog, Garmer, who had left St. Hilaire along with Ian's mom and younger brother. I wondered if Willow had gotten a pet. She didn't seem the type. To my relief, after an even longer pause, I realized that the sound was coming from the *Ghost Killers* EMF meters, which had begun going off, one after another. A symphony of squealing electronics, each vying for attention, made my head feel as though it was going to explode. I resisted the urge to put my hands over my ears.

From the expressions on the faces of the Mullens, this was obviously not what they expected to happen. On the show I'd watched with the Corps members, their meters, at most, made little clicking sounds that faded into silence, not this explosion of noise and confirmation.

There was a flurry of activity as Asher's parents and Rick tapped on the equipment faces and checked the plugs. It was clear that they'd never once considered St. Hilaire might be able to beat them at their own game. *Serves them right.*

I took a step to the left, which was enough to allow me to see Asher watching his parents with an unreadable expression on his face. Next to them, Rice was barely concealing a smile.

The electronic squeal grew louder, the floodlights brightening with each screech. But there was still no Ian.

"Your stupid dead boyfriend better not ruin everything," Willow said, not taking her eyes off the Mullens.

"He'll be here," I said out loud. *At least I think he will*, I thought to myself. Before she could offer some argument, there was a loud *pop* and then there was Ian, looking tousle-haired in that deliberate way he had. I watched as he scanned the room, his blue eyes landing on me, barely a hint of a smile on his lips, before gliding over to the Mullens with confident steps.

"Right," he said, clapping his hands in front of him. "I've never been much good at cartwheels; do I need to tell a joke? Dance?" He leaned in toward Paula Mullen. "Or do you prefer to be scared?"

I managed to stifle a laugh behind my hand. Or maybe I didn't quite stifle it because I felt Rice's heavy glare fall on me.

"Some people do, you know," Ian said to Mrs. Mullen, "prefer to be scared. But that's not my style. I'm more of a lover than a fighter." This time he turned toward me and winked, which, mixed with the herbs in my system, made me feel as if I was floating over the room. I looked at the floor and hoped Rick's lens wasn't trained on me.

When I glanced over to make sure, he was fiddling with some switches on the side of the camera. I was super curious to know what he saw on the monitor. Did Ian show up? Did he look half as frighteningly sexy on the screen—with his rock-star hair and his arrogance, his painted-on jeans and shockingly white shirt—as he did, standing a few feet in front of me?

Martin Mullen took a decisive step forward. "You," he said, pointing his index finger at Ian's chest. "I know you."

Ian cocked his head in his ghostly way. "That's interesting. How can you say you 'know' a ghost when you don't even believe I exist?"

The meters went silent. Rick must have cut them off. What would the Mullens do now? Would they air a show that proved their entire life's work wrong?

A chair squeaked, drawing my attention. Asher was standing now. His face pale and absolutely blank. I couldn't tell if he was watching Ian or his father. The serum was making it oddly difficult to focus my anger. I didn't want to feel sympathy for Asher, but I did and couldn't explain why.

Now that the monitors had been cut off, everything in the room was eerily silent. It felt like everyone was holding their breath. For his part, Ian was standing in front of the Mullens, arms crossed. He was opaque enough so as not to make anyone doubt how present he was, but transparent enough to prove the point that he wasn't exactly alive. No one could ever accuse Ian Mackenzie of not being good at his job.

My heart raced with excitement. Had we won? Was this it?

Somehow it all seemed too easy. I'd expected some explosion. Some huge…something. But all that happened was Paula Mullen taking a step forward to stand next to her husband. She reached out a hand but stopped short of touching Ian.

"Are you real?" she asked quietly. "Prove you're not a trick of light or a projection or…"

Ian reached out a hand to meet hers, and she recoiled as soon as he touched her. I had no problem imaging the chill she felt when their hands met. I knew how cold Ian could be.

"As real as it gets," he said.

"You were that medium we came to see," she said after a beat. Her husband put an arm behind her to shore her up. "And now you're…"

"Dead. You can say it. It's nothing to be ashamed of."

"My daughter…" Asher's mother seemed to be on the verge of tears but he still stood in front of the red chair taking it all in.

"Mrs. Mullen," Ian said in the voice that put customers at ease, sucked up to teachers, and made just about everyone else swoon, "I promise, I did my very best to contact her. She just wasn't there. It's a good thing actually. Not everyone needs to stay around." He paused and gave her the comforting and conciliatory smile I'd seen many times before.

"But *you* did. Stay around, I mean," Martin Mullen said. I couldn't figure out if it was a question, statement, or accusation, and it didn't matter because Willow came out of nowhere and pushed her way between the Mullens and Ian.

"You can stop filming now," she said to Rick. He shuffled awkwardly and looked at the Mullens for instruction.

When they didn't react, he asked, "Why would I do that?"

Willow examined her fingernails as if she was trying to decide what to order for lunch. "Does the name Christine Allen mean anything to you?" she asked in a way that made it clear she already knew the answer.

Rick paled. "I don't… I mean…"

"Yeah, that's what I thought," Willow said. She turned to

the Mullens, "Did you know that your cameraman had an unfortunate incident a few years ago involving a boat and a girl who died? She was...how much younger than you?"

"What the hell do you want?" Rick barked at her. I couldn't tell if he was going to be sick or if it was anger that was turning his face a bright red.

"The tape," she said. Then she leaned over to examine the side of the camera. "And that memory card, too, please."

The Mullens looked at each other, and for a second I wondered if they were going to do something stupid to try to stop Willow but then they turned to Rick, and Mr. Mullen said, "I don't know what this is about but it isn't like we can use this footage."

Rick's hands were shaking as he retrieved the card and handed it to Willow along with the long reel of film. How had she even talked to the girl's ghost without a séance?

"Did you...did you hold a séance to talk to her ghost?" Rick's tongue tripped over the last word.

"No, idiot," she sneered. "I looked you up on the internet."

"Okay, Willow, are we done here?" Ian asked.

Willow threw the film into the corner of the room and pocketed the memory card, before turning toward Ian. "Oh no. You and I are just beginning." The two of them stared at each other, some sort of unspoken challenge going on that I didn't understand.

"What's going on?" I asked.

"Your boyfriend," Willow said, drawing the word out without looking my way, "has an outstanding debt with me."

Something dark flashed in Ian's eyes. "Our deal was that I'd show up, and I've done that. You wanted me to insist we do this in your loft, and I've done *that*. My debt to you is paid."

"I'm glad you think so." Willow smiled in a way that made my head hurt. Then she turned to me. "Right. Well, I told you he asked me to check in on you while you were…" She glanced at Clive Rice, and I had no doubt at all that her glance was a deliberate reminder of how easy it would be for her to ruin my future. "Indisposed. Do you think I played his errand boy because I was concerned about you?"

Ian ran his tongue over his teeth. "Actually, she played errand boy because *I* was concerned about you."

He knew better than to make deals with Willow. But it was clear by the way he'd said "concerned" that he'd been worried enough to put aside whatever common sense he had. And, of course, what he'd been concerned about was me using my grand-mother's serums. I'm sure he was pissed at me now, given that I could feel myself swaying slightly from side to side. At least I knew he wasn't going to get on my case in front of everyone.

"And what is it you want from Ian?" I asked her, aware that I was over enunciating. She didn't seem to notice or care.

"What I've always wanted," she said with a terrifying glint in her eye.

"And what is *that*, Willow?" Clive Rice demanded.

Willow flipped her hair behind her, and for a minute, I thought she was going to say she was joking and offer everyone something to eat and then we'd all head our separate ways. But then she said, "It's amazing how no one really listens to me."

And I knew, in a heartbreaking instance, exactly what she wanted.

chapter forty-one

RUSS

"You want to send him back," I said.

"You what?" said Rice just as Willow said, "Gold star for Russ Griffin. Glad I haven't been wasting my time with you after all."

I glanced at Ian, hoping he'd remember our conversation about Willow believing that mediums existed to "free" spirits from their connections to the living. I hoped he had some sort of Ian-like plan for dealing with her.

"Willow," Ian said more calmly than I would have expected. "Let them go. Then we can talk about this." He waved toward the Mullens. And toward Rick who looked like he was hoping the walls would swallow him. Asher looked weirded out, and I had to wonder which he was more freaked out about: ghosts really existing or me having a ghostly boyfriend.

"Ian," I cautioned, stumbling a step closer to him.

"There's not much she can do to me. I'm already—air quote—'living' on the other side," he said, narrowing his eyes at my uncharacteristic clumsiness.

"You should have stayed on the other side," Willow said. She unlatched the door to the wooden cabinet I'd assumed held dishes or books. It was completely empty. "And I *want* them to see this. Maybe then they'll gain some proper respect for what we do."

I tried to catch Ian's eye, but he was staring unblinking at the cabinet. "What's that?" I asked.

"Yes, Ian," Willow said in a singsong voice. "Please share your knowledge of my work."

Willow's voice was all wrong, and it was making the hair on my arms stand up. Ian was doing nothing to put me at ease. When I lived in Chicago, we'd had a brownout. It was the product of one of those storms that seemed to blow up once a decade or so. Streets flooded so high that houses filled with water. Trees were down everywhere, and before we lost power for what ended up being three days—but which felt like a year—the lights dimmed. The entire neighborhood was murky and gray. When we looked at the apartments across the way, they were bathed in an almost romantic glow, all the lights at half power.

That's what Ian looked like. Something at half power. It was the first time he was fully recognizable as a spirit. As a thing that was no longer living. As no longer a person. I thought back to the meeting in Rice's office and about how long Ian had been able to hold his form. Somehow I needed to get this over with so that he could go rest up.

"Wait," I said. "Let everyone go first. Come on, Willow." I

stepped toward her, confident for no discernible reason that she wouldn't fight me.

When she didn't, I caught Asher's eyes. "Get them out of here."

Asher froze, looking more shocked by the fact I was speaking to him than by everything that was going down. "Please," I said, although I'm pretty sure no sound came out of my mouth.

I thought the Mullens would also put up a fight. But then Ian looked at them and said, "Go," and I guess when you're trying to prove that ghosts don't exist and one tells you to leave, you listen.

After they left, only Ian, Willow, Rice, and I were left in the room. "So, this is your way of asking me to leave and never come back," Ian said to Willow, with less snark than usual. "But honestly, I can't see why you care. Am I stealing your crown or something?"

"Oh, your memory can't possibly be that short," Willow cajoled. "Give everyone the backstory. You always did know how to spin a good yarn. Entertain us. Your audience is waiting."

Ian closed his eyes as if he didn't have the energy to keep them open and speak at the same time. He looked murky now. Transparent. I was terrified to look away, afraid that if I did, he'd disappear.

"I found Dec a block away from the car wreck that killed his parents," he said in an odd ghostly monotone. Then he opened his eyes, looking directly at me to ensure I understood. "After the party."

"The police came," he continued in an odd, sad voice. "Then the Guild. And then I was left alone with only the bloodstains

272

on the concrete. I couldn't have come to you, Griffin. I had nothing to say that you would have wanted to hear that night."

His words made their way to the base of my spine where they settled with a painful knot. I wanted to grab him and tell him to stop talking, that it didn't matter anymore. But that would have been a lie. It still mattered. I just didn't want it to.

"I know," I whispered. "But what does it have to do with… that?" I point at the cabinet.

Ian nodded his head in a distracted way. To my eyes he seemed to be glowing.

He launched back into his story. "I came here, after…" His voice broke, and he looked at me as if something inside him was breaking as well. "I told you that Willow had been the one to ask for my help in saving the Hamptons. I didn't know where else to go. Besides, she'd said she'd been working on a way to vanquish ghosts. And I was having a problem with one."

"You mean Sarahlyn Beck?" I asked.

"You never should have made Sarahlyn your problem," Willow said.

"Willow," Rice warned, his voice coming from far away. "Enough. It isn't our place to play God; we can't go around sending people's spirits on just because someone has upset you and you've found a way to do it."

Willow gave Rice a withering look. "And *you* should never have double-crossed Sarahlyn in the first place." When Rice didn't say anything, she looked at Ian, "Continue," she commanded.

"I asked Willow to let me see the cabinet," he said. "I'd never heard of anything like it before. But she'd left out some crucial information."

"Yes, always keep an ace in your pocket." Willow laughed. And then she shrugged at Ian and said, "Although to be completely honest, I didn't know."

Ian stared at her and I stared at him. "Didn't know what?" I asked.

It felt like everyone in the room inhaled at once. Everything, including possibly time, simply stopped.

"I didn't know that the cabinet works on the living too," Willow explained as if it was something simple and insignificant.

Her words were clear, but still I had to ask. "Works?" Things started to fall into places I didn't want them to.

"Did you know I had been passed over to lead the Youth Corps in favor of Ian, even though I was Guild family?" she asked quietly. "You see, Father and I have some fundamental differences, but that didn't mean I was less fed up with hearing about the Guild's golden boy."

"You *killed* him?" The words stuck in my throat like glue. Things happened in St. Hilaire. Strange, horribly sad things. Somehow this was more.

"You know what he's like," she continued. "I was showing him the cabinet and he said something snotty, and I simply closed the door on him. I had no idea that it would… " She let her words trail off. "He just vanished, but it was Ian. I assumed he'd figure out some way of coming back. I didn't even know he was *dead* until he'd been missing for a while and Father tried to contact him. Not that he answered."

Ian, already dimmed, stumbled and sank to his knees and bent forward, hands on the floor. I rushed over to him. "What's happening to you?"

"And here I thought you didn't care," he gasped as he attempted a joke. His hands balled against the wood.

"You always knew better," I said, which might have been the most honest thing I'd ever told him.

He took my hand and squeezed it in a spasm. It was surprisingly solid but I was pretty sure if I touched his back my hand would go straight through to the floor below. He didn't let go, and I felt an odd draining rush that made me dizzy. Ian, though, looked a little more solid. Somehow he was draining energy from me. *Take it all*, I thought. *Take everything you need.*

Ian pulled himself up and moved toward the cabinet. "I didn't realize at the time that you were worse for St. Hilaire than even Sarahlyn," he said to Willow. "But I'm a quick study and have learned a lot since then."

The room grew cold and a horrible roar emerged from the cabinet.

Ian caught my eye, and I saw a warning in his stare. Whatever was going on came as no surprise to him.

Without any another word, he threw open the door to the cabinet. The whole room shimmered with gray fog. Smoke but not smoke. Solid but not solid. And then the gray began to make an explosion of horrible noises. Screams, and shrieks, and something that sounded like gears grinding.

As the fog began to surge, alternating between one giant mass and individual entities, I saw ghostly body parts that formed and then faded back into the whole.

The mist swirled again and then assembled itself into individual ghosts. A lot of them. All ages and from all eras. I'd rarely seen more than one ghost at a time. Séances weren't group events. Ghosts each had their own reasons for staying connected to the living, and that rarely overlapped with the trauma of other spirits.

Was Ian somehow calling these ghosts here? That would explain what was using up all of his energy, but how was that even possible? Even the strongest living medium couldn't maintain that sort of connection. I was so cold I couldn't concentrate on the question. Every beat of my heart sent ice through my veins. My vision swam and cleared in alternating beats.

"Do you recognize these spirits, Willow?" Ian called out over the horrible bellowing of the specters. "Because they know you."

"Willow," bellowed Clive Rice. "What have you done?"

The blood drained from Willow's face, and I realized it was the first time I'd ever seen her scared. "Why are you here?" she called into the mist of bodies.

The spirits spoke as one when they said, "You do not get to decide who moves on and when."

"I've been busy," Ian said. "I've been rounding up all of these ghosts who you think you sent on. But see, that isn't how it works. All you did was slam the door so that they could never get closure. You didn't free them. You didn't make them go away. You just put them into an even more horrible type of limbo."

She shook her head as if she couldn't believe her ears. "But that isn't what I was trying to do."

Ian stepped over to me, standing between me and the crowd of ghosts. "No, you were trying to siphon their power so that they were trapped for all eternity. But you still think this is about you?" he said to her. "You have a lot to learn."

Ian stepped back as the ghosts formed a circle around Willow. They began to pull together moving closer and closer to her. Then, as one, they turned, with her still in their center, toward the cabinet.

The dreadful noises they were making got louder and more pained before surging into a sickening *pop* as they crammed back into the cabinet, Willow still in their midst. Before I could even register it, Ian slammed the door and, with a flash of light, they were...gone. Willow was gone. The room, calm.

Clive Rice sank to his knees, looking deathly pale. "Ian Mackenzie, what have you done?"

Ian glared at him. "Hopefully I've straightened out some of her screwups. Well, me and each of those souls who just gave up any chance of closure in order to free St. Hilaire of Willow Rogers. But when I was rounding up all of the spirits she'd trapped, I realized something else. You know, we don't get therapy in the afterlife, so it took me a while to figure it out on my own." There was more than a hint of Ian's sense of humor in his voice, and I hoped it meant that the worst part of this day was over. Ian could regroup and get his strength back. I just wanted to sleep for about ten hours.

Then Ian said, "All this time, I thought it was Sarahlyn I was so angry with. But really, who can blame her? You were the one who had been trying to use her to make money for you. She was a means to an end, isn't that right?"

Rice was still on his knees. Sweat was pouring down his face. "Now, Mr. Mackenzie...please don't do anything rash," he begged.

Ian barked out a laugh. "Rash? I've had over a year of being dead to figure out how to make you pay for choosing your greed over the lives of the mediums you were sworn to protect. There is nothing you can do to regain my trust. Nothing you can do to bring back the Hamptons or the other mediums you've hurt."

"Wait, we can discuss this," Rice whimpered.

"No," Ian said calmly. "No, we can't. But there is someone *else* who would like a word with you."

The air in the room shifted and a shrill sound like nails on a chalkboard came out of the cabinet. Then, before I knew it, the door opened and Sarahlyn Beck stood in front of Rice. She was taller than I'd imagined, her edges hazy and barely defined. I hated her in a way I'd never hated a spirit or even a living person, but I couldn't do anything other than watch things play out.

"Sarahlyn," Rice begged. "Now, please. I know you wanted to save St. Hilaire as much as I did."

"I did not. Want. To. Be. Used," she howled. "This town. I built this town."

"I know, but…"

"You didn't have the right."

Sarahlyn was more fog than body, and her voice was piercing and distinctly not human. I guessed that's what happened to ghosts who had been around so long. Too long. I wondered if whatever had happened to her would happen to Ian too, someday.

"I think it's time," Ian said to her.

I tried to catch my breath. It was suddenly difficult to figure out who the true villains were. Willow was gone. Rice and Sarahlyn…well, they deserved each other.

It felt like a tornado was ripping through the room as she moved toward Rice. Wind and thunder and lightning surged, and I couldn't tell if it was coming from outside or here in the loft and I watched, dumbfounded, as the swirl made up of ghost and Guild president moved toward the cabinet and then, as Ian again closed the door, were gone.

The room was silent again. Deathly quiet. Ian and I were the only ones left, and for the first time, I didn't know what to say to him.

chapter forty-two
IAN

I knew I would die young because ghosts had spoken to me for as long as I could remember and every single one of them had said the same thing. *You will die young.* That hadn't left a lot of room for speculation.

Spirits had often told me things they shouldn't. People had too. I was a robber baron in the currency of knowledge. And in St. Hilaire, knowledge was power. It worked for me.

I'd never shared these predictions of my early demise with anyone. In fact, I'd rarely dwelled on the prediction itself. But as I'd gotten older and had to accept that the present snippet of time was all there was for me, I found myself taking more and more risks, simply because there was no reason not to.

And then I learned that I enjoyed taking risks.

When I was alive, I prowled at night. Wandered through town. Attended parties. Tried to release the pressure in my chest to *do* something. To *be* something. To *create* something. To leave a mark.

When I was alive, every moment in which I avoided acting was a moment wasted. Life was short. Mine would be shorter. It would be the most indulgent kind of gift to be given time to squander. Time for small talk and watching sunrises and binge-watching bad TV shows just for something to do. I thought that once I died, I'd have all endless time of another sort. But that turned out to be a fucking stupid assumption.

As a medium I thought I'd understood ghosts and their obsessions and often single-minded focus. I'd contacted spirits who had stayed around for all the reasons they'd taught us in school: Guilt, Hate, Obsession, Selfishness, Terror (GHOST). But all those reasons could be boiled down to revenge and regret, fear and love.

All could be attributed to me and why I had haunted St. Hilaire:

I had a plan to avenge Robert and Marian Hampton's deaths.

I was still working through the regrets that lingered from some miscalculations during my last year alive.

Where once I'd been afraid of wasting time, I found myself afraid of losing myself in the sheer vastness of it.

Love, though, was a loaded term. It was what people wrote horrible songs about, a word they bandied about without thinking. I thought it had nothing to do with me.

In different ways, I had cared, still cared, about my brothers.

I cared about the youngest, Alex, the way one might care about a three-legged puppy abandoned on your doorstep. I cared about my middle brother, Colin, the way one might care for an unreliable weapon that might go off if it wasn't cleaned precisely every three hundred and twelve days. If anyone had the courage to push me for an answer, I'd admit I cared, at some level, for my absentee father and my impatient mother, but no one would ever ask, particularly them. But love wouldn't have entered into any of those connections.

What relationships I'd had were fleeting because I knew I wouldn't be around to see things out. And there was always something—someone—else pleasurable right around the corner. Also, I got bored easily.

Even when I was alive, I hadn't been the Hallmark-card type.

Once I'd stopped needing to sleep and didn't feel pressured to *live* anymore, I felt the stifling weight of time, its endless nature. Its surprising, eternal darkness.

Russ Griffin was a light who kept pulling me back.

In those moments when I would have sought out noise and spectacle and bodies to reassure myself that I was alive and would stay that way for one more night, I began to look for a different kind of kick.

I was better behaved as a ghost than I'd been before. When I haunted Russ, I limited myself to his room's dark corners. No matter how much I longed to reach out to trace the mountains and valleys of his shoulder, or how hungry I was to examine the tattoo on his wrist, I held back knowing that Russ, who was leery of being touched, would find the gestures as something invasive rather than affectionate. Somehow, I'd kept my hands to myself.

Still, I'd wanted to pick up where Russ and I had left off so long ago as much as I'd wanted to understand and push the boundaries of this thing I had become.

Spirits remained tethered to the world of the living for revenge and regret, for fear and love. I had to accept that, for me, all of these to varying degrees involved Russ Griffin.

I'd waited for Russ and masochistically relished the pain of waiting. Then he had called to me and my waiting was over. We'd carved out a little time. I wanted more. But, as the song goes, you can't always get what you want.

"And that, Griffin," I said, breaking the silence, "is how you put on a show."

Russ sank to the floor and put his head in his hands. I'd been draining energy from him in order to make it through the day. Calling on a large group of spirits was difficult even when you were one. I sat down and joined him.

"What the hell just happened?" he asked. "Why didn't you tell me about Willow?"

"You mean about how I died?" I asked and laughed even though it took too much of my remaining strength. "You're still on about that?"

"Sorry," Russ said somberly. "I just…"

"I had work to do. Had you known, you would have been fixated on that and nothing else. I wanted time. With you."

Russ pushed back the hair out of his eyes and worked his face into a smile. "We have it now."

His words hit painfully somewhere in my chest. "Anyhow, I

think you got your wish," I said, changing the subject. "Destroy that cabinet and then, with Willow and Rice gone, you'll be able to help set St. Hilaire back on the right path."

"Well, *we* will," Russ said and took my hand in his warmer one. I'd been cold since I'd died. But all I felt now was numb. It wasn't a pleasant feeling. I stared at our intertwined fingers and then at Russ's face, which contorted in thought. "But if destroying the cabinet means Willow and Rice can't come back, what about you?"

I inhaled. It was hard work but it felt meaningful. It felt like the last sip of beer in a glass or the last piece of candy in the pack. It felt like something to savor since it was slipping away. "About that…" I said, my voice cracking in my ears.

Russ would hate me for a while. I got that. I kind of hated myself too. Things were ending just as they should have been starting. We'd wasted too much time and I'd chosen to go out on a high note by paving the way for Russ to save St. Hilaire.

I focused what little energy I had and forced it into my arm, which I put around his back, pulling him to me. "There are so many things I want to say to you," I whispered into his hair. Uncharacteristically, I was struggling to put any of those things into words.

"Ian?"

I could feel anxiety radiating from him. It was tangible, terrible, bitter. Knowing.

"Yeah," I said, hoping I could confirm his fears without having to say it out loud. Growing up in a town of spirits meant knowing that endings weren't necessarily final. But I'd pushed beyond the limits this time even for ghosts. Every one of those spirits who came through Willow's cabinet needed power—more power than she'd left them with. I hadn't had much to spare, but I gave them everything I had. What would it have mattered had things not been resolved with Willow? What would the point have been?

For the first time I didn't know what would happen next. If I just stopped. If there would be enough of me left to remember what it felt like to hold Russ close like this.

I didn't know how to say goodbye.

He stared straight ahead, and I watched a tear silently fall down his cheek and land on my sleeve.

"You know this shirt is dry clean only, right?" I quipped, trying stupidly to make him laugh.

We should have felt powerful and content. After all, everything I'd organized had gone exactly as planned. Maybe that was because I could never quite picture this part of the story. I probably hadn't tried very hard.

Russ snuffled and rubbed his eyes against his arm. Then he looked at me, eyes huge and full of a million things at once: pain, regret, fear, and still something else underneath, something that was destroying my non-beating heart.

"I'm sorry," he said. "For all the times that I didn't or couldn't…"

"Love means never having to say you're sorry. Isn't that how it goes?"

"Love?" he asked, choking a bit on the word.

"Do you think I would have stuck around all this time for less?" I swallowed, fighting against the darkness that would soon force me to fade into fog like Willow's vanquished ghosts.

Well, screw it. It would have to wait. At least for a moment. Still, I said, "I can't stay, simply because I want to. I'm out of acronyms."

Russ gave me that wide-eyed look he always did when he thought I was joking around to avoid the subject at hand. Could I take the memory of that look with me wherever it was I was going and capture it in rock or amber like some fossil?

"You can do it," I said, on the verge of tears myself. "Unscrew the Guild. And while you're at it, get rid of that shit of your grandmother's. I swear if you kill yourself with that stuff, I'm going to find a way to send whatever is left of Willow after you and make you miserable for all eternity."

"I will," he whispered.

"And…" I thought of something else. "What's that kid's name? The Mullen son."

"Asher," Russ said, puzzled, but not enough to ask why I'd brought him up now, of all times.

I hoped he'd be able to climb out of his grief someday. It would be easier if he weren't alone. "He was watching you the whole time he was here. I think, you know, you could do worse."

"Ian…"

"Just sayin', life is what you make it." I shuddered. I was pretty sure death was also what you made it. It was unfortunately also lacking in many things I still wanted. I tried to sigh, but I didn't have control of those muscles anymore. Time was slipping out of my grasp.

I put a hand out in front of myself and watched it morph from solid to transparent and back again. I bumped my shoulder into Russ's and said, "This would have been kick-ass in the clubs."

Russ rewarded me with a laugh but it quickly turned into a sob. He was shaking now, tears pouring down his face silently. It isn't often that you knew you were creating a moment for someone. A last moment that would define every memory they had of you. I couldn't screw this moment up.

This was perhaps the hardest part of leaving someone you cared about. Loved. Thinking about how he would be after the shock had worn off. I hoped he'd take my advice. All of it.

We'd gotten everything we said we wanted. Clive Rice gone. Willow too. Sarahlyn wouldn't be back again so that whole story was put to rest. Our unspoken desires had been the high price we'd had to pay.

I was tired in a way I wouldn't have been able to fathom when I'd been alive and had seemingly endless energy to draw upon. I forced myself to stand, pulling Russ up with me. Outside, the rain picked up, pelting the roof of Eaton Hall. I watched the cabinet to see if it was going to open and claim me, but it sat, solid and quiet as a coffin. That was fine. I didn't want it any more than it apparently wanted me.

My knees buckled and I stumbled. This was it.

"One more thing, Russ," I said, sinking into his arms.

"Anything," he breathed out.

"Remember me," I said and kissed him until I turned into smoke.

chapter forty-three
ASHER

I grabbed a tie from the back of my closet because it seemed like the right thing to do, given the occasion.

My parents had walked into town for dinner, the first step in an effort to repair their marriage. It seemed as if the whole thing in St. Hilaire had scared them into being nicer to each other and to me. Maybe it would even last.

I thought about driving my dad's SUV into St. Hilaire but decided to walk because the sky was sparkling and comfortingly clear and I could always come back and get the car if we needed it. Also, I had to get into the right headspace, even though I wasn't really sure such a thing existed.

I hesitated before stepping up to St. Hilaire's gate. This felt like a rite of passage. A point of no return. I knew what I'd seen up in that loft—I wasn't stupid enough to disbelieve my eyes—I just wasn't eager to see it again. If I walked through these gates, I knew I was signing myself up for something I never would have imagined before.

"Asher Mullen," I said to the girl manning the gate. "I'm"—I took a deep breath—"here to see Russ Griffin."

The girl nodded and checked me off a list. Then she pushed a button and the door to the town swung open.

I looked around as if I'd never seen St. Hilaire, wanting to view it with fresh eyes. As if I'd never watched a ghost appear and talk to my parents.

Incense smoke seemed to being coming out of every window. The houses had a charm all their own, and if I listened, a melodic mix of wind chimes rang out from multiple buildings.

I follow the directions Russ had given me to his house, and once I got there, I stopped, feeling everything at once. I hadn't seen him since the filming even though we'd talked almost every day. I was excited but terrified as well, so I lost myself in the spinning of the wind chime on their porch, its colors hypnotic and calming.

"Here goes nothing," I said to myself. I was trying to talk to Mari less these days, not because there was anything wrong with it, just because I was trying to stop relying on someone who wasn't here for me to lean on.

Besides, I was learning that it was kind of nice to talk to someone who talked back.

I forced myself up the two steps to the front door. It opened before I could knock.

"Hey," Mr. Griffin said. He looked different here than he did when he was working at the train station, definitely more relaxed. "Come in. I think Russ is almost ready."

I parked myself on an overstuffed gray sofa, feeling jittery and full of misplaced energy.

"Do you want something to drink?" Russ's dad asked.

"I kind of want to get this over with, Dad," Russ called, coming down the stairs. "But thanks."

He was dressed, as always, in his long jacket and dark jeans. For a second I thought maybe wearing a tie had been too much. But then he stopped in front of me and smiled. "A Pluto tie. I like it," he said. I blushed.

"Let me know if you need help," Mr. Griffin said.

"We're good. But thanks," Russ squeezed his dad's arm. I wondered if my dad and I would ever be as close but figured that we probably wouldn't and that would have to be okay.

Russ gestured for me to follow him through the kitchen and out the back door. "How did you get it here?" I asked.

"Youth Corps. What good is a title if I can't leverage it?"

He flipped on a floodlight. I'd expected to see the cabinet standing in his yard like the TARDIS in *Dr. Who*. Instead, the yard was littered with various smashed-up piles of wood.

"What happened?" I asked, looking around. I'd seen pictures on the internet of storm damage that resembled this mess with pieces of wood and paper everywhere, and a couple of tools thrown in for good measure.

Russ kept his eyes on the wood and said, "I borrowed an ax from my dad. It was a good way to work out some feelings."

I knew Russ had a lot of feelings to work out. I watched as

he started merging the wood into a single pile. It felt odd to be here. Odd to be invited into St. Hilaire, odd to be seeing Russ again in person with all our secrets on the table. My secrets, anyhow. I suspected Russ might take a little more time to share his.

I cracked my knuckles and took a deep breath. Then I wandered over and picked up some errant twigs to add to the pile. When Russ first told me his plan, I'd assumed that the whole town was going to turn out but he said he wanted to do this on his own. Then he asked me to join him.

I'd been turning that over in my head for days, beyond flattered that he didn't consider me some outsider.

"I'm glad you're here. It meant a lot that you came," he said.

"It meant a lot," I said back, "that you asked me."

I took my tie off and draped it around the banister near the deck. We worked in silence, aside from the sounds of wood hitting other wood and the crickets starting their evening song. The Griffin yard smelled of herbs—lush, deep, and earthy. How was Russ going to avoid being pulled back to using them when they were so present?

"What did you decide to do about your grandmother's book?" I asked, not looking at Russ. When he first told me about the shots he'd been taking, I did my best not to freak out, glad we were on the phone and he couldn't see my face. But he said he'd made a promise to Ian to quit and this time he needed to keep it. I believed him.

"I'm taking your advice," he answered. I'd told him I thought he'd regret losing something his grandmother had obviously put so much work into even if he wouldn't be able to look at it for a long, long time. "I gave it to my dad and asked him to lock it away somewhere."

I smiled but I wasn't sure he saw since he had procured a Firestarter from somewhere and was standing with it and a small blow torch, staring at the pile we'd created.

"That's a lot of wood for just that cabinet of Willow's," I said. "It didn't look that big back in the apartment."

"It isn't only that," he explained. "My dad had a bunch of stuff he wanted to get rid of. Old blueprints and such, so it seemed like a good opportunity."

He held the torch up but hesitated. I took a step closer, knowing, at the very least, he had to be thinking about Ian dying in that cabinet. Russ didn't talk about Ian much but I knew he was still trying to sort out a lot of things. I was just glad that he let me be there in his silences. I was willing to wait him out.

"Do you want me to go inside and let you do this alone?" I asked, wondering if I was the cause of his hesitation.

It took a minute but he shook his head. "No. It's time." He lit the starter and threw it into the pile. The wood burst into flames as Russ returned to my side. The fire sent orange sparks high into the sky, and the thick smoke filled the air and covered the moon.

Russ shivered even in the heat. I wanted to reach out to comfort him somehow, but it was too soon or possibly not soon enough. Definitely the wrong time, either way.

"I'm glad the Guild didn't stop me from doing this," he said. "I was up all night worrying that they might want to keep it around in case they needed Clive Rice back for anything."

The fire crackled like a witch. If you stared into it long enough, it looked like figures were dancing in the flames.

"Are you okay with all of this?" Russ asked out of the blue. It wasn't like we hadn't discussed what had happened in the loft. We'd discussed that, my parents, *his* parents, his relationship with Ian, my feelings of guilt about Mari. We'd discussed everything, really. Everything except whatever there was between us. If there was anything left between us to discuss.

When I didn't answer, he said, "I know you accept the ghost stuff. As much as you can. And I know you get that this is all going to take me a while to sort through, if I even can. But I hope…" A wave of sadness swept across his face and he tried to fight it off.

"Russ…" I started.

"I want to warn you. Because this place is weird and there's so much work I have to do to make it less weird, and I'm kind of a mess and kind of…"

I reached over and grabbed his hand before I could talk myself out of it. "Wonderful," I said. I looked down at our intertwined hands, my rings settling on top of his owl tattoo like a crown. "You're kind of wonderful."

I held my breath, waiting for him to react, but to my surprise and relief, he began to laugh. "That'll come back to haunt you," he said, rolling his eyes and squeezing my hand. "Don't say you weren't warned."

"Is this what it's going to be like now? All ghost jokes?"

"Well, now that you know…" He turned toward me, the fire reflected in his dark eyes. "I do mean it. This is a lot. *I'm* a lot."

"Wow," I said. "Two weeks of therapy and you're already so self-aware," I chided him. I knew he'd gone to a couple of support group meetings in Buchanan. He obviously wasn't talking about the ghost stuff there, but like he told me, he had enough other issues to work out to keep him busy for a while.

He laughed, still shy, I guess, about someone knowing his personal life.

"Yeah, okay," he said, leading me to the deck. "Come look at this. I want to see what you think." He bent into his backpack and pulled out a bit of metal a little larger than a bookmark. "My dad had one of his friends from the train yard make it."

He held it out to me and I took it, surprised at its weight. I flipped it over and read the inscription. IAN MACKENZIE. ALWAYS REMEMBERED.

"I like that," I said. "Where are you going to hang it?"

"There's a bench near the fountain in the town square," he said. "I know it's cheesy, but I think Ian would appreciate it."

We stayed quiet, each with our own thoughts as the fire burned hot. It was easy to assume that Russ was thinking about Ian. And, of course, I was thinking about Mari.

"You know there are supposed to be shooting stars tonight," Russ said, staring at the smoke that obscured the sky. "You can't wish on them if you can't see them, though, is that right?"

"How did you even know that? Am I turning you into an astrophile, Russ Griffin?" I was so grateful for the darkness, hoping the fire wasn't bright enough that he could see the smile I couldn't keep off my face.

"I saw a flyer up in Hub City Books that talked about when you could see the most shooting stars. And they have a ton of books about space. I didn't realize there was so much you could *say* about stars."

"I'm *so* proud of you," I said, trying to sound like I was joking. I wasn't joking, though. I was so freaking happy to be standing here next to him, and even though there was so much sadness in the occasion, I felt the promise of something I never thought possible.

I took Mari's ring off my finger and rubbed the shooting star engraved inside for luck. Impulsively, I tossed it to Russ. "Here…you can see this one," I said. "Make a wish."

His eyes opened wide as he caught the ring and slipped it on. Then he laughed, a solid laugh unlike I'd ever heard from him. "I don't know what to wish for," he said. "I think I might be on the way to getting everything I want."

chapter forty-four

RUSS

There was a hole inside me. How long would it take before I stopped looking for Ian around every corner? Would that time even come?

Asher kept telling me it was okay to miss Ian. That he would never stop missing his sister, and while I often reminded him that Ian was *not* my sister, he said it didn't matter. That I needed to feel what I felt. It was a part of me.

I took a deep breath and rubbed the owl on my wrist. I was trying to focus on the future, now that I was really starting to believe I could have one.

Before I left the house, I lit the candle on my desk and took a jar from the shelf. Basil. I crushed the herb in my hand and released it over the flame. The room filled with the scent of the herb. Basil was good for focus and opening yourself up.

My walk into town felt deliberate. Things were changing and I had to let them. More, I had to let myself change with them.

I paused when I got to the bench. I'd invited Colin, but he'd never replied, and, last I heard, he was leaving St. Hilaire, which made me oddly sad. I pulled the plaque out of my bag and nailed it on. Then I looked over at the statue of Sarahlyn Beck. Was it ironic or just a coincidence that the two memorials were so close together? I hoped Ian wouldn't be pissed about their proximity.

I wandered the long way to Eaton Hall, through the fairy garden and around the wishing well. My thumb went to Asher's ring on my finger. It wasn't *that* sort of ring, but it surprised me how grounded I felt every time I noticed it was there.

Asher was waiting for me at the door. We were going to go see a movie, which seemed mundane, and normal, and wonderfully indulgent.

He pulled his jacket open to expose two boxes of Raisinets sticking out of his pocket and whispered, "I've got the goods. Don't tell anyone."

I laughed and shook my head. Eaton Hall felt, as it always did, important. But with Clive Rice gone, and Willow too, to be honest, things felt lighter, fresher. Even the old trees in the courtyard had been trimmed to let the sunlight surround the building.

"Russ, hold up." I turned to see Cindy Hale running toward me. "What in the world is up with all this freaking paperwork?" she asked.

"Oh, did I forget to warn you about that when you took over?" I smiled. Cindy was filling in as interim leader of the

Youth Corps while I got my head straight. Then the plan was that we would chair the group together.

"Humph," she said as she went in, but I could tell she was smiling too, and I knew she would do a great job.

I glanced at Asher. Was this what happiness really felt like? This feeling that everything made sense and might actually continue making sense for a while if only everything stood still for a minute?

I took Asher's hand as we turned to leave, but then I stopped and turned around. "Wait. There's something I need to do."

The old wooden plaque that held the Guild's rules hung crooked upon the door. I straightened it out and then dug in my bag for a Sharpie and corrected the text.

RULES OF CONDUCT FOR MEDIUMS

TRY NOT TO ~~NEVER~~ CHANGE THE COURSE OF THE FUTURE through the sharing of information. **But by all means, look after one another.** ~~This includes scenarios of life and death.~~

~~MEDIUMS PASS ALONG MESSAGES FROM THE departed. We do not read minds and any attempt to insinuate otherwise will be met with censure by the Guild.~~

NEVER READ A FELLOW MEDIUM OR SUMMON A SPIRIT to that end **without their permission**. ~~Mediums who have passed on may only be contacted with explicit Guild approval.~~

NEVER USE YOUR GIFTS FOR SELFISH GAIN.

NEVER MISLEAD THOSE YOU COULD HELP.

ALL WISHING TO MOVE TO ST. HILAIRE WILL BE TESTED. **We exist as a community of mediums, but welcome all who wish to call St. Hilaire home.** ~~A full half of any family must be able to pass tests as certified mediums and be able to support themselves as such.~~

ALL HIGH SCHOOL SENIORS WILL **HAVE THE OPTION TO** serve in the Guild's Youth Corps during that school year. **Guild membership from that point forward will be determined through community-wide elections.** ~~In the likelihood that a student shows special promise, there exists the option for a one-year position as Student Leader within the Corps, leading naturally to a permanent Guild position upon completion.~~

HAVE A NICE DAY.

THE GUILD, GOVERNING BODY OF ST. HILAIRE, NEW YORK, REESTABLISHED ~~1870~~ **2022**.

ACKNOWLEDGMENTS

It's said that writing is a solitary activity. If that's true, then writing (or publishing) during a pandemic takes this adage to its extreme.

To those who read a draft of this book and offered helpful feedback, even while it felt as though the world was crumbing, I am infinitely grateful. Shawn Barnes and Tom Wilinsky are rock stars, treasured friends, and immensely talented writers. I hope they each know how very much I value them. Beth Hull is literally a book-saver, multiple times over. I have no idea how her brain works, but I'm so grateful that she continues to share her magic with me. ALL the ponies!

My agent, Lauren MacLeod, is the kindest force of nature I know. Plus, she's queen of gifs and brainstorming. What more could a writer wish for?

To all at Sourcebooks, particularly Annie Berger, Jenny Lopez, Cassie Gutman, Rebecca Atkinson, and their teams, as well as Erin Fitzsimmons and Nicole Hower for this amazing cover, and Danielle McNaughton for the internal design, thank you. I'm incredibly grateful to be partnering with you.

To anyone who has read any of my books, THANK YOU, THANK YOU, THANK YOU. It is a special type of privilege to launch the characters who live in my head into the world and have them find a safe haven with you.

To those I love who may think they have nothing to do with my writing but whose support holds me together and allows me to tell these stories. I would be remiss if I didn't thank: Macon St. Hilaire and Laurin Buchanan, who also, once again, loaned me their names, as well as Mari Sitner (did you know your dad let me use your name?); Suzanne Kamata, for long-distance cheerleading; Laura Richards, for always having my back; Lisa Maxwell, for being the best kind of sounding board; Emilie Richmond (because we always knew, didn't we?); Ron Goldberg (who will probably never read this book); and Joe Chiplock (who hopefully will), for allowing me to live vicariously through their New York shenanigans and for giving me someplace to vent and kvell (often simultaneously) while making me laugh and then cheering in all the right places. And, always, my dad, Harold Baker, my first and most ardent fan.

Finally, to Keira, for letting me steal her cow joke (even though I didn't ask permission), and to John, who will one day realize all of the Easter eggs I leave for him in my books, I love you both!

ABOUT THE AUTHOR

Photo © Stephanie Saujon

Helene Dunbar is the author of *We Are Lost and Found* and *Prelude for Lost Souls*, as well as *Boomerang, These Gentle Wounds*, and *What Remains*. Over the years, she's worked as a drama critic, music journalist, grant writer, and marketing manager. She lives with her husband and daughter in Nashville, Tennessee. Visit her at helenedunbar.com, on Twitter @helene_dunbar, or on Instagram @helenedunbar.

FIREreads

—————— 🔥 #getbooklit ——————

Your hub for the hottest young adult books!

Visit us online and sign up for our
newsletter at FIREreads.com

 @sourcebooksfire

 sourcebooksfire

 firereads.tumblr.com

CPSIA information can be obtained
at www.ICGtesting.com
Printed in the USA
LVHW102101100622
721011LV00005B/104